PRAISE FOR
DRUSILLA CAMPBELL'S NOVELS

WHEN SHE CAME HOME

"Like Barbara Delinsky, Campbell entertains as well as informs as she wraps a novel around a timely social issue... Campbell puts her own spin on it by telling a PTSD story from the point of view of a female Iraq War veteran...Plenty of contemporary food for thought."   —*Booklist*

"A heart-wrenching novel that deals with a number of important social issues, including the actions of private contractors in war, the treatment of women in the armed services, domestic violence, and school bullying."   —*Kirkus Reviews*

"This gut-wrenching novel will strike a chord with many veterans, both male and female."   —*National Examiner*

"Carefully researched and skillfully crafted...poignant and deeply human. *When She Came Home* will be of special relevance to military women and their loved ones, but, just as importantly, to all of us who seek insight into the serious issues that such families face."   —BookReporter.com

"Compelling, emotional, and very realistic...I recommend this book because it's so true to today's world...[The] story tugged on my heartstrings and made me cry a few times."

—LongandShortReviews.com

LITTLE GIRL GONE

"An unflinching portrayal of life in emotional and physical captivity. Campbell has a powerfully understated voice and resists the easy path of sensationalizing the story. Instead she provides authentic drama rich with complex psychological composition. The result is a novel that is hard to read, but even harder to put down."   —*San Diego Union Tribune*

"Campbell's latest has full-blown appeal for teen readers, echoing stories of abduction in the news (à la Jaycee Dugard and her memoir, *A Stolen Life*) or popular fiction (think of Emma Donoghue's Alex Award–winning *Room*)."

—*School Library Journal*

"*Little Girl Gone* peers insightfully into the lives of people easily written off as monsters. With an economy of style, vivid details, and grace of expression, Drusilla Campbell has written a novel well worth staying up late to keep reading."

—Laurel Corona, author of *Penelope's Daughter* and *Finding Emilie*

"Campbell writes with deceptive simplicity all the more impressive for the psychological currents simmering below the surface of a barren terrain...a novel that celebrates the power of friendship and the freedom to make one's own choices." —CurledUp.com

"*Little Girl Gone* is a fantastic exploration into domestic violence and the power of courage in the face of tragedy."
—BookFinds.com

THE GOOD SISTER

"Should be on everyone's book club list."
—*Publishers Weekly*

"A novel about motherhood, sisterhood, and even childhood...In a novel that examines the sometimes devastating effects of postpartum depression, Campbell has managed to humanize a woman whose actions appear to be those of a monster rather than a mother. Through her sister's eyes, we are able to understand and even empathize with Simone Duran, a woman who has failed as both a wife and mother."
—T. Greenwood, author of *The Hungry Season*

"Can you have sympathy for a woman who attempts to murder her children? The way Drusilla Campbell tells her story, yes, you can. Even more important, in this unflinching look

at family relationships, postpartum depression, and the complex lives of the characters, especially the women in this book, you can come to understand how such an unthinkable act can happen. Make no mistake, *The Good Sister* is a painful story, but it is also a story that will carve away at your heart."
—Judy Reeves, author of *A Writer's Book of Days*

WILDWOOD

"The pull of family and career, the limits of friendship, and the demands of love all come to vivid life in *Wildwood*."
—Susan Vreeland, *New York Times* bestselling author of *Girl in Hyacinth Blue*

Also by Drusilla Campbell

When She Came Home

Little Girl Gone

The Good Sister

Bone Lake

Blood Orange

The Edge of the Sky

Wildwood

IN DOUBT

Drusilla
Campbell

GRAND CENTRAL
PUBLISHING

NEW YORK   BOSTON

Grand Central Publishing
Hachette Book Group
237 Park Avenue
New York, NY 10017

www.HachetteBookGroup.com

Printed in the United States of America

RRD-C

First edition: August 2014
10 9 8 7 6 5 4 3 2 1

Grand Central Publishing is a division of Hachette Book Group, Inc.
The Grand Central Publishing name and logo is a trademark of Hachette Book Group, Inc.

The Hachette Speakers Bureau provides a wide range of authors for speaking events. To find out more, go to www.hachettespeakersbureau.com or call (866) 376-6591.

The publisher is not responsible for websites (or their content) that are not owned by the publisher.

Library of Congress Cataloging-in-Publication Data

Campbell, Drusilla.
  In doubt / Drusilla Campbell.
    pages cm
  ISBN 978-1-4555-1033-7 (paperback) -- ISBN 978-1-4555-1034-4 (ebook) 1.
Women lawyers--fiction. 2. Teenage boys--Fiction. I. Title.
  PS3603.A474I53 2014
  813'.6--dc23
                                        2014013082

For Angela

The place of pain is the place of promise.

Larry A. Parker

IN DOUBT

1

For a long time he believed that everyone felt as he did. He assumed that the constant clench of his stomach was part of being human—like the burn behind his eyes and the dreams that woke him, wringing wet and trembling. In school he began to understand that he was different, others were not as he was. Eventually he named what he felt: anger.

One morning a few months after he had left school and begun working at Roman's Gardens he became aware that the anger had subsided and become no more troubling than a mosquito bite. He felt a new freedom, and for almost two years he was happy.

But now the anger was back and during the hiatus it had put on muscle. His time in the gardens had freed something in him. A fantasy of liberation had slowly taken shape. As the line separating his dream and his reality became harder to distinguish, he was often frightened by where his imagination took him. He swore off violent thinking, but the fantasies drew him back. When he imagined what he could do, what he *might* do, the tightness in his gut relaxed a little.

Though the revolver was an inanimate metal thing, it felt warm and alive in his hand, a natural extension of himself with connections to his arm and back and shoulders. After he left the garden and moved home, the first thing he did every morning was check to see if it was still where he'd placed it in his bottom dresser drawer, swaddled in a white T-shirt. Since he'd installed locks on the door and windows, his bedroom was perfectly secure, but there was always a possibility that she had found her way in and taken it while he slept.

He tenderly unwrapped the gun, flipped the cylinder and counted six bullets, then laid it on his pillow. The innocuous T-shirt's metallic odor emboldened him as he pulled it over his head. After checking the safety, he tucked the revolver in the waist of his jeans as he'd seen done on television. Pulled down, his shirt covered it. The steel was hard and warm against his bare skin, a part of him.

Looking at his reflection in the mirror on the closet door, he did not see a handsome seventeen-year-old with his life before him. Looking back at him he saw the anger, which had become like a friend, an ally in an interminable battle.

2

Hey, what're these for?" Carmine Giraudo stood in the middle of his sister's office surrounded by cardboard boxes in various stages of unpacking. He held out a set of three keys on a plain silver ring. "What's the car key? Not your 4Runner."

"I'll take them," Sophie said, reaching.

"First tell me whose car this belongs to."

"I don't remember." Sophie shook her hand in his direction. "Just give them to me, okay?"

Laughing, he held the keys above her. "You got something going on I should know about, shortcake?"

"Don't I wish."

"A beach shack down in Malibu? A hot little car hidden in a garage somewhere?" He tossed her the keys. "I know you've got secrets; I just haven't figured out what they are yet."

"And you never will." He thought she was kidding.

Sophie laid the key chain in the lower left drawer of her desk beside two glasses and the bottle of Dewar's she kept there.

"Maybe you've got a storage unit in LA. Is that where you hide the bodies? An old car and a couple of castoff lovers?"

Tuning her brother out, Sophie stood, hands on her hips in perfect imitation of her mother and grandmother, surveying the jumble of furniture and boxes, tilting stacks of unread magazines and journals, legal books, and miscellanea cluttered around her. The office suite smelled of fresh paint, and the big items—a new carpet, her two desks, the file cabinets, bookcases, couch, and chairs—were in place. Tomorrow someone would come and hang blinds on the windows that overlooked the courthouse corner of Mission Park. She could manage the rest on her own.

"You must have lots to do, Carmine. It's almost time."

"What's so secret about a set of keys?" He was hurt that she would not confide in him.

"I'll tell you when I'm old. You can drag the truth out of me then. My dying words."

He sucked in the corner of his mouth and looked at her sideways, their grandmother's skeptical expression. She gave him the same look back.

"Suit yourself, shortcake."

She pretended not to notice the nickname they both knew she hated. She had always wanted to be tall and willowy, a runway model instead of short and curvy like every other woman in the Giraudo and Marsay families. She had once made the mistake of telling Carmine that in her next life she would be six feet tall, athletic, and flat chested. A Valkyrie. He had never forgotten.

Though she had trained herself not to react to his goads,

it was hard to trust someone—even a brother—who thought it was good, clean fun to poke fun at her for the pleasure of watching her flinch. Her ex-husband, County Prosecutor Ben Lansing, had also been a tease, though in the beginning his jibes had seemed good-natured and affectionate.

Carmine said, "You can sit with me and Jeannie."

"I'll watch from up here."

"Are you pissed about the key thing? I didn't mean anything." He looked so innocent. "You're welcome to your secrets."

"I'm on edge, Carmine. That's all. I've got so much to do."

"You've got a lot on the line here." He looked around the office. "It's a nice place, Sophe, but I don't see how you'll ever make enough—"

"And thanks for the good wishes."

"You're gonna have to work like a motherfucker to make the rent."

"Really?" She slapped her forehead lightly. "I thought I was getting it for free."

"Jeez, you're bitchy. No wonder you never get a date. You scare 'em all away."

Like their mother, Carmine thought being family excused rudeness.

"Listen," he said, "I want you to be a success. I'm hoping you'll be a famous criminal lawyer and get a movie made about your life. But not all your cases are going to be big ones like Orlando Cardigan. It's not like there's a lot of crime in SanSeb."

Did her brother really think she was unaware that her defense of Orlando Cardigan's son had been almost a fluke: a big retainer and her fee at the end *paid on time*? Cardigan had taken a chance on her because she had once been a kick-ass prosecutor. And now, because of her success defending his son, she had been able to move from a dismal cubbyhole next to a supermarket parking lot to this suite in one of the town's historic buildings, near the courthouse and overlooking Mission Park.

She shared a general receptionist and copy machine with four other attorneys, but her three-room suite had its own small outer office and, off it, another space the size of a walk-in closet. She had already hired a fledgling paralegal, Clary, and eventually she hoped to generate enough business to hire an associate and a full-time investigator. Right now she was doing her own bookkeeping and housekeeping, and whoever was in the office answered the phone.

Even with the furniture in place, the pictures hung, and the packing boxes disposed of, her office would probably always be untidy. She might have changed addresses, but she was still Sophie Giraudo.

From the window she watched the courthouse corner of the park fill up, but she wasn't thinking about the gathering crowd. She loved her brother, but he knew how to get to her. She couldn't stop thinking about the keys stowed in her desk drawer. What did it mean that she had held on to them after all these years? What would Carmine say if he knew where and how she'd come by them?

Her brother had followed the rules all his life and never

seemed to mind being under the controlling thumb of their mother. In contrast, Sophie had fought her way out of her mother's womb in a difficult thirty-two-hour labor, almost strangling herself on the umbilical cord in the process. Ever since, she'd been in some state of mutiny, often her own worst enemy. Carmine was like their easygoing father, content to go along, letting the women in his life run the show. Contentment and self-satisfaction seemed to be part of her brother's DNA in the same way that rebellion, risk taking, and self-doubt were essential to hers.

In a few minutes Carmine would be in the middle of the party to celebrate Governor Maggie Duarte's birthday. Known and liked by everyone, he had a wide circle of friends, remembered names and faces, and could shake hands like a politician. As the high school senior guidance counselor and athletic director, he was frequently called upon to shepherd and chaperone school groups, and today he was in charge of getting the glee club through the crowd and into place on the risers. A senior girl with a scholarship to Juilliard would sing the national anthem.

The old glass in the sash windows tinted Sophie's world a cool underwater blue and slightly rippled her view of Mission Park, a four-block rectangular expanse of grass and trees and playgrounds with a creek running through it. Like almost everyone in SanSeb, Sophie regarded the park as the heart of their big, thriving town. Too many coats of paint had long ago sealed her windows shut, but the vents at the top were open, letting in the fragrance of *carne asada* from grills set up in the street in front of the courthouse. The congregation of St. Mary and All Angels would soon be selling chili bowls, hot dogs, and tacos for a buck apiece, a steal on this special occasion. Flags—stars and stripes and golden bears—flew from rooftops and hung from the windows of the buildings around the park. An immense banner across the front of the courthouse declared HAPPY BIRTHDAY, MAGGIE! in case there was a soul in town who didn't know the reason for the festivities.

Though her family had known the governor since she was a little girl, Sophie's parents, Anna and Joe Giraudo, had chosen to remain at home. Apart from Carmine, Sophie saw no one she knew in the crowd, which was not surprising considering how rapidly San Sebastian's population had grown in recent years. It was sometimes hard to recognize it as the quiet Central Coast town in which she had been born and brought up.

In recent years, the town's mild climate and its location near the coast and midway between San Francisco and Los Angeles had made it attractive to the mostly affluent newcomers. They had remodeled the Craftsman and Victorian houses along Diamond Back Street and St. Ann's Road or built mansions in the oak-studded hills and down the long, sloping plain to the sea. There were new condos and apartments out by the university and along Peligro Creek they had displaced the struggling five and ten acre ranches. SanSeb's tax base had almost tripled in the last ten years, making the stores on Maine and Mission Streets more interesting and expensive than in the old days, when every shop owner knew Sophie by name. As a lawyer, she was well-known and respected, but she had never been popular like Carmine. The gene for easy friendship had been left out of her DNA. She had a crowd of acquaintances, but her only true friend was Tamlin, whom she'd known since high school.

Orlando Cardigan had become something of a friend over the course of his son's trial. Before Will's trouble, she'd known Orlando only by reputation, as one of a consortium of benefactors who had raised the millions required to repair the Mission San Sebastian and restore the gardens around it. The abandoned canneries along De Anza Creek had been demolished, and the old buildings replaced by sleek, clean industries surrounded by more gardens and landscaped parking. Enrollment at the university was up, a new community college was under construction, and all of this was good.

The small town of Sophie's childhood had become a big town and might even be a city one day. Maybe then she would feel less cornered by her identity: Joe and Anna Giraudo's rebellious daughter, Carmine's sister, Sandrine's granddaughter, Delphine Marsay's great-granddaughter.

Sophie watched the crowd in the park grow: a trio of men dressed like Spanish friars, a conquistador, women in ruffled Mexican costumes, picnickers with blankets and folding chairs, strollers and excited dogs straining on their leads. Moving in and out among the townspeople, unrecognized, there had to be undercover agents and law enforcement officers because no matter how popular Governor Maggie Duarte was in some parts of the state and especially in her hometown, there were other places where the enmity against her was voluble, and violent rhetoric blurred the lines between free speech, hate speech, and criminal threat.

Not only was she the state's first female governor; she was the first Mexican American governor and an outspoken advocate for minority rights, immigration reform, free choice, and higher taxes for the top one percent. In California, no one was neutral about Maggie.

3

Floating in the unanchored waters between sleeping and waking, Iva Devane dreamed of a voice, a softly sexless voice repeating the same badgering demand.

Open your eyes, Iva. See, see.

She obeyed and saw that she was alone, again. Beside her, the bed was cold. Riga, a large brindled Cane Corso, rested her jowly muzzle on the edge of the bed and stared at her. *You beautiful creature*, she thought, reaching out to touch her. *My guardian angel.*

A mile away an excited coyote pack yipped after prey. Beneath Iva's hands, the dog's skin rippled.

Until recently Iva had been an easygoing woman who slept through the night without stirring, but recently a bony restlessness had elbowed its way into her dreams, where it jabbed her constantly. Even during the day, discomfiting emotions surfaced and demanded her attention: uneasiness, dissatisfaction, doubt. She wanted to talk about this with Roman, but he rarely had time for a serious conversation. Half-asleep, she dropped her defenses and the truth rolled in:

she was tired of waking up in a cold bed and no longer wished to share her husband with a gang of adolescents who doted on him, fed off him, and competed for his favor. For a little while at least, she wanted his undivided attention. Tears warmed the orbits of her eyes, ready to fall, only awaiting permission.

She didn't cry.

She pushed the bedcovers back and sat for a moment on the edge of the bed. Beneath her feet, the cold hardwood floor reminded her that although Roman's Gardens was already wild with new growth, it had been a cool and unpredictable spring. She walked to the window and looked through the sheers at the yard between the house and the largest barn. In dawn's gray light, the greenhouses, damp with dew, shimmered like silver. Behind them, the bunkhouse and sheds were shadows without detail.

During their first years on the property, before the house was restored and modernized, Roman had built an apartment for them at the back of the barn. It was called the clubhouse now. It happened occasionally that he fell asleep back there. The sign on the door, BOYS ONLY—NO GIRLS ALLOWED, was a joke at the same time that it was not. Iva stayed away because Roman said boys who had never had anything to call their own needed a place where their privacy was respected. A flat space outside the clubhouse door had been cleared and laid with asphalt for a basketball court. Last year, lights had been installed at more expense than Iva had been comfortable with, though Roman had argued her over to his side,

reminding her that lonely boys, angry and confused and way-
ward boys, any and all kinds of boys, could not resist a ball
and a hoop.

Each year, Roman's training and education program,
Boys into Men, enrolled youths from troubled homes who
disliked school and resented authority. Some of these were
day boys who worked from nine to five and returned to
their homes at night; others lived in the bunkhouse. Both
groups were paid a minimum wage. A few favored boys
lived in the house, and when they weren't learning the
nursery trade, Iva prepared them for the California high
school equivalency exam, a job she found challenging because they were rarely motivated to learn. She despaired of
their vulgarity and abysmal ignorance, but Roman told her
to be patient.

She fed them and taught them and did their laundry. Roman counseled and consoled them and was the father none
of them had ever had. He taught them to play basketball
whether they wanted to learn or not because basketball focused the mind, taught teamwork, and was a game they could
play all their lives. Boys into Men gave them a start in the
world.

She went back to bed and pulled the blankets up under
her chin. In the rafters a spider had slung a web between
two beams. Once she would have attacked it with a broom,
but lately she'd lost heart and could not be bothered. It
was easier just not to look at it. Her favorite of Roman's
boys, Donny Crider, had confided once that his mother ob-

sessed about housecleaning. Mrs. Crider supported the two of them by running a day-care center out of their home, and as Donny described it, she followed the children with a damp rag, wiping their fingerprints off the walls and doorjambs. She wouldn't tolerate a cobweb or finger smudge, not one, not anywhere in the house.

The other boys called Donny *pretty girl* and from the kitchen window she had watched them grab their crotches and make kissy-faces at him. Iva had complained to Roman, but he said the taunting would toughen Donny. She thought that was harsh, but if there was one thing her husband knew, it was boys.

"You're awake." Roman entered the bedroom, carrying a tray. "I brought your breakfast."

"I should get up."

"Stay where you are. You've been running yourself ragged lately."

Maybe overwork explained her peculiar mood.

He propped an extra pillow behind her back.

She said, "You didn't come to bed."

"I was up before dawn. Cobb had another nightmare. I found him out on the porch bawling his eyes out."

"Is he okay now?"

"I fixed pancakes and he ate the whole stack, half-asleep. You know how the newbies are. Homesick as all hell, but I don't know for what. His mother's a jailbird." Roman cupped Iva's cheek. "How did you sleep?"

She didn't complain, but he knew. This man knew everything about her.

He chuckled. "I should teach you to play basketball. It'd help you unwind, get the kinks out."

"I was thinking about Donny," she said, deflecting the conversation from herself. "I wish you'd reconsider, Roman. Couldn't you stretch the rules a little this one time? Poor Donny." To have such a selfish mother.

4

One day during the previous week Iva had been supervising the boys while they took a reading comprehension test, a simple two pages about a man and a motorcycle, which she'd let them read and then asked them to summarize for her. Donny Crider had just that week received notification that he had passed his general education exam, the equivalent of high school graduation, and for this reason he no longer attended class but worked a full day in the gardens. It was a significant milestone, and Iva was pleased and proud of his achievement but sorry for herself. He had been the bright spot in her teaching routine.

It was late in the morning of a mild, blustery day and she was dividing her time between the boys in the dining room and making soup in the kitchen when she heard the dogs barking. Looking out the window over the sink, she saw them tugging on their chains as a woman got out of a car, slamming the door. She had smooth dark hair and wore a well-pressed and tailored denim pantsuit, sturdy shoes, and plain gold earrings that gleamed across the yard. Immediately Iva thought she was a real estate agent.

At least once a week, agents dropped by on fishing expeditions, the dollar signs flashing in their eyes as they imagined the vast gardens flattened, dozens of homes and hundreds of apartments rising in their place. She was about to go out and tell the woman that they were not interested in selling when Roman came around the corner of the barn, yelling at Riga and Laz to stop their infernal noise. Donny was behind him. He stopped when he saw the woman.

She ignored Roman. Iva heard her say to Donny, "I told you to be home yesterday. We had an arrangement. I had to leave the sweeties with the neighbor. You know I don't like that. You made me come all the way out here."

Iva hurried onto the front porch. She heard Roman saying hello, saw him smiling. For a moment she wasn't worried.

"It's always a pleasure," he said, "when a boy's family pays us a visit."

"This isn't a social call, Mr. Devane. I'm taking Donny home."

"Oh, I hope you'll reconsider that." Roman had a wide smile and large gleaming teeth. "We've been working on a project. One of the greenhouses has a tear in it, and with a breeze like we've got going today, it's only going to get worse. How 'bout I send him home after we get the job done?" Roman looked over at Donny, who was crouched between the two mastiffs, his hands resting on their muscular shoulders. "You can catch a bus, can't you? Maybe Mr. Gotelli'll give you a ride."

"He didn't tell you, did he?"

"Tell me what, Mrs. Crider?"

"He's through here."

Iva stepped off the porch. "You can't mean that. Why?"

Elena lifted her hand to smooth her hair. On her wrist she wore a watch designed to look like a bracelet. Iva knew that it was gold, like her earrings.

"What's the point? He has his GED."

"He lives here," Iva said.

"His home is with me, Mrs. Devane. It's not that I don't appreciate what you've done for him, but he has responsibilities."

"Mrs. Crider," Roman said, "your son is doing so well at the gardens. He's very talented—"

"At what? Digging?" She laughed. "Donny, come here. Now!"

When Riga and Laz were puppies, Roman trained them using the same kind of obey-me-or-else voice. Donny patted the dogs, and then, as if his legs wouldn't work unless his shoulders led the way, he slouched across the yard. It was not the way he'd walked that morning when he left the house after breakfast to work in the greenhouses or yesterday when he loped out to the truck, his tool belt bouncing on his hip, on the way to set up the fruit stand out on the road. He passed Iva with his eyes down. Behind her, she heard him clomp up the porch stairs and the squeak of the screen door as he opened it.

Elena was saying something to Roman in a lowered voice. Iva hurried closer.

"I don't want to make trouble for you, Mr. Devane. I'd just as soon Donny didn't know anything about this."

"What kind of trouble?" Iva said.

Elena ignored her. "We could have avoided all this if he'd left when he was supposed to, but you know the way he is. Not the most reliable boy."

"He's been a good worker for me, Mrs. Crider."

"I haven't got a complaint in the world," Iva said.

"I'm sorry to see him go. I wish you'd reconsider."

"Please," Elena held up her hand. "I don't want a scene."

"Why would there be a scene?" From the kitchen window Iva smelled the soup she was making, beef with barley. Someone needed to turn down the gas under the pot before it burned, but she couldn't leave the yard.

"I'm a busy woman, Mrs. Devane." As if Iva wasn't, as if she spent her days lolling on the porch. "I need him to help me."

"Will he go to college? At least he should take some courses. He's smart enough and so interested in horticulture. He knows the Latin names of all the plants."

"Really? Well, I'm sure that will take him far." Elena shifted her weight to her hip. "We're not rich, as you know. And I think Donny knows that if he goes to college he'll need to study something more practical than a dead language."

Not thinking, Iva said, "It's not fair."

"I beg your pardon?"

"What my wife means is that Donny is a natural plantsman. I've come to depend on him."

"I'm sure you have." Elena looked back and forth at them,

her chin high and her eyebrows raised. "You're not fooling me. I know what goes on here. How many boys have you got on this property? A dozen? Maybe two dozen? Oh, my goodness, it's quite a little scam, isn't it? I hate to think of all the laws you're breaking."

"What are you talking about?" Iva asked.

"Most of the boys are just scum, aren't they? Dregs? You get them from the courts or the schools and no one cares what happens to them. Then you pay them next to nothing and work them seven days a week. Well, you made a mistake with Donny. He has a mother who loves him. I feel sorry for those other boys, but at least Donny'll be free of you."

"There's nothing criminal going on here." Roman was a large man, big around the middle, wide in the back and shoulders, and as strong as a plow horse. Iva had seen him angry and hoped he'd manage to control his temper this time. There was no truth to Elena's accusations, but she seemed like a woman who would take pleasure in making trouble.

"I could report you to the county or the sheriff. You'd be shut down and lose your business license. I wouldn't be surprised if you were called up on charges of abuse—"

"Abuse!" Iva cried.

"These boys are children and they have rights under the law. You can't use them like slave labor."

It was so outrageous that Iva could think of nothing to say. She looked at Roman.

"Go, Iva. Help the boy pack."

"But, Roman, it's not true. You can't let her say these things."

He walked her to the porch, speaking quietly. "I know it's not true, but she's jealous, Iva. Jealous people say crazy things. She wants her boy back and she knows he doesn't want to leave the gardens."

"Donny's almost eighteen. He has a right to choose."

"You know that, I know that, but she's one of those smother mothers."

"Did you see his face?"

"Of course I did."

"He looked like he was dying."

"But he isn't. And, Iva, believe me, we don't need her kind of trouble. We've got a fine business here and we're doing real good for these boys. Donny's had the benefit of the program. I think the best thing is to let him go."

"He's like our son."

"But Iva, honey, he's not. He's not." He put his arms around her. "That woman's his mother and it's her choice."

"Could he come back after he's eighteen, maybe work for us? He's a natural with plants; you've told me that a dozen times."

"I don't want to cross this woman."

"But we've done nothing wrong!"

"Some people are just mean, Iva. It gives them pleasure to cause pain." He smelled of the soil, of what was strong and permanent and safe. "Go help him now. Let's not prolong this thing."

When Iva entered the little room at the back of the house, Donny stood in the middle of the floor staring at the bed, onto which he'd dumped the contents of his closet and bureau.

"I don't want to go."

"I know." She stood behind him, her hands on his shoulders.

When he first came to the gardens he'd been a scrawny kid, but in the almost two years Iva had known him, hard work and healthy food had built him up.

"Get your backpack," she said, taking charge. "And here are some plastic bags for the rest of your stuff. You're only going across town."

"Can't I stay here? Please?"

"Roman says no."

"I'd work really hard. I could move into the bunkhouse and you wouldn't have to pay me or anything."

"I begged him."

"Roman said no?"

Gently, she turned him around. "Look at me."

His sea-green eyes were awash and his mouth twisted as he struggled not to cry.

"Give it a little time and then come back. I don't know why your mother's so upset, but people have moods. That's probably all it is. Come back in a few months and I'll convince Roman to give you a job. After you're eighteen it won't matter what your mother wants."

He shook his head.

"Donny, you've got your whole life ahead of you. Roman will give you a great letter of recommendation. You'll be able to work anywhere." For his sake, she tried to sound upbeat. "And there's your graduation gift. You've got a hundred dollars coming to you. Put that in the bank. Make it the start of your college account."

"You don't know her. What she's like."

"If you were my boy I'd want you living at home too." Saying this, she felt a sharp sensation in her chest, as if something had taken a bite out of her, and as much to comfort herself as him, she took him in her arms, something she had never done before and never would again.

5

Five days a week Elena Crider's house was full of children, her little sweeties as she called them. Six or eight boys and girls, babies, toddlers, and school age, who came to her for breakfast and often stayed until after dinner. They had grubby little fingers that left prints on walls and cabinetry, shoes that tracked mud across the floor of every room, a body odor that turned her stomach sometimes. Still, with a reliability she considered heroic, Elena had cared for other people's children, rarely missing a day. Year after year. This day was special, however, a holiday to honor Maggie Duarte, her astral sister. The parents of the little sweeties had to make other arrangements.

Years ago, Maggie Duarte had returned to San Sebastian to visit her parents after living for some time in Washington, DC. She and her family had attended the busy ten a.m. Mass at St. Mary and All Angels, where, puffed up with pride, Father Peña stood in the center aisle and announced to the congregation that Maggie was leaving her job in Washington, coming home to California, and running for Congress representing the Central Coast, where she had always maintained her legal residence. Spontaneously, the congregation stood and applauded.

Later, in the parish hall, Elena shook Maggie's hand and wished her success. As their fingers touched, she had looked directly into her eyes. What a moment it had been! Elena had never doubted that Maggie, too, felt the charge between them. Such a powerful connection could not exist in one direction only.

Over the years, Elena had written dozens of letters to the governor, always with news about the town and All Angels. Mostly, though, she wrote of her own life, exaggerating a bit to make it more interesting than it was and to bring a little fresh air into Maggie's pressurized existence. On the birthday they shared, she sent flowers and a special card, and in her notes she reminded Maggie that they shared not only the same special day in April, but very nearly the same *time* of birth. They were astral sisters, she said, and Maggie never contradicted her.

Perhaps today she would acknowledge how much the cards and letters meant to her. She might see Elena in the crowd and introduce her to her family. In turn, Elena would introduce Donny, and the governor's eyes would widen when she saw how handsome he was.

The previous evening after the sweeties had been picked up, she'd gone to the hairdresser and had her hair cut and colored in a way she knew made her look even more like

Maggie Duarte than she just naturally did. Afterward, she'd stopped at Long's Drugs, where the pharmacy assistant who rang up her purchases said the angular cut made her look just like the governor. *You might as well be sisters.* The girl said it without prompting and Elena had pretended to be surprised, but she couldn't resist telling her that she and Maggie had been born under the same astrological sign and only a few moments apart. Maggie was older, of course. They were both Aries.

"You're saying it's your birthday tomorrow, Mrs. Crider? How're you going to celebrate?"

"We'll be at Maggie's party," Elena said, as if she and Donny had been invited to a private affair as well as the festivities in the park.

"You know the governor?"

Elena lowered her eyes demurely. "We keep in touch. She's so busy, of course. You can't imagine the pressure she's under. It never lets up."

"And your son, is he going too?"

"Of course."

Since he was a small boy Donny had been her escort to movies and summer concerts in the park, and when she could afford it, a nice dinner out. She had taught him gentlemen's manners and how to calculate a tip, and she even let him sign the bill sometimes. Her handsome little husband.

Now it was the day of the festivities, and he was saying he didn't care about the governor and wouldn't go.

"What else have you got to do?"

"Stuff."

"What kind of stuff?"

"None of your business."

"You never had such a mouth before you went out to that garden place."

"Let me go back."

"Absolutely not, Donny. I won't consider it. One person in this family has to know what's right. Roman Devane was exploiting you, taking advantage of your strong back, you and the other boys he's got out there. If I wanted to, I could call the sheriff and he'd close the place down. I was looking out for your best interests and someday you'll understand that."

A muscle in Donny's jaw rippled. Elena did not remember ever having seen that before.

She said, "I must be insane to care what happens to you. I should let you go to the devil and be done with it, except that's not the kind of person I am. Not like your father. He walked away from you without a second thought, but I didn't. I could have gone off, I could have had a career, but I knew what was right to do. And I did it. For once I'd like to see a little gratitude."

She changed her tone, wheedling down the sharp edges.

"Why do you have to make everything so difficult, Donny? You know how important this day is to me. You *promised* we would go together. We talked about it weeks ago."

"I never promised."

"Don't contradict me. And why are you wearing that ragged old T-shirt when you've got a closet full of nice things?" A sour, metallic odor came from his body, filling her with disgust. "I hope you'll take a shower before we go."

"I told you—"

"I know what you said, Donny. I have ears. See them here, on the side of my head? Unlike yours, my ears work perfectly well. And I also have a memory. You made a promise to me." She lowered her voice. "You're not a cheat like your father, are you?"

The way his jaw moved, Elena imagined there was something tucked in the pocket of his cheek, something alive that he was going to spit at her.

"It's time you got your priorities straight. You have a family to think about."

"I don't have a family. I have you."

"Go ahead, be as cruel as you like; I know you don't mean it." She patted her pursed lips with her first finger. "Give me a kiss now. Momma needs some kissy-kiss, Donny."

He stepped back.

"You don't need me," he said.

"That's not the point. *I want you.*" She cocked her head to the side and smiled as she thought Maggie Duarte would. "Where do you have to go that's so important?" She grabbed him above the elbow, pinching hard, but he didn't wince. He'd grown strong working at the nursery and shook her off, jarring her arm in its socket. She had never seen such a look on his face, as if she meant no more to him than a night crawler he'd dug out of the earth, as if he could cut her in half with the edge of a spade.

Elena changed her tone.

"Sweetheart, here's an idea. We can meet in the park, by the fountain. That'll give you a little extra time on your own."

At five or six years old he had sneaked out of the house and gone by himself to the fountain in the park. Stripped down to his underpants, he'd left his clothes in a neatly folded pile and jumped in the water. The police had brought him home to her, and it had amused them to tell her what he said when they fished him out, his fists full of pennies and nickels off the bottom. He'd been helping his mama. *Mama doesn't have any money.* They'd all had a good laugh together, but afterward Elena punished him for humiliating her.

She sugared her voice. "It would be much better, though, if you came home in time to shower. If Maggie wants to talk to me—"

"Why would she want to do that? Who the fuck are you to her anyway?"

Elena pretended not to hear his foul mouth. Laying her palm against his chest, she felt heat radiate off his body.

"You look so nice in that blue shirt with the little white stripe. The one I gave you for Christmas? If you'd open your door I could iron it, make sure it's crisp looking, and I'll just bet your good shoes need polishing. I'm happy to do it. Why do you want to have a lock on your door anyway?"

Elena understood that a seventeen-year-old boy typically required some privacy, but Donny was hardly typical, and more to the point, what did he have hidden in his bedroom that he didn't want her to see? He had installed the lock the day he moved home from Roman's Gardens, and neither cajolery nor commands had been enough to make him remove it or even let her in to clean. It was hygiene and not secrets that concerned her.

Beneath her palm, through his grubby T-shirt, she felt his racing heart. Didn't she know her son? Wasn't her boy as clear to her as a bright penny? She heard a soft expulsion of air from his lungs, and his shoulders dropped an inch.

There now, she thought. *That's my good boy.*

"Kissy-kiss, Donny."

6

Sophie wiggled her toes in her expensive new carpet, thinking it was so thick and soft, she could take a nap on it. She thought about the money she'd spent furnishing and decorating this office, and the muscle between her eyes tightened. The salesman had promised her she would never regret the expense, and she didn't, not yet anyway. But money in general worried her.

Like every other attorney she knew, Sophie was still paying off law school loans, and she owed her parents an additional sum for staking her in private practice when she left the prosecutor's office. Joe and Anna had offered to forgive her debt, but Sophie insisted on making a monthly payment. If she didn't she would see disappointment and criticism in her mother's expression for the rest of her life.

Until that afternoon, no one had come right out and criticized her—not directly—but she knew her family thought the new office was extravagant. Carmine's comments were just the beginning. Eventually her mother and grandmother would start in, as if she needed them to tell her it wasn't necessary to have the office suite painted before she moved in or to buy expensive carpeting. She could have lived with vinyl cunningly stamped like knotty pine and area rugs woven in China, designed to look like they came out of Persia on a camel's back. For that matter she could have stayed where she was in the one and a half rooms she had occupied since leaving the prosecutor's office.

She calculated that she had enough cash remaining in checking and CDs to keep the office going for the rest of the year if she was careful. But without a SanSeb crime wave between now and 2011, she would have to start taking divorces and custody cases, the kind of lawyering she had once sworn she would never do. Maybe her family was right. Maybe the chunk of money she'd made from the Cardigan case had made her even more reckless than she naturally was.

Compared to Sophie's family, which had been in SanSeb since the Depression, Orlando Cardigan was a newcomer, one of the entrepreneurs taking advantage of the area's electronics and pharmaceuticals boom. Along De Anza Creek he had built condos and apartments for the population employed by the new high-tech companies, and west of the 101 he had erected rental housing for students at the growing university.

His son, Will Cardigan, aged fifteen, had been expelled from yet another eastern prep school and began hanging with lowlifes. He was arrested and charged with peddling crystal meth for the Bleeker brothers, Darwin, Gaylon, and Junior, a trio of small-time criminals operating from the east county.

At Will's trial Sophie had convinced the jury that the

man who identified him in a lineup was not a reliable witness and that the rest of the prosecutor's evidence was equally flimsy. She had succeeded in shifting the focus of the trial from Will to the Bleekers, on whom neither the sheriff's department nor the SanSeb police had been able to make charges stick in the past.

Though they were believed to be involved in most of the county's small-time illegal activities, the brothers were cautious and media shy. On the few occasions when they required the services of an attorney, they had been represented by a woman from one of Los Angeles's most respected firms. None had ever done time.

After her victory in the Cardigan case, Sophie's friends and family, particularly Carmine and Ben, had warned her that she'd made serious enemies. The Bleekers were unpredictable and clever and could make her life miserable if they chose to.

Bring them on, she had thought, pumped by victory.

She watched Carmine herd the glee club onto the stage. The kids were fidgety and looked small-town hokey in their royal-blue robes and satiny white stoles, Old Glory and the California golden bear flapping in the breeze behind them. Maggie was going to love it. Despite her progressive politics, she was an in-your-face patriot who never missed a chance to wave the flag and talk about what she called All-American Values. Hers was the Technicolor immigrant dream of America, and she wanted Californians to remember it.

Her parents had illegally crossed the border from Mexico,

trudging through the mountains near Tecate and down into San Diego County with Maggie, a nursing infant, papoosed in a bedsheet across her mother's back. Her father had been in some kind of trouble in Mexico, and in pursuit of a new beginning the family had struggled tirelessly. Maggie had picked tomatoes beside her mother in the fields around Santa Susana and strawberries south of Oxnard. Her mother cleaned motel rooms, and on weekends her father worked construction for cash under the table. Eventually they saved enough to buy a truck and a square of land outside SanSeb. They had raised a family there and become citizens when amnesty was offered.

The high school band emerged from a school bus parked at the courthouse corner and wandered toward the bandstand, resplendent in blue-and-white uniforms with red tasseled epaulets. Carmine arranged them in their places and soon the sounds of their tune-up drowned out the mariachis.

Just when it seemed to Sophie that the confusion had reached its tipping point and chaos was inevitable, the band director raised his baton and the musicians launched into a robust Sousa march. The crowd went quiet for a moment and then began cheering the governor's name as she and her husband, Robert Cervantes, and their nine-year-old son, Robert Jr., entered the park accompanied by the bully-chested mayor of SanSeb and members of the city and county councils.

Maggie stepped onto the stage and the crowd burst into the birthday song, which the mayor silenced by lifting his arms and patting down the noise. He talked over the singing until it faded away, accompanied by a few good-natured boos and some laughter.

"Hold on there, folks. Let's not get ahead of ourselves." The sound system squealed and there was another smattering of laughter. "I know I speak for all of you when I say how happy I am to have our very own Maggie Duarte here today to celebrate her birthday, but we want to do this thing right, so before we get on to the party, let's take off our hats, put our hands on our hearts, and honor the country we all love." He signaled the choir director and a moment later a tall girl, her straight blond hair like a golden helmet in the sunlight, stepped to the microphone.

From the depths of Sophie's purse across the room, her cell phone rang.

It was her mother, Anna. "Has it started?"

"Just now, Ma. You should be here. It's huge. Can you hear the singing?"

Sophie switched the phone to speaker mode and held it up. At that moment, the anthem was interrupted by three gunshots in sharp succession. She dropped the phone and ran to the window in time to see the governor collapse. In the park there was a moment of stunned silence, and then the screaming began.

7

In the days that followed, San Sebastian became the focus of state and national media attention. Overnight, the town was full of strangers—the curious, the sympathetic, and the ghoulish. They stood in the park and stared at courthouse corner, the scene of the crime; they pointed to where the boy identified by police as Donny Crider had stood when he shot the governor. Journalists and photographers descended and filled up every hotel and motel room as far north as Atascadero.

On the sidewalks, in offices, coffeehouses, bars, and restaurants, the shooting of Maggie Duarte, the senselessness of the act and its suddenness, was all anyone talked about. Some gossiped that the shooting was a hate crime. Others said terrorism. No one wanted to believe that it had been a random crime, an act of violence without meaning. And how could it happen in San Sebastian, the Garden City of the Central Coast, the best place in the world to live and raise a family? Parents hugged their boys and girls tighter; they locked their doors and kept watch from their windows. They were shocked and ashamed that this tragedy had happened in their town, that a boy from the local high school, apprehended without resistance in the parking lot behind Sophie's office, had put three shots through the heart of San Sebastian.

There was a rumor that he'd said he was sorry, but what good was sorry?

At some point it was noted that in the sliver of time before the second shot, Carmine Giraudo had leapt onto the stage and taken down the blond soloist, who stood frozen, an easy target. He had covered her body with his own and the press called him a hero. His photo appeared on the front page of the *San Sebastian Sentinel* and the second page of the *Los Angeles Times*. It was learned that in his position as head of counseling at SanSeb High School—the irony was stunning—Carmine had advised Donny Crider not to drop out of school when he turned sixteen. The *Times* did a long editorial piece about the link between school dropout rates and gun violence. Carmine was interviewed on television.

A.J. Boyd, one of the nation's foremost defense attorneys, announced that he had been retained to defend Donny Crider. In the space of hours he and his staff moved into a half dozen rooms in the elegant Hayes Ranch Hotel, where he immediately held a press conference to announce that his client would plead not guilty. Ben Lansing told reporters that Donny would be charged as an adult with attempted murder with premeditation and assorted minor offenses. Ben was going for the maximum sentence.

Remarkable in its swiftness, a change came over the town.

Despite all the activity created by the shooting, the streets and shops and particularly the park seemed empty. Wherever Sophie went she thought she heard an echo. When friends met they either wrapped their arms around each other or avoided eye contact as if they, not Donny Crider, had done something shameful.

Maggie would live, the doctors said, but she would never walk again and what recovery she could hope for would take a long time. Some said she would have to resign as governor; others were sure she would eventually be able to perform limited duties, though, of course, that would not be enough. It was a foregone conclusion that the political career of Maggie Duarte was over.

To the residents of San Sebastian, the beneficent spring sunshine felt like a taunt. It was as if nature were daring them to enjoy themselves. The paths and lawns and playgrounds of Mission Park remained eerily vacant, and pedestrians walked the long way around to avoid crossing the courthouse corner. In Sophie's mind the park came to represent the shame the town felt. Litter from Maggie's party—paper cups and napkins and greasy paper plates—spilled onto the grass from the unemptied trash cans. In better times the park department would have quickly dispatched a crew to clean up, but no one seemed to care.

One morning early, Sophie saw from her office window a half dozen dogs ransacking the overflow from a trash can and knocking over others. She could not remember when she had last seen dogs running wild in the park or anywhere in town. She called animal control but they were a long time coming.

8

A few days after the shooting, Elena Crider walked into Sophie's outer office.

"Do you know who I am?"

Sophie, on the floor connecting a new printer, recognized Elena immediately. Her picture had been on the front page of the *San Sebastian Sentinel* several times. She got to her feet, brushing the dust off her pant legs.

"Ms. Crider, let's go into my office. Don't mind the mess." There were still unpacked boxes stacked in one corner. "Obviously, I'm just moving in."

Elena's dark hair was cut in a smooth, angular style that emphasized her broad cheekbones and high forehead. She reminded Sophie of someone.

"I've seen you at All Angels, haven't I?"

"Yes," Elena said, sitting in the chair opposite Sophie, her hands knotted on her lap. "We—my son and I—we've been members for years. Not as long as your people, of course. Everyone knows the Giraudo family."

Too true.

"How can I help you?"

"I want to know where he got that gun. I don't keep a gun. How did he even know how to load a gun?"

She didn't give Sophie time to answer, but went on, re-capping the facts of the case as if they were not well-known to everyone. Donny's first shot had been wild and high; the second hit Maggie in the lower back as she turned to shield her son. The third bored into the dirt to the left of the podium.

"Are you listening to me?"

"I am, Ms. Crider, but I still don't know how I can help you."

"Donny wouldn't hurt Maggie, not on purpose. He knows there's no person on earth I admire more. Or ever hope to. He might as well have shot me." Without pausing, Elena shifted the conversation to herself. "That day, it was my birthday, too. Do you follow astrology, Ms. Giraudo? Well, Maggie and I are both Aries, you know. She was born at 4:03 a.m. I was born at 4:04. She's older than I am, of course, but apart from that, we're almost twins. It's insane to think Donny wanted to kill her."

Sophie remembered her grandmother, Mémé, telling her that she had to listen hard to hear the intuitive voice of her heart, but listen she must, if she wanted to be a good attorney.

Now a flutter of intuition at the base of her throat warned her to be wary of Elena Crider. Sophie recognized her type. She was the witness who would pick anyone out of a lineup before she would admit she didn't remember if the perp was black or white, tall or short.

"You have counsel already, I believe. A.J. Boyd is a fine attorney."

"I fired him." Elena's lips tightened. "All he cared about was getting his face on television. I tried to tell him things—and I do have some things to say, believe me—but he wouldn't listen; he talked right over my words."

"Even so, you might want to reconsider. It's not necessary to like your attorney. The relationship has nothing to do with friendship. Mr. Boyd has years of experience and knows how to handle the media, which will probably be an important factor in this case. He's the attorney who can help your son."

"I saw on the news how you kept that other boy out of jail."

"Will Cardigan was a very different situation."

"I don't care. I still want you."

The State of California versus Donald Crider would be a huge case with plenty of business-generating headlines. It would devour her time and resources. It could make her famous. Sophie sat back and crossed her arms over her chest. She had to think about this. Sophie was no different from any other defense attorney waiting for the big case that would distinguish her. If she turned Elena Crider away, who was to say she'd ever get another opportunity as good?

She trusted her intuition, but it seemed misguided to reject a possible client because his mother put her on edge. Donny Crider couldn't help who his mother was, and in the law, liking and disliking were irrelevant on both sides of the equation. He had the right to solid representation, and Sophie knew she could provide that. She had a total of almost nine years of experience, six in the prosecutor's office trying drug, arson, assault, burglary, and robbery cases. She knew how the courts worked; judges and juries generally liked her.

More important, Donny was precisely the type of client Sophie had entered the law to defend, a young man standing alone before the full power of the judicial system and terrified, regardless of guilt, innocence, or motive.

"You think I can't pay you." Elena rummaged in her leather bag. "Well, here, this is your retainer. I didn't give it to Mr. Boyd."

Sophie looked at the amount on the check. Twenty-five thousand dollars was a drop in what was likely to be a bottomless bucket.

"If it's not enough, I can get more, but I expect you to be frugal."

She could at least try to get him out on bail.

But Elena didn't want this. "I want him to stay in jail."

"Are you afraid of him?"

"Of course not, but I have to be practical, don't I? I operate a day-care center in my home. It's a lot better than most of them because I take good care of my little sweeties. I most certainly do not expose them to killers."

"Your son isn't a killer." She'd never laid eyes on the kid and already she was defending him.

"I'm a realist, Ms. Giraudo. Donny did what he did and now I'll do what I must to hold my life together. My business has to come first. What can I do for him if I'm destitute? The boy will understand."

"Have you seen him yet?"

"People are so quick to judge. And parents, when they think about their children's safety, just a hint of scandal—"

"Have you seen him?"

"No, and I don't mean to."

"His morale—"

"He should have thought about that before he pulled the trigger. He should have thought about me. Since the shooting? I haven't had a single child come to my home. And no one so much as called to say they weren't coming in except Mrs. Belknap and she couldn't wait to hang up. I told her Donny wouldn't be coming home. And I reminded her that he never had anything to do with the care I gave her children, not directly. It's not as if she can find anywhere better in SanSeb. Give them time and they'll be back, begging me to take their children again. And I will, of course. But in the meantime I can't allow even a touch of Donny's crime to soil me."

Gripping her handkerchief in a stranglehold, Elena continued. "I've spent years building a good reputation in this town, and he wiped it out in a moment. Less than that. I just don't understand. Couldn't he have shot someone else? Why Maggie of all people?"

Sophie wondered the same thing.

9

The officer on duty, Kravitz, stood outside the barred door of Donny's cell combing his hair with a neon-green comb.

"You know what I'm doing tonight, Crider?"

Donny, lying on his cot, didn't know or care, but there was no point in saying anything. Less than a week in jail and already he knew to keep his mouth shut.

"First I'm goin' home and I'm gonna take a long hot shower. Wash off the crud of this place, know what I mean? Then I'm taking my girl to Outback for a steak and a big plate of fries. You like fries, Crider? Ever had 'em with mayonnaise? That is some kind of good, lemme tell you. Her and me'll have a couple of drinks, watch some basketball, and then go back to her place and fuck 'til we pass out. You ever fuck a girl, kid, or d'you just like to shoot 'em?" Kravitz laughed as he stuck his comb in his back pocket. "Another day gone and still no visitors. You're so popular in this town, Crider, you must have bird flu."

Donny didn't know how many days he'd been listening to

Kravitz's taunts. He had no clock, and in a world of artificial light, time had no clear edges. Food was his clock. At some point a tray of breakfasty stuff was pushed through a slot in his barred door; later came white-bread sandwiches and then ground meat in a gravy served over rice or mashed potatoes with green beans. Once there had been strawberry gelatin mixed with fruit.

It was never dark in his cell, and for some reason his eyelids no longer shut properly. There was always a line of light below his eyelashes, and the lids quivered. He stared at the acoustic-tile ceiling and tried to ignore Kravitz's voice telling him about a serial killer of children who'd been visited by his mother every day until his execution.

"So what's wrong with you, Crider? How come your old lady don't like you?"

She loves me, Donny thought. *She loves me more than anyone in the world.* She had sacrificed her life for him and he had shamed her. He deserved to be punished. He had it coming. Love and punishment, they went together. She had told him this a thousand times. His father had not punished him, though Donny knew he had done something unforgivable because he never said a word to him on the day he left, not even good-bye.

Donny was three and sitting on the front steps watching Mr. Pucci wash his car across the street. He heard his mother yelling, and after a minute his father came out the screen door and ran down the steps with her behind him. The corner of his suitcase banged into Donny's shoulder. He let out a yelp of pain and his mother told him to shut up, but he couldn't, and she slapped him across the back of the head so his mouth shut hard and he bit his lip. Donny remembered almost nothing of his childhood, but that day when he was three was clear and crisp. He wanted to bang his head into the cell's cement floor until his brains scrambled and he couldn't remember it anymore.

His friend Jenna had persuaded him to find his father up in Salinas. She hadn't nagged him exactly, but she kept saying it was important for him to know his father, and finally he said okay, as much to quiet her as from any compelling desire on his part. Whatever his father had to say to him, Donny knew it wouldn't be good. Jenna told him not to think so much.

"And don't call ahead. Don't make an appointment. Just walk right in. Surprise him and he'll have to see you." She rode in the elevator with him. It was the only time they ever held hands.

Donny would have recognized his father anywhere, in any crowd of men. Looking at Brad Crider in his office was like seeing his own image reflected in a mirror.

"What are you doing here?" Brad pushed aside the papers on his desk and stood up. "What do you want?"

Donny's suddenly parched throat ached and his tongue stuck to the roof of his mouth.

This is your father. This man is your father.

"Is she with you?" Brad sounded breathless. Without waiting for Donny's reply, he left his desk and walked to the office door. Seeing Jenna in the waiting room at the end of the hall, he asked, "Who's that?"

"My friend. Jenna."

"Your mother's not with you?"

He shook his head.

Brad expelled a long breath and closed the door. He leaned against it for a moment, his eyes closed.

He's like me, Donny realized, amazed. All his life he had wondered about his father, how he looked and the kind of man he was. Now he knew. He was a successful business- man; his fancy office showed that. But, like Donny, he was uncomfortable with emotions. He liked situations that were forthright and simple.

"What do you want?"

It was the kind of direct question Donny appreciated, and he knew that he should be able to answer with equal di- rectness. But he couldn't say anything. He didn't know why he'd come except that Jenna had said he should, said it often enough so he finally agreed.

You left me behind. You left me alone with her.

Would it be enough to say that he had come because he was curious about the kind of man who would do that?

"Did she send you for more money?"

"Who?"

"Your mother. Does she want more money?"

Donny had lost track of the conversation.

"She wants to bleed me dry."

She. His mother.

He knew that his father was telling him something, a completely new piece of information.

"You give her money?"

"Of course I do."

"No," Donny said. "You don't."

"Did she tell you different?"

"You're lying."

"You come to my office, don't even say you're coming. I haven't seen you in fifteen years and now you're calling me a liar? Like you know anything at all?"

Your father didn't want you, never wanted you, I've sacrificed and done without all my life so you can have a decent home, but that man's done nothing.

"I've given her eighteen hundred dollars a month since you were three years old."

"You never came back."

Brad's face dropped open like a trapdoor giving way. Two pink spots appeared on his cheeks and his forehead shone with sweat. He looked aside. "It was her; she didn't want me near you."

Be glad you don't know him. He heard his mother speak as if she were in the room, standing at his side. *The man's no good, a weakling. You're better off without him.* He slammed his palms against his ears, but that only made her voice more strident. *You don't need him. You have me, Donny. I'm all you need.*

He left the office without saying good-bye and charged down the hall and across the waiting room to the elevator, where he banged his palm against the down button.

"Donny, you'll break it!"

He couldn't wait for it to come and ran for the stairwell, barreling forward with Jenna behind him.

"Stop, Donny, tell me what happened. Talk to me."

On the drive home she begged him to talk about what had happened, but he couldn't. He tried not to think, but there was nothing he could do to silence the noise in his mind. His father's voice and his mother's chorused inside him, a screaming discord that made him want to open the car door and throw himself out into the traffic if that was what it took to silence them. Eventually the words became indistinct, a dull ache of sound, a blur of noise. Later, when he was alone, he wanted to remember what his father had said, but the memory had broken into bits he could not arrange in a way that made sense. He knew only one thing. He'd been lied to all his life.

Beginning that day, Donny's memory had gotten worse. Whole chunks of time—the day before, a week ago—disappeared as if they had never happened. Maybe he recalled bits and pieces of something for a minute; then the thought vanished or faded in and out, never sticking around long enough for him to get a fix. His memory was like a mosaic now. Bright bits and shiny pieces without a central design or mortar to hold them together. Donny thought this might be what it felt like to go crazy.

When he couldn't sleep, he liked to think about Jenna. They had met in a science class, and she probably never would have noticed him except that the teacher made them lab partners. If she had something she wanted to say, she had a soft, persistent voice, but she listened better than anyone when he talked about being a plantsman and traveling all over the world. She laughed a lot but never at him. He liked her in a way he'd never liked anyone before.

Often he had sneaked out of the house and met her at the Denny's restaurant near the 101. The waitresses kept the fries and soda refills coming while they sat in the back booth and did their homework. Jenna was good in English and history; science was simple for Donny. Jenna said that together they equaled one honor roll student.

His mother called him a potato head, but Jenna said he was smart. Depending on the day, he believed either his friend or his mother. Thinking back over the events of the last week, Donny had to admit now that his mother was probably right. Only a potato head would shoot the governor and not know why. If there was ever a reason, it was in the locked house of his mind, in a locked room, in a locked box inside a locked drawer.

Kravitz left and the night hours passed.

From time to time the night guard checked on him. He always had a dog with him, a big German shepherd with a spiked collar. His toenails clicked on the cement floor, reminding Donny of the way the crickets sounded from his bedroom window at Roman's Gardens. Some of the boys at the gardens were afraid of the Devanes' two big dogs, Riga and Laz, but Donny had always liked dogs. He'd begged for one when he was nine. Elena had taken him to the pound and he thought they were going to get one, but instead she explained that most of the dogs they saw and petted would not live out the month. She said they were victims of boys just like him who had promised to care for them and then had not done so properly. Donny had been aware that she seemed to take pleasure in the details as she described how the animals were crowded in a small windowless room, the door slammed shut, and while they barked to be set free, poison gas poured in on them. She said dogs were innocent creatures that had to be protected from careless boys like him.

Donny supposed that he slept, but he did not feel rested. Breakfast was scrambled eggs so pale they were almost white and a pancake sodden with sweet brown syrup. Kravitz was back.

"Hey, buddy-boy, you finally got a visitor."

10

Sophie was a first-year law student, twenty-two years old and an unpaid intern in David Cabot's San Diego law office, when she attended her first jailhouse interview. The client that day had been a woman with a long, tired face, crisscrossed by lines and yellowed by tobacco smoke. She was accused of vehicular manslaughter, and drunk or sober, she looked mean enough to do what she was accused of: killing her husband's girlfriend with her battle-scarred Jeep Cherokee. Sophie sat a little behind David's associate during the interview, taking notes. Though she tried to appear lawyerly, it was hard to concentrate and harder still to distance herself from the crime the woman had committed.

In the same way, Sophie was distracted by Donny Crider's movie-star good looks. According to the stereotype, a teenaged shooter was supposed to be a pimply geek who lived in his bedroom, glued to a computer, but Donny was a knockout, with a fine, straight nose, smooth olive skin, dark hair—a little long, a little curly—and black-lashed sea-green eyes, accented by thick, straight brows. The kind of kid likely to be pursued by a posse of gawking, doting girls.

The fact that this Adonis had tried to kill Maggie Duarte made the crime even harder to understand.

Ankles chained, his hands cuffed in front of him, he shuffled into the room dressed in the regulation jailhouse uniform, a blue jumpsuit too large for his sapling body. The guard shoved him onto the chair across the table from Sophie, making him stumble.

"Go easy, okay? What's with the ankle restraints?"

"Talk to the boss."

That would be Chief Joe Spiteri, a SanSeb High football hero when Sophie was a ninth grader. Like every other man in town between the ages of thirty and fifty, Joe was a buddy of Carmine's.

Donny stared at the table in front of him, not acknowledging her. She introduced herself.

"Your mother has hired me to defend you. She decided the other attorney, Mr. Boyd, wasn't right for the job."

He nodded, still not looking at her.

"Do you understand that you're being tried as an adult? You can choose your own attorney. You need to understand that. If you want Mr. Boyd—"

"I don't care."

"Well, you should. Wake up, Donny. You're in big trouble."

As an intern with David Cabot and later as a prosecutor, Sophie had worked with a few teenagers. To understand them better she had read books about adolescent development and psychology. She did not expect to get much from Donny in this first interview.

He clicked his thumbnails against each other, a crickety sound. Elena hadn't said anything about him being slow-witted, but, then, she'd been more eager to talk about herself than her son.

"Do you understand the charges against you?"

"I'm not a retard."

"I'll make a note of that."

Sophie reminded herself that if congeniality was what she wanted, she'd be better off teaching first graders. She pulled her electronic notebook out of her briefcase and typed in her password.

"Are they treating you okay?"

"I guess."

"Just so you know, Donny, you've got a few rights. Even if you are in jail. You can take a shower every day. And exercise. I can get you books if you want them."

"There aren't any windows."

"Sorry, I can't do anything about that."

He slumped in his chair and picked at a hangnail.

"Let's talk about your visitors list. I've put your mom on it, of course." Sophie did not believe Elena meant it when she said she wouldn't visit. "Anyone else?"

"She won't come."

He sounded so sure that for an instant she believed him. But no matter how ashamed Elena might be, he was her son. She might make him suffer for a while, but eventually she would come. Murderers, pedophiles, gangland assassins: they all had faithful mothers.

"What about friends?"

He shook his head. Sophie wondered if he was always so reluctant to talk. Quite a contrast to Elena, who seemed to like nothing better than the sound of her own voice.

"No one?"

"Mr. Devane maybe."

"Who's Mr. Devane?"

"Ms. Iva."

"How do you know these people? I have to put something down on the form."

He rested his forehead on the table.

"Are they neighbors?"

"Nope."

"Teachers? At SanSeb High School?"

"Boys into Men."

During the hour they'd spent talking in Sophie's office, Elena had spoken disparagingly about the program Donny enrolled in after he dropped out of high school, but Sophie had called around to social service contacts and heard only good things.

"Tell me about the program."

Donny looked up, and for the first time, there was life behind his eyes. "Roman runs it. You know Roman's Gardens?"

She'd seen the sign about three miles from town on Dry Creek Road.

"She helped—"

"Who is 'she'?"

"His wife. Ms. Iva. She helped me get my GED. Me and her worked together sometimes with the plants. Mostly vegetables. Organic. We sold 'em at the stand out on Dry Creek."

He showed a little animation when he spoke of Iva Devane. Handsome boy, farm woman. Sex behind the fruit stand? Was it possible in real life or only in the movies? And if it was true, what did it have to do with the case?

"You like her."

He clicked his nails.

"You *don't* like her?"

He clicked his nails.

After years of questioning clients and witnesses, Sophie had known all kinds. Some couldn't stop talking. To get them going, she had only to look receptive. Some needed a question or two, but for a few, like Donny, the sullenness ran deep.

"Why didn't you just stay in high school? Why'd you join Boys into Men?"

"It's not like the army. You gotta get admitted."

Donny had felt special because of Boys into Men. Was that why Elena was so averse to the program? Was she jealous?

"Why'd you leave school?"

He ducked his head away from her as if embarrassed. "I like plants."

"Okay."

"He was teaching me. To be a plantsman."

"You mean a gardener?"

"You're like my mother," he said, glaring. "You don't know anything. A plantsman doesn't dig around or weed or stuff like that. I mean, he can, but it's not the main thing; anybody can do that. *You* could do that. A plantsman really knows stuff. Soil chemistry, the Latin names of plants and how they're related to each other in, like, families. Flowers and bushes and all, from everywhere. Even China."

"It's not a word I've ever used."

"Anyone can be a gardener."

"If you were so happy at Roman's Gardens, why'd you leave?"

"Who told you I did?"

"Your mother."

He pressed his lips together.

"Donny?"

"Can I go now?"

"Why did you leave the program?"

Carmine had once told her about a boy he'd counseled who could sit in the chair opposite him and not speak a word for a whole hour. Sophie didn't have the patience for that.

"Okay, listen up. The district attorney has charged you with attempted murder. That carries major time." She watched his face for a reaction and saw none. "By the time we get to the preliminary hearing, he's going to hang so many other charges on your case, it'll look like a Christmas tree. He wants to put you away for a very long time, and I think he can do it. More than a thousand people were in the square. They saw Governor Duarte get hit. The police apprehended you in the parking lot with powder burns on your fingers. You let them arrest you. You weren't even running when they got to you. It's in the police report that you said you were sorry. Do you remember saying that?"

He brought his cuffed hands up to his forehead, pressing the heels against his eyes.

"I'm the only chance you've got, so you better talk to me. Why'd you do it?" He shrugged. "Did someone tell you to do it? Who told you to shoot the governor?"

"Nobody."

"You did this on your own, then? It wasn't someone else's idea?"

"I said already."

"Where did you get the gun?"

The apple in his throat moved up and down as he swallowed. "Took it."

"From where?"

"Him. Mr. Devane."

"Where was it when you stole it?"

"I forget."

It was such a bald lie, she would have laughed if she hadn't been sick of trying to get anything out of Donny Crider.

When Donny first started at Boys into Men, there had been a bumper crop of plums at Roman's Gardens, and hundreds of them hung heavy on the trees, weighing down the branches. Those that had fallen smelled winey and swarmed with yellow jackets. Roman had dispatched a picking crew, but they couldn't do it fast enough, and those that fell split and lay in the dirt and the heat of the sun. The wasps flew in circles, drunk on fermented juice.

Ms. Iva had asked Donny to help her make plum ketchup to sell at the fruit and vegetable stand. They'd stayed up most of the night cutting and then cooking down the fruit, stirring the sugary syrup constantly so it would not catch and burn. Next morning he was up at seven hauling brush with the other boys. By dinnertime he was too tired to hold his head up.

He felt like that now, sitting opposite the lawyer, listening to her talk about what would happen to him. He wished she would come right out and say the truth. That his life was over. He would never travel to China or up the Amazon in search of new plant varieties. He'd never own a nursery or go to college to study botany. He'd probably never even dig in the dirt again or feel the sun on the back of his neck.

He might as well be dead.

Sophie wondered what thoughts were going through Donny's mind that made him look so resigned.

"Did you steal the ammunition too?"

"The gun was loaded already."

Roman Devane kept a loaded gun in a house full of boys.

"Where was it?"

"I don't remember."

Bullshit.

"Why did you want to kill the governor? Were you making a political statement?"

"I don't even know what that means."

"Are you angry at the government, Donny? Are you a terrorist?"

"Me?"

"You, Donny, I want to know about *you*. You have to help me or I can't help you."

"Why?"

"Why what?"

"Why do you want to help me?"

The truth was that she didn't want to, not in her heart. But he deserved a fair trial no matter what his crime. She told him this.

"You liked what you were doing with Mr. Devane. You had your GED. You had a bright future as a *plantsman*. It doesn't make sense for you to steal a gun and ruin it all."

On the day Sophie's father supervised the planting of his olive trees, she had joked about how small they were. "Will any of us be around to see them bear fruit?"

"Gardeners are patient people, Sophia. And optimistic. We believe in long life and a productive future."

She recounted the exchange to Donny. "If you're a real plantsman, it doesn't make sense to throw everything away. You must have had a really powerful motive."

His eyebrows came together as he studied the tabletop.

"Why did you do it, Donny?"

"I don't know."

"And another thing that doesn't make sense. The *way* you did it. Why would you plan the shooting but not your getaway? You must have known there were cops and security guards all over the place. It's like you planned on getting caught. Did you hope they'd shoot you? Is that what you wanted? Did you want to die?"

He rolled his shoulders forward and back, his head from side to side.

"You've got to give me something to work with."

"I'd win then?"

"Win? You want a trial?" She had to be honest with him. "Donny, there's no point in it. Any jury, anywhere, is going to find you guilty. The evidence is overwhelming. And one day the gun's going to turn up and it'll have your fingerprints on it. There was powder on your right hand. You're right-handed, aren't you?"

He nodded.

"Let me walk you through how it happens in the real world, okay?" She measured each word so there would be no misunderstanding. "If we go to trial, I can't pull a rabbit out of the hat. The evidence against you is so strong that you're for sure going to be found guilty. You could spend most of the rest of your life behind bars, Donny. That's the truth."

"I don't want to go to jail."

"You're already in jail. Enjoy it. You're headed for prison, and this place is a five-star hotel compared to that. If you want a trial, it's your right to have one. I'm your attorney and I'll give you the best I've got. But *as* your attorney, I would strongly advise against it."

She had taken his case because she believed in every de-fendant's right to the best possible defense and because she knew what it was like to be powerless, with no one to defend you. Even if he was surly and uncommunicative, it was Sophie's job to see that his rights were served.

"At your arraignment Mr. Boyd entered a plea of not guilty. In a few weeks we'll go before a judge again. The prosecutor will show the judge why he thinks you should be tried; he'll present evidence and maybe some witnesses as well. I can tell you, he's got everything he needs. He wants to go to trial. He wants to be a hot shot and grab headlines. He thinks you're going to *make his career*. Before that happens, I believe you'll want to change your plea to guilty. If you do that, I can go to the prosecutor and bargain for a lesser charge."

He wasn't looking at her; his attention was fixed on the ceiling. She couldn't tell what he was thinking or if he was even listening to her anymore.

"Tell me why you shot the governor. What do you have against her?"

"You already asked me that."

"And you already didn't answer." She waited. "Had you ever met her?"

He shook his head.

"Your mother feels really connected to her."

Now he nodded.

"Do you feel connected to her too?"

He blinked and squinted at her. Between rows of black eyelashes, his green eyes shone like sun-spangled water under the fluorescent lights.

"She's politically progressive. Is that what bothers you? "

He shrugged again. One time too many as far as Sophie's patience was concerned.

"What does that mean? That shoulder thing you do? Either answer me or don't, but quit shrugging." She wanted to give him a good shake. "This is your life we're talking about here, Donny. Are you actually saying you don't know why you shot her?"

He shrugged again.

She tossed down her pen. "You really don't want to have this conversation, do you?"

Violence did not just happen. Sophie knew there was always a reason. Unless she had met the one-in-ten-million exception to the rule. And maybe pigs could not only fly but haul a banner across the sky announcing *Free Bacon for All*. Motive was in the interview room with them. Sophie felt it dodging in and out of their conversation.

She stood up. "One thing about me you ought to know. I'm stubborn and I'm going to keep coming back here every day, asking the same questions. Eventually you're going to have to talk to me."

"Okay."

"What's that mean? Okay what?"

He shrugged.

11

It was five p.m., dinnertime. Iva clanged the iron bell hanging from a hook outside the kitchen door, feeling as she always did, like Auntie Em in *The Wizard of Oz*. How was it that she had gone from youth to middle age as seamlessly as one movie scene bled into the next? Here she was at the end of the day, forty-one years old, as frumpy and drab as a black-and-white movie. She rang the bell again, harder, and from somewhere near the greenhouses a voice yelled a response.

The bell signaled the town boys that their day was over. Some would be picked up at the end of the driveway; others walked a mile and a half to the bus stop. Mr. Gotelli and the other men employed by Roman had left for the day a half hour earlier, and she had already sent dinner out to the boys who lived in the bunkhouse. By five fifteen, Roman's Gardens would be quiet.

After clearing away the litter of that afternoon's home class, Iva had set the dining room table, leaving empty Donny Crider's place next to Roman. When she thought of the shooting and how he would pay for it with the years of his life, the tragedy of it took her breath away. Half a dozen times that afternoon she had wanted to sit down and never get up again. Soon Milo, a tall boy with the tattoo of a cross between the index and middle fingers of his left hand, would also be gone, but she wouldn't miss him. He had recently taken and failed the test for his GED, afterward showing no inclination to try again. He brushed off his failure and joked about his ignorance, letting everyone see that he didn't value the opportunity offered him by Roman and Boys into Men. For this alone Iva disliked him.

Donny had passed the test easily. Not only was he intelligent and a gifted plantsman; he was a kind boy, willing to help where the others would rather play basketball or hang out in the clubhouse. Shooting Maggie Duarte had been an act of violent stupidity, in no way like the beautiful boy Iva knew.

The boys washed their hands at the spigot outside the back door and filed through the kitchen into the dining room, taking their assigned seats at the table, with Roman at the head like the father of the family. Milo came in rubbing his hands on his grimy jeans to dry them. He went immediately to the place that had been Donny's. As he was about to sit, Roman shook his head and pointed to the end of the table, then offered Donny's place to Cobb, the newest boy. Milo tried not to show that he cared, because if the other boys knew, they would rag on him. The teasing that went on among the boys was merciless, and it took all of Iva's self-discipline not to intervene.

To be accepted into the program, a boy had to be sixteen.

Cobb, short and narrow shouldered, looked like a bewildered twelve-year-old, with blond curls and canted blue eyes empty of expression.

Roman told him, "This is your seat now, son."

At the end of the table, Milo clenched his fist around his knife, but when Roman asked him to say the grace, he let it go and bent his head respectfully. In Roman's presence the boys behaved themselves or they didn't last long. During class they were respectful and obedient enough, but beneath their superficial good manners, Iva sensed an undercurrent of nastiness sloshing among them. It floated in their eyes, and she heard ripples of it in their laughter. Still they tried to stay on her good side, for all she had to do was complain to Roman and an hour later a boy would be out on the road thumbing a ride home. No GED, no certificate of completion or letter of recommendation from Roman, no better off than he'd been the day he came to the gardens.

She set the big casserole dish full of chicken, pasta, and vegetables on the table in front of Roman.

"What have you made for us tonight, honey?"

As far as Iva knew, Roman had never been farther east than Merryville, Arizona, but he spoke like a man who had spent his life working livestock in west Texas. It was a friendly kind of speaking, he told her. *Boys are drawn to it.*

"Chicken fricassee."

The boy on Roman's left snickered. In their rooms that night they'd be calling it chicken fuckasee and laughing like jackasses.

Roman addressed the boys at the table. "Y'all listen up.

When the time comes for you to get married and settle down, I want you to recollect Ms. Iva here. Lemme tell you boys, Ms. Iva's the kind of woman you want for a wife."

Iva blushed. She knew the images that were running through their overheated imaginations.

At first she had argued against having boys live with them in the house. That was a time when, despite the doctor's discouraging words, she had still hoped they might have children of their own to fill the many bedrooms. Roman reminded her that the world was full of needy boys hungry for a chance to grab the carousel ring. Of course, he was right, and in the time since that conversation, dozens of boys had lived in the big house with them. The years passed in the independent way they did, like guests slipping away from a party unnoticed, until you looked around and the room was empty.

She was happy to eat her own meal in the kitchen while Roman quizzed the boys on what they'd learned that day. The kitchen was her favorite room, and next to gardening, cooking was her favorite occupation. When she was growing up, her father had prepared the same meals over and over: hot dogs and hamburgers, canned spaghetti, and a mélange he called "gravetta" made of ground hamburger, onion, and frozen peas, thickened with a little flour and water and served over instant mashed potatoes or boil-in-a-bag rice. Her father seasoned gravetta with a product called Accent. Many years later Iva learned that it was this ingredient, monosodium glutamate, that had so often given her a headache in the evening. Her own food was seasoned with salt and pepper and the herbs and spices she grew herself. She still had migraines, but there was nothing she could do about them.

Fog had crept up the long wedge of sloping land between San Sebastian and Mars Beach and now it hung over the gardens like Spanish moss. On summer evenings Iva liked to work outside for an hour or so before bedtime. The year before, Donny had been a great help when every tomato, bean, and zucchini ripened at the same time. This year he had helped her transplant tomato seedlings, cupping them in his palm and murmuring as he placed them in the cultivated earth. *You'll be fine here, you'll like this garden.*

After dinner Roman and the boys went out to the clubhouse.

"You make them study," she called as they crossed the yard between the house and barn. "I'm giving them a spelling test tomorrow and I expect everyone to pass. That means you, Milo."

In the upstairs room that served as Roman's office she rewrote and transcribed his handwritten blog and posted it on the Boys into Men website. It was her job to make sense of his jumbled logic and misused words. His punctuation was so individualistic, it made her laugh out loud to see the way he used a semicolon. She read the finished product through to herself and felt a sense of satisfaction that she had made his meaning clear. As much as she might sometimes yearn for a traditional family life, she was proud of what they were accomplishing together. As he said in his blog, they were making a difference in the world, one boy at a time.

She filled out a bank deposit slip and put it and several checks in her wallet, looking forward to the next day's errands. She had never been particularly gregarious and a quiet life suited her, but she tried to get away from the boys for an hour or two every day. Almost always she had a good reason to go into town as she would tomorrow, but sometimes she just drove to Mission Park and watched the people.

The park was the center of life in San Sebastian, the scene of high school graduations, weddings, fairs, and countless play dates. Iva didn't like to admit it, feeling disloyal to Donny, but he had ruined the park for her and for everyone.

By the time she had finished working in the office, Roman was already in bed, propped against her pillows as well as his own, reading one of the many e-mailed newsletters she printed out for him every week. He looked up and smiled as she began to fold the clean laundry she had dumped earlier in the day from a basket onto a chair where she would not be able to ignore it.

"I think it'd take another Hurricane Katrina to stop your forward progress, Iva. What I said about you to the boys tonight? I meant every word." He patted the bed. "Take a breather. Sit beside me."

"If I sit, I'll collapse."

"I've been watching you, taking you in. Are you not feeling well?"

"I'm fine, Roman."

"Is there something troubling you?"

It was as if there were a space inside her waiting to be filled, a hollow dug into her being, waiting for something to be planted.

"I'm fine."

"I reckon you're still fretting about Donny. We all are. I know the boys keep asking why he did it, and I hardly know how to answer them. Who'd have thought a quiet boy like him would have that violence inside."

"You think?"

"Well, don't you? He shot Duarte. And I'm pretty sure he used my gun to do it."

She stopped folding. "Yours?"

"Now, don't take that tone, honey. We're just talking here, husband to wife. I didn't want to tell you, but around the time he left, my revolver went missing."

"Roman, I've told you I don't think there should be guns in the house."

"It's a right we have, and you know what happens when we don't—"

"And you certainly don't need to teach the boys how to shoot."

"It's part of being a man, Iva, knowing how to manage firearms. Feeling comfortable around guns, knowing they can protect themselves. It gives the boys confidence."

She knew that arguing was a waste of breath, for on the subject of guns, Roman was adamant. He taught the boys to box and wrestle, to play basketball and shoot a gun. It was all part of the program.

She said, "It's lucky his aim was terrible."

"Well, now, that's the peculiar thing. Donny was a good shot."

"Even luckier, then." She picked up a sheet and put it down again. "Did you report it stolen?"

"Immediately. Police'll find it somewhere, and then I suppose we'll have cops all over the place asking questions."

"But you didn't do anything wrong, Roman."

"I'm not worried, Iva. You shouldn't be either."

The fog withdrew to the coast and a pearl moon climbed the sky, lighting the bedroom with a white glow. Iva loved the garden year-round, at all hours, but in the growing season it was best after dark, when the soil released its fragrance and the cool air gave heart to the plants so they stood taller and straighter than they did in the heat of the day. Donny had come upon her once, down on her knees picking worms off the tomatoes, dropping them into a bucket of water.

"I saw the light," he said, indicating the miner's hat she wore. "I thought someone was stealing vegetables."

"You should be in your room. Why aren't you asleep?"

"Moon's too bright."

"You better get back where you belong."

"Before I came here, I used to help the man across the street in his garden. Sometimes at night."

"Bet his garden wasn't as big as mine." Almost an acre of edibles laid out in lines as straight as notebook paper.

"It was peaceful same as this."

She wondered why a boy Donny's age wanted to be peaceful, but she let his comment go. The next night she stayed in, but the one after that, just before sunup, she found him on his hands and knees with a bucket and trowel.

"It helps to stir up the soil a bit," he told her. "That's where they hide."

"Roman's going to be so mad—"

"You won't tell him. Will you?"

She never did.

12

Before they heard it on the evening news, Sophie wanted to tell her parents that she was representing Donny Crider.

She had been thirteen and in the eighth grade at All Angels Academy when her family moved from the apartment over the market to the house where her parents still lived. Its advantages were proximity to the market and half an acre facing southwest, perfectly suited for the olive grove Joe wanted. A year ago, he had decided to devote himself to the trees full-time and turned the market over to his brother, Delio. It was one of the rare times Sophie could remember when her father took a stand against Anna and refused to budge or compromise.

At the back of the house, she parked the 4Runner next to her father's truck and entered the kitchen from the laundry room, as all the family did. Only strangers came through the Italianate formal garden and rang the bell at the front of the house, where the heavy drapes were kept drawn every day, all day, for fear the sun might fade the upholstered furniture on which people rarely sat and no one ever felt comfortable. The remodeled back of the house was where the family lived, in the kitchen and family room.

Anna Giraudo, small and trimly built, with dark springy hair and large eyes the color of strong coffee, was drying dishes from a rack beside the sink. She stared at Sophie as if she didn't know her.

"Holy Mary, Mother of God. What were you thinking?"

"Hi, Ma. I'm fine, thanks."

"Carmine's up in the trees telling your father now." She crossed herself. "Pray God, he doesn't have a heart attack."

Carmine and Joe were helping the arborists with the last of the yearly pruning required to let sunlight into the heart of the trees. The huge fees charged by the arborists meant that Joe Giraudo's small olive oil business would never see a profit, but if the trees made her gentle father happy, Sophie thought it a small price to pay.

He wasn't a businessman and had never wanted to own a market, but as the eldest boy in the family, he had inherited it when Joe Sr. died: a corner store then, a cramped little mom-and-pop. It was Anna who loved the business, and under her guidance it had expanded by many hundreds of square feet to become an essential part of northside life. Delio, Joe's baby brother, ran it now with the help of his wife and boys.

"You couldn't call?" Anna asked. "You wanted to hit me with a two-by-four?"

"I'm here now, aren't I?"

"You'd do this just to get your name in the paper? You need clients. Carmine tells me that."

"My brother has a big mouth."

"Forget Carmine. Remember: I spent my life in business. I see what I see, Sophia, and I put what I see together. One thing plus one thing equals another thing. You got a fancy new carpet in your new office, but you still drive that old truck. Just now, I knew you were coming. I heard you a block away. If you were making money, you'd get a new carpet *and* a decent car."

"I love the 4Runner. I'm never getting rid of it."

She'd been in the house for five minutes and already the walls were closing in.

"Carmine says Ben's going to throw the book at your client. Good riddance."

"He's a boy."

"That's how you defend him? You want a boy killer out on the street? I'm telling you, Sophia, no one's going to speak to you if you do this. They probably won't speak to me either. What kind of a daughter did I raise?"

"Gotta go, Ma." She put her hand on the doorknob. "I only came by to—"

"Don't be such a prima donna, for goodness' sake. Stop trying to escape."

"I'm not trying to escape."

"Listen to what I'm saying. Maggie Duarte might be governor, but she's a friend, too. Even a lawyer doesn't turn her back on a friend. Or maybe they do but they shouldn't. Maybe that's why nobody likes them. And this isn't a big city. This is a town, your hometown. There are things you just can't do."

"Stop right there, Ma. She's not your friend. You haven't seen Maggie since Orlando Cardigan bought the farm and turned it into condos."

"That one! Another friend of yours. What is it about these creeps that you like so much?"

"Will Cardigan was found innocent."

"Yeah, rich man's son."

"He was a patsy, Ma. I proved that to the jury. It was the Bleeker brothers—"

"Then why aren't they in jail?"

"They will be, Ma." She had wondered herself why the police were moving so slowly when Will Cardigan had given them valuable, damning information about the Bleekers' drug operation. "These things take time."

"If I were you, I'd put double locks on my doors."

"If someone wanted to get me—"

Anna chuffed, blowing a puff of air out from between her closed lips. "Like the circus guy said, 'There's one born every second.'"

"Minute. 'There's one born every minute.' And it was P.T. Barnum."

"Well, now I know why we sent you to college."

After thirty minutes of listening to Anna, Sophie ached all over from holding back a scream.

Following law school she had been tempted by a great job offer from her mentor, David Cabot; but ignoring what she knew about Anna, that she was a dynamo both urgent and continuous in her control and criticism, and believing that she had outgrown her renegade spirit and could live happily in the same town with her mother, Sophie had allowed the pull of family, old friends, and community to draw her back to SanSeb. She loved her family, even gossipy Carmine, the many overbearing aunts and uncles, nephews, nieces, and cousins who were in and out of the house all week. She had returned to SanSeb to be present for all the celebrations and crises and hiccups of their lives and to see how their stories played out.

On the kitchen counter, Carmine had left two bags from Joe's Northside Market. Anna grabbed cans of soup and beans out of them and slammed them onto the pantry shelves. Sophie lifted out a half gallon of milk and opened the refrigerator. Anna took the carton from her, shoving her aside with her hip as she did.

"You don't put things in the right place."

No question about it: domesticity brought out the worst in her mother.

Anna had been the first person into the market in the morning, out on the dock ordering vendors around, and almost always the last to leave after tidying her desk and touring each aisle to check the temperature gauges in the odd assortment of coolers and freezers installed over the years as the market expanded and adapted to the growing and increasingly sophisticated northside neighborhood. It had been dark when Anna came upstairs to the apartment, and if the family had depended on her for dinner, they would all have starved.

Sophie's grandmother, Mémé, had been the family's live-in cook and cleaner, a job she relished because it put her in charge of the kitchen, the heart of the family. They had eaten well in those days, for Mémé put nothing on the dinner table that was not delicious. If she had to, Anna could cook a meal, but she complained the whole time.

"Why don't you get a job, Ma? Get out of the house. All Angels Academy can always use a volunteer." Sophie was amused by the thought of Anna making life miserable for the little girls in sky-blue and navy uniforms. She draped her arms across her mother's shoulders and pressed her forehead against hers. "Everyone in town knows you. There's a dozen places you could work. Or you could learn about olives."

"Olives." Anna pushed her away. "I know enough about them already."

"You're young, Ma. Not even sixty."

"Good as."

"And you've got more guts than anyone I know."

"The words you use."

Sophie laughed. "I give up. You win; your life is over. I'll stop at Carboni's on the way home and order your coffin."

"You make jokes, but just wait, it'll happen soon enough."

And so it went.

Sophie was walking out to her car when she encountered her brother coming around the side of the garage.

"Hey," he said, "Dad's trees are doing great. You should go take a look."

"You couldn't wait." Sophie stood with her hands on her hips. "You had to rush up here with your big news."

"I wasn't rushing. I was on the way home."

"And you made a little detour."

"I always bring groceries."

"Whatever. Who told you?"

"Guy at the jail told Ben; he called me."

In San Sebastian, Sophie could not move without someone reporting on it.

"Where do you get off telling Mom I'm defending Donny for the publicity? That is so out of line."

"It's true, isn't it?"

"Are you serious? You think I'm that kind of lawyer? And even if it were true, it's none of your business."

"It's family, Sophe. If you'd for once come out from behind that wall—"

"I am not defending him for the money. Got it? Okay?"

"Okay, okay. Shit, you're a bad-tempered broad." Getting into his Honda, he said, "Go see Dad. Show some interest in his trees. Act like you care." He slammed the door before she could think of a comeback.

Joe was washing his hands at the spigot outside the shed where he stored his tools and to which he often retreated to avoid his wife when she was in one of what he called her "presidential" moods. His expression brightened when he saw her and immediately Sophie felt guilty about not visiting more often.

"Sweet girl," he said and kissed both her cheeks. "Are you staying for dinner?"

"I've got to go back to the office, Dad. I just wanted to see how you're doing."

"I'm fine, the trees are fine. The arborist is a pirate."

She laughed. "What else is new?"

They walked toward the house along a pea-gravel path bordered on either side by lavender bushes humming with bees.

"How're you doing for oil, Sophia? I've got some of last year's left."

"I still have half a bottle, Dad."

He shook his head in mock concern. "That's not a good sign."

"You know me; I don't cook much."

"I'm surprised you haven't moved a bed into that new office. You'd save gas money. Retire that old wreck."

Even her father, as mild as he was, could not keep from voicing his opinions regarding her lifestyle; but his comments were easier to take than either Carmine's or her mother's.

"Carmine told you?"

"He did."

"Ma wants me to bail on this kid. Is that what you want too?"

Sighing, he stopped on the path and brushed his palm over the lavender so the smell of the flowers filled the air.

"What I want is for my girl to be happy."

"And I am. Happy."

"You're busy. You're committed. You're ambitious." He pulled down on the brim of his baseball cap, keeping the sun out of his eyes. "I don't know, Sophia, is that the same as happy?"

13

Sophie's ex was sitting on the front steps of the condominium that had been her share of their divorce settlement.

"I almost gave up," Ben said. "It's after ten. Where've you been?"

She'd gone back to the office after seeing her parents and, as was often the case, lost track of the time.

"Thanks a lot for blabbing to Carmine." In the kitchen she opened the freezer and put a bottle of vodka on the bar. "Help yourself."

"Can I smoke?"

"You always ask me that and I always say the same thing."

"You used to smoke."

"I used to do a lot of things."

They'd been married for five years, but she'd never been tempted to tell Ben much about the years before they met.

He grabbed two glasses and walked ahead of her across the living room. At the time of their divorce, she had directed him to take what he wanted, and he had surprised her by wanting a lot. In the three years since, she'd had neither time nor sufficient inclination to replace the love seat and coffee table. On the walls, which were in need of painting, she still saw the outlines of his framed NASA photos of galaxies a jillion miles away. On the dining room table he'd been good enough to leave her, several days' worth of mail lay in piles beside a half-full glass of water and a coffee cup from that morning. Or the morning before.

The condo was built on a slope, its front entrance and garage at ground level. A wide deck at the back extended over the hillside down to Peligro Creek. In the summertime Sophie and Ben had lain in bed listening to the bullfrogs. Tonight the fog was so thick they couldn't see the cottonwoods and sycamores that grew along the banks of the creek, and the frogs were silent.

"Why are you here, Ben?"

With the cigarette clamped at the corner of his mouth, squinting to avoid the smoke, he poured a vodka shot and handed her the bottle. "I never should have let you have this place."

Ben was one of those smokers for whom smoking was a sensual pleasure as much as an addiction. He inhaled and let the smoke out slowly, watching it cloud before him or drawing it back in through his nose. It irritated Sophie almost to distraction, the luxurious pleasure he took from poisoning himself.

"It's a good spot," he said, "but you're vulnerable. A woman alone, not even a dog. On a night like this someone could come up from the creek..."

She had thought about getting a dog but didn't want the responsibility. Sophie liked to think of herself as free to come and go, though in fact she hadn't taken a vacation since her friend Tamlin had convinced her to fly to Cabo to celebrate her divorce.

Ben was talking about alarm systems, a security guard, and a case in Monterey County involving an accused rapist, but Sophie had tuned him out. She was remembering the vacations her family took when she was a kid. Neither of her parents had cared to be away from the market for long, so they went for holidays to Swiss, a wide spot in the road a few miles north of Mars Bay where they rented a house across the highway from the beach. They had done this every year in August for two weeks. And every day Anna or Joe would drive back to SanSeb to check on things at the market and return with deli food for dinner.

"When you took on Donny Crider, you made yourself a world of enemies."

"So I'm told."

He tossed back his drink and poured another. "Why'd you do it, anyway? To piss me off?"

"That's all I ever think about, Ben."

"Sarcasm is verbal aggression. I learned that in a psychology class. Dr. Willets. He had a glass eye."

"So you've told me." Many times.

"This isn't going to help your career. After we lock him up, you'll be stuck defending nothing but drug addicts and wife beaters. You'll never get the slime off you." He continued in this vein. Again she tuned him out.

They were the same age, thirty-five or nearly, but cigarettes and irascibility had lined Ben's face prematurely. He was going to look permanently grumpy in a few years. By then he would be a judge with no need to charm juries. Laying down the law came to Ben as easily as breathing, making him a natural for the bench. He was also stubborn and controlling. Tamlin had once pointed out that when Sophie married him, she had married her mother plus testosterone. Since their split Sophie had tried to move him to the fringes of her life, but SanSeb's legal community was a small one and Ben was like one of the sycamores along the creek. Even after a long drought, he wouldn't budge.

Over the years of their marriage, Ben had grown too sure that he was one of the good guys, one of the *few* good guys. Paranoia had crept into his thinking, and a jaw-jutting, them-against-us attitude that helped his career but not his personality. To get away from him and because it was easier to work on the law than go home to a man she felt trapped with, two cats in a cage, Sophie had stayed late at the office. On three or four occasions she'd found company away from home, with strangers. She wasn't proud of breaking her vows and knew the marriage had failed in part because she didn't bother to make it work. She still felt guilty, which helped explain why she couldn't just turn him out and send him home.

He crushed his cigarette under his heel and put the butt on the table between them. He'd done that when they were married, left little piles of crushed cigarettes on the deck for her to clean up. Sophie was so glad not to be married to Ben

Lansing anymore; there were no words to express how glad she was.

"I'm here to tell you that I'm not going to deal on this one, Sophe. I'm going to charge the SOB with everything I've got. I know you don't like him any more than I do and you're only defending him because you've got highfalutin liberal ideas about the law. But if you're planning on a plea, forget it." He leaned forward and she smelled the cigarettes on his breath. "Maggie's our girl, right? Nobody shoots our girl and gets away with it."

In the beginning arguing had been part of the chemistry between them, a kind of verbal foreplay. They were well-trained lawyers and disputation was their comfort zone, so every disagreement was a challenge in which each had believed there was a chance to bring the other around. Occasionally that happened, but not often enough. As it turned out, their differences were too basic. By the time they separated, neither could admit when the other was right.

"I'm just going to ask you to be humane, Ben."

"Like he was to Maggie? He's a fucking assassin." He reached for the vodka again.

She stopped his hand. "Go home. Please."

"You're giving up that easy?" Grinning, he took the bottle back and poured what was left of it. "When I'm done with your kid, he won't get out until he's drawing social security."

"If you won't deal, I'll take it to a jury. He's an appealing kid." She was bluffing, but he was easy to mislead. He couldn't read her tells; he told friends she didn't have any.

"The jury'll be out for ten minutes," he said.

"I'll bring in every expert who ever wrote for *Science* magazine. I'll find character witnesses and show baby pictures. I'll have the jury bawling before I'm through, Ben. You know I can do that."

He flicked his tongue against his lower teeth, a mannerism that told her he was not as confident as he wanted her to believe. She'd seen it in trials and in poker games when he was deciding what to do with a mediocre hand.

"You wanna have a pissing contest?" He stood up and pretended to open his fly. "Just hang it over the railing and show me what you got."

"You're drunk. Go home."

"I'm being your friend here, Sophe. You're going to need all the friends you can get when you've alienated ninety-nine percent of the town."

"Only ninety-nine?"

"You need someone to keep an eye on you. Let me move back in here. Why do you have to be so stubborn?" After too much vodka his arguing had taken on a note of complaint. "I'll sleep in the spare room. Do my own laundry. You won't even know I'm here unless you want to." He lit another cigarette.

"You have to stop smoking, Ben."

"You wouldn't say that if you didn't care."

"You can't drive."

"I'm okay."

"It's Friday night. There's traffic."

"I'll walk. Pick up the car tomorrow. It's not far."

"Don't fall in the gutter."

"The cops love me. They were all at my bachelor party, remember?"

"Good night, Ben."

Closing the front door behind him, she rested her forehead against the wood and shut her eyes, expelling a long breath of relief.

She would always love Ben Lansing. Bellicose, arrogant, and controlling, he was a man with a dozen bad habits he would never change, but she had never loved anyone before or after him. She just couldn't be married to him. Sometimes she believed she had lost her taste for love, become allergic to it or outgrown its allure. Love meant vulnerability and that meant danger. Any risks she took now, she took on her own terms.

14

Looking back, Sophie knew she'd been a little crazy when she was thirteen, in the spring of her eighth-grade year. In college a psych professor had told the class that the adolescent brain was, basically, the brain of an insane person. He'd been one of the stars of the department, so she believed him.

Change was in the air that spring and with it a disconnect from previous years. On the stretch of lawn outside Sophie's eighth-grade classroom at All Angels Academy, the jacarandas did not bloom. It was as hot as midsummer, and the nights were scarcely cooler than the days. In March the Giraudos moved from the air-conditioned apartment over the market where Sophie had lived all her life to a house a mile away on a property large enough for a small grove of olive trees. In the house, built in 1910 with spacious, high-ceilinged rooms and big windows, Sophie could not sleep for thinking of the people who had occupied the house before them, whole generations of strangers who had slept in her room, their smells and sweats, their prowling germs and bacteria.

Overnight Anna became impossible, as if until she saw Sophie in a fresh environment, in her own bedroom and no longer sharing a room with Mémé, she had not realized that her little girl was a teenager with breasts and hips and stormy eyes. After years of lovingly benign neglect, Anna made Sophie the target of her attention. *Tuck your fanny in, you look like a pigeon. Keep your back straight, don't eat fatty foods, chocolate gives you acne, don't play with your hair, pick your face, or move your hands so much.* All at once, Anna cared who Sophie's friends were and where she went. *Stay away from that boy, I know his father. Don't hang out at the Sweet Shoppe. Come straight home. Have you been smoking cigarettes?*

It never stopped.

Though the house was large enough for all the lively personalities of her extended family's particular mix of American, French, and Italian cultures, Sophie felt trapped, unable to escape her mother's relentless harrying.

Don't open the curtains, you'll fade the furniture. Don't put your feet on the bed, that spread cost fifty dollars.

A vast and passionate restlessness rose in Sophie and consumed her, a need to be on the move, a feeling that the skin she wore belonged to someone she didn't know. No place fit her anymore; no place could hold her. Temperatures spiked into the nineties for most of April and May. She couldn't sleep or lie still, and the only relief was to be up and out in the night.

She moved from shadow to shadow and if she found a gate unlocked and no dog barked an alarm, she slipped into the backyard, where she sat in strangers' lawn chairs, drank Cokes from their outdoor coolers, and pretended that the house and the pool and the backyard trees were hers. She was ruled by the compulsion to walk into someone else's life and assume an identity other than her own. Escape was what she wanted, to be anyone but Anna Giraudo's daughter for a single night, a few hours. She wasn't a thief. Never a vandal. More like a shopper trying on shoes she would never walk in.

If she were caught the consequences would be serious, but she couldn't find it in herself to care what happened beyond the moment. Her mother would be mortified and maybe that would be good; maybe then she would leave Sophie alone.

One night at dinner, Anna said that she'd seen the man who lived across the street from the market loading his SUV with bikes and kids. His wife had come in for sandwiches and bottled water and told Anna that the family, dogs and all, was spending a week at its Lake Tahoe condominium, taking advantage of the unusual weather.

At two a.m. the air was warm and the neighborhood was dark and quiet. Occasionally a dog barked. The security gate was locked across the front entrance to the market, its large square windows darkened by blinds that hid the lights in the refrigerated cases. Across the street, as if to welcome Sophie, the wooden gate with a bell shape cut in the arched top had been left unlocked. A motion-sensitive light blinked on over the back door, revealing a messy yard. The dogs had dug up the lawn and there was a faint smell of shit in the air. She climbed the back steps and, standing on tiptoe, looked through the small square window into the kitchen, illuminated by a night-light beside the sink. Her shoulder nudged the jamb. Reflex-ively, she stepped back as the door slowly swung open, and she stood frozen on the threshold for a long moment before she told herself that people who went on vacations and left their gate and door unlocked were just asking for trouble.

The dinky old-fashioned kitchen had a countertop tiled in yellow-and-white ceramic. Standing in the middle of the room, she could touch both counters with her outstretched hands. A row of canisters lined up under the cupboards in descending order of size: *Flour*, *Sugar*, *Tea*, and *Coffee*, each labeled in fancy, old-fashioned script. The aging refrigerator opened with a foot pedal, revealing half a dish of dried-up tuna casserole, peanut butter, the remains of a package of English muffins, and a bottle of Welch's grape juice. She un-screwed the lid and took a sweet, sticky swallow. Upstairs there were three bedrooms. The larger of these had an air conditioner in the window. She turned it on and lay on the bed in its cold draft, stripped to her bra and pants.

In the new house, Anna did not believe in air-conditioning.

The houses Sophie entered that spring were always empty—she was careful about that—but even so, she knew that the more often she trespassed, the greater the chance of being caught. As the stakes rose, each excursion was more thrilling than the one before it. Sitting in class at All Angels the morning after one of her adventures, she regarded her classmates with disdain, the well-behaved little girls in their sky-blue and navy uniforms with their perfect penmanship and saccharine good manners, raising their neatly manicured hands: *Yes, Sister; no, Sister; please, Sister, may I?*

Occasionally Sophie was tempted to break the rules of deportment, stand and proclaim her individuality, but instead she remained at her desk with her knees together and ankles neatly crossed, relishing the masquerade, the sense of a secret life held intimately close. While Sister Josepha lectured the class on the government's system of checks and balances, Sophie remembered the winey taste of old grape juice.

That spring Sophie tacked to the wall above her desk a poster of a surfer at Cortes Bank slicing through the curl of a wave that was immense beyond belief. She had never been a surfer, but the picture captured a feeling she understood.

She met Tamlin at the dead end of the school term when she had swiped Carmine's skateboard and taken it around the corner from the house to practice jumps where her mother wouldn't see her and tell her to clean her room. She sat on the board and from across the street watched a moving van unload in front of a blue-and-white Victorian with a sagging front porch and a skinny citriodora growing beside it. In the heat she could smell the tree like a simmering lemon. At dinner she told her family that the new neighbors were an Asian woman, an African American man, and a girl with black hair all the way to the middle of her back.

A skinny girl with straight black hair. Sophie disliked her on sight, but a week later, when she and the girl were in the same advanced swimming class at the YMCA pool, she heard her cuss fluently about the smell of the bathroom and the crappy thin towels the club furnished. Her insolence won over Sophie, especially after she'd seen that straight hair tangled up under a stupid-looking bathing cap just as easily as her own wiry curls did. Loving rules and conformity, the coach said they couldn't go in the water without the caps and made them swim punishment laps when they claimed theirs had been stolen. She threatened to call their parents if their attitude didn't improve. They were good swimmers and didn't need a bossy college girl telling them to breathe "with maximum efficiency." United against a common enemy, they cut class and hung out.

Over the summer, Sophie's imperative to escape the house diminished. Tamlin's strict Vietnamese mother was every bit as domineering as Anna, and having an empathic best friend made all the difference. Maybe if Anna hadn't grounded Sophie for a month when she found cigarettes in her top bureau drawer, or if, at dinner, she hadn't been on Sophie's case about the way she dressed, skirts too short and tees too tight, if Anna hadn't said that her hair looked like a bird's nest; maybe if a lot of things had been different Sophie would not have gotten out of bed and pulled on her shorts and cotton sweater and walked through the hot August darkness to the house on Mariposa Street.

One last excursion. It was risky—it was *always* risky—but that was the rush; that was the roar.

The houses on Mariposa Street were new, two storied, big and expensive, and set back from the street on spacious lots with old oaks. Sophie had been watching one house in particular for several weeks, enchanted by the handsome father and pretty blond mother and their always happy little boy.

Daddy drove a sporty car; Mom had a gleaming morning-glory-blue SUV. Every evening both cars were in the driveway, side by side. And then one night they weren't.

The red Miata convertible was all by itself, shining under the streetlight. Seeing it alone so late meant to Sophie that the family had gone somewhere overnight and the house was empty. She tried the back door, found it open, and should have known that it was all too easy.

The interior was like no other house she had ever been in, one immense room without walls between the kitchen, dining room, and a big living room space. The floors were some kind of white stone and there wasn't much furniture, just a few simple pieces. No books or magazines or knickknacks, no baskets or pillows or lap rugs. Two or three large abstract oil paintings hung on the white walls, but there were no photos anywhere, not even a snapshot of the happy little boy stuck with a magnet on the refrigerator. The refrigerator had glass doors. Looking in, she saw cartons of nonfat milk and yogurt and cottage cheese, blue-lidded plastic deli containers stacked like cement blocks.

She was halfway up the staircase when she heard a sound on the landing. Looking up, she saw the man standing at the top of the stairs wearing shorts and a T-shirt.

Her brain stopped working.

"You're the girl who's been checking us out." He had silver-blond hair like his little boy and he spoke in a slightly amused and matter-of-fact way, as if encountering a stranger on the stairs in the middle of the night were nothing out of the ordinary. "I noticed you last week. You're not too subtle.

As a spy." He stepped toward her. "Don't worry, my wife's not here. She took the boy up to Santa Rosa. We're alone." He stopped. "You don't have a gun or anything, do you? I don't like guns. Guns make things so complicated."

He smiled and passed her on the stairs. She thought his shoulder would touch her but instead she felt only a brush of warm air.

"I'm going to watch a movie. Keep me company."

The man wasn't dangerous. How could he be when he lived on Mariposa Street and had a small son and a pretty wife? Sophie didn't care for the way the house looked inside, but no one ignorant or dangerous would live in a place so clean and uncluttered. And what a story it would make for Tamlin. She couldn't wait to tell her all the details, the slightly floral smell of the man's cologne and especially the refrigerator with glass doors. The voice in her head told her to get home immediately, but it was Anna's voice and easy to tune out as she followed him across the living room and through a door made to look like part of the wall into a room with books and CDs and a big-screen television set. Only when she heard the door close did she realize that the man was wearing boxer shorts.

"I have to go home."

"Why? My wife won't be back 'til next week." He opened a cabinet and a bar swung out. "What do you like to drink? A screwdriver maybe? I've got some really good tangerine juice." He held up a bottle of juice Sophie recognized. "This stuff is the best. My wife gets it at your market."

She didn't like that he knew who she was.

The glass he offered her was cold and moist with condensation. It almost slipped from her hand.

"Easy there, Sophia. I don't want to clean up after you. I like your name, by the way. It has a beautiful sound." He said it again, releasing the syllables on a languorous sibilant breath. *Sopheea*. He raised his own glass. A clear liquid poured over ice cubes. "Thanks for coming. I was feeling lonesome. Drink up."

She obeyed without thinking, tasting only the tart sweetness of the tangerine juice.

He put on a movie she'd never seen. It had subtitles that were hard to follow because the man sat next to her on the couch, talking.

"You like the night, don't you? I know you do because when you watch the house, I watch you. My wife sleeps like the dead, eleven to seven every night, but I only need three or four hours and then I'm up. I catch a movie or go online. I've seen you standing in the shadows over by the Wilsons' house. Three times. I never would have known your name except I'm in Joe's Northside four or five times a week. Sometimes you work the deli counter, right? I asked the checker who you were. He said he was your brother."

"I have to go home."

"That's what you said."

She stood up, saw stars, and sat down again. She didn't remember drinking the tangerine juice, but the glass in her hand was empty. "I shouldn't be here." Her tongue felt thick and spongy.

"You're right. You shouldn't. A girl your age should be at

home all tucked up in bed with her stuffed animals. I hate to think what your mother would say if she knew what you get up to at night." She moved away from him a little. "Don't worry, Sophia. I'm not going to tell anyone."

He took her glass and set it on the table beside the couch. "I like secrets, Sophia. I know you do too."

She stiffened as he ran his fingers down her bare arm.

"How old are you? Maybe fourteen? Just starting to think about things, aren't you, starting to wonder how it all works?"

She didn't look at him.

"I bet you have fantasies, don't you? It's all right. It's normal. You're a hot little girl, Sophia. I can tell that when I look at you." He put his other hand on her knee and tried to spread her legs. She pushed his hand away, but he was strong. "So here's our secret, Sophia. I promise I won't tell anyone that you broke into my house and tried to steal—"

"I never."

"I don't want you to get in trouble, Sophia. Burglary's a serious offense." With one hand under her chin, he pushed her head back against the arm of the couch and moved the other up between her legs.

"I'll scream."

"That's okay. The room's soundproofed. You won't bother anyone."

"I didn't try to steal. I never—"

"Be nice now and I'll never tell your mama what a nasty child you are. It'll be our secret. Forever and ever."

Between her legs his hand was hot through her shorts. She squirmed and jerked away. The movement made her head swim. She thought she might throw up. She wanted to throw up. He grabbed at her shorts' elastic waist and yanked them down in a sudden movement that made her squeal. She drew her knees up and twisted away, but he held her with his fingers between her legs, rubbing and then entering her, moving them back and forth. She prayed to throw up. Instead she began to whimper and then to cry. Hating him, she hated herself more for being stupid and weak. When he removed his fingers, she sobbed with relief but then she felt his penis shoving into her and that was much worse. The weight of him held her down. His face pressed into the hollow between her neck and shoulder and she thought her body would split up the middle. She screamed and he covered her mouth with his hand. She bit his palm but he didn't seem to notice. He smelled like gardenias. What kind of a smell was that for a man?

When he fell away from her afterward, she straightened her clothes and escaped. In the kitchen she stopped and listened to make sure he wasn't coming after her. Why should he when he was perfectly safe in the certainty that she would never tell her parents anything? The only sound in the house was the murmur of the movie in a foreign language and the hum of the refrigerator.

She was sore but it was a tolerable pain. Already the specifics of what had happened had begun to fade from her mind, and in the years to come she remembered most clearly the smell of gardenias, a fragrance that would always sicken her. But she never forgot the sensation of powerlessness as physical as a gag over her mouth, as terrifying as a wave breaking over her.

A set of keys lay on the kitchen counter. She knew they were his. Two house keys and the key to the Miata. Without thinking why, she grabbed them and ran out the back door. In the driveway she stopped beside the red car. Her hand did not tremble as she pressed the point of the key against the car door, as she dragged the serrated edge down and up again, around and down at an angle. *Rape*.

15

Lorne Hampstead, the private investigator recommended by David Cabot, arrived in Sophie's office to find her taping a piece of cardboard across a windowpane.

"Someone threw a brick in here last night. Watch your step." She indicated the glass on the carpet. "Who are you?"

"Lorne Hampstead."

"You got here fast."

He held the cardboard while Sophie secured the tape. "Any idea who did it?"

"One of my many admirers." She told him how angry the town was with her decision to defend Donny Crider. "I had seventy-one e-mails this morning." She made air quotes. "'You are a slimy shyster and if someone shot you in the face I'd dance on your grave.'"

"He'd dance until he needed you."

"Until *she* needed me. That bit of poetry came snail mail on pink stationery. Fancy handwriting." She sank into her desk chair and ran her fingers up through her thick hair. "You're not seeing me at my best."

"David said you needed a PI, not a bodyguard."

Hamp saw her frown and guessed that he had insulted her by implying—inadvertently—that she couldn't take care of herself. Already he could tell that she was an arm's-length kind of person, the sort of woman who would rather fall on her own than ask for help. There didn't seem to be any *right* thing to say at that moment, so he kept his mouth shut.

She handed him a sheet of paper. "I worked this up for you over the weekend. It's a fact pattern. Read it and you'll know everything I do about the case, which you can see isn't a whole hell of a lot."

David Cabot had told Hamp that Sophie was the best student intern he'd ever had, tough and knowledgeable about the law, honest and intuitive. "She cares about people," Cabot had said over the phone. "The clients matter." Even without this recommendation, Hamp would have taken the job. He'd been in Ventura for long enough.

By now he had walked all the beaches to the north and south dozens of times and talked to the surfers, drunk beer with them, told the tall tales that were expected of a gray, a scarred-up old-timer whose best surfing days were behind him. Everywhere he went, he showed the picture of Bronwyn standing by the long board in Hawaii the summer before she disappeared. She was seventeen and as beautiful as a miracle. He searched each face for a sign of recognition. The only clue he'd had in two years he got from a couple of boys with drug-addled memories who called her Brownie and claimed to have been in the Malibu lineup with her a few times. For a time he haunted the scene down there hoping for a substantial lead, but there was nothing. Late at night when he couldn't sleep, he wondered if his daughter had found the edge of the world and surfed off it.

As he read the fact pattern, he was aware of Sophie watching him. He knew what she saw.

He was a familiar type found in every Southern California beach town. What surfers called a "gray," a man who had logged too many hours in the sun and salt. Hamp wore his hair long, tied back with a bit of rawhide. His eyes had squinted down to bright-blue slits, and days in the sun had tanned his skin to the color of a deep golden leather, tattooed with coin-sized sun freckles. A thick white coral scar marked his right arm from funny bone to wrist, and half of his left earlobe was gone. The worst damage didn't show: six-plus concussions from too many dives to the ocean floor and the rocks he didn't see coming.

He'd always been a hotshot, daring the waves to dump him. Now he was a cliché, and that suited his purposes. The people to whom he showed his daughter's picture wouldn't remember him. He and the brief exchange of question and answer would drop out of their memories and that was okay. Hamp didn't want Bronwyn to know he was combing the beaches from Baja to NorCal.

He looked up from reading. "Short on hard facts. Long on hunches."

"You may as well know that about me, Lorne."

"Hamp. I'm not the Lorne type."

"I trust my intuition."

"David told me that." In Ventura he had been investigating insurance claims for a firm of personal injury lawyers. The job got old after the first week. "I'm glad for a change."

"There's something going on in this case that no one's talking about. I don't know what it is, but if you want to help, you've got to take my guesses and feelings as seriously as I do. If you can't, then it's good we know it now. Save us both a lot of time." She counted on her fingers. "I've got a shooting without a motive, a perp who barely talks, and a mother who's a bitch. That's all I know for sure."

She was spiky, maybe in over her head, but fighting hard not to let it show.

"David says you're a good lawyer."

She half smiled and rocked her hand from side to side. "I was a good intern and I won lots of cases when I was prosecuting, but as a defense attorney? The jury's still out on that."

"I did a little research about you, read up on that other case. What's his name, like a sweater?"

"Will Cardigan."

"That's the one. What kind of name is that anyway?"

"I don't know. English? I never heard it before."

"So, d'you think somewhere there's a kid called Will Pullover?"

He wanted to see if she had a sense of humor. At least she smiled.

"You got him off by convincing him to sell out his pals to the cops. They've got to be pissed at him. And you."

"Will's back east with his mother, well beyond the reach of the Bleeker brothers. I doubt if they could find Massachusetts on a map."

"But could they find you?"

"They're east-county hoodlums. More interested in drugs and stolen cars than me."

Hamp wondered if this was bravado or if she really believed it. "You've got nerve, Sophie, taking that case and now this one."

Her cheeks turned pink.

"Where do you want me to start?"

"There's a little office out front," she said. "Actually it's more like a big closet. I put a desk in there over the weekend. It's all yours."

"I travel light."

The possessions most people valued—furniture and mementos, a well-oiled omelet pan, a photo album—these were entanglements to Hamp, seaweed that dragged him down. Since his daughter's disappearance he'd stored almost everything he owned in a facility in San Diego and lived in residence motels and friends' spare rooms. When he found Bronwyn he would have to move fast.

"Right now, this case is a fishing expedition, okay? You can start by finding out about Donny's father. Brad Crider. It was a long time ago, but I'd like to know the circumstances of the divorce. What kind of a guy is he? He's not a deadbeat; I know that much." She handed him another sheet of paper. "I got this off the Internet. He owns a bunch of office buildings. I want to know why he never sees his son. Looks like there's plenty of money, but he's never paid a penny of child support?"

"She take him to court?"

Sophie shook her head.

"And this would connect to the shooting, how?"

"Who knows? Probably not at all, but you put the hook in the water and wait for something to give it a tug. Isn't that how fishing works?"

He reread the paragraph about Elena Crider. "Where'd she get the twenty-five thou? Maybe the ex?"

"Maybe, but how did she get him to part with that much when he hasn't sent a penny to his son in fifteen years? And why would she not tell me where it came from? I asked her and she told me"—Sophie quoted with her fingers—"'I have one or two resources.'"

"What about this guy…" Hamp checked the fact pattern again. "Roman Devane?"

"Donny says he stole his gun, but the little bit he told me, it doesn't make sense."

"Has the gun been found?"

"Not yet."

"I'm not a lawyer, Sophie, but I've been in this business a while now, worked with a lot of lawyers good and bad. Let's say we find out a pile of stuff about Donny and his history and his family—"

"I don't know what I'll do with it." She stood up and walked to the window not covered by cardboard. From behind, her straight back and firmly squared shoulders communicated a determination that Hamp liked.

"Maybe the government'll give you a good deal."

"Maybe, but it's not likely. I used to be married to the prosecutor. Ben wants to be appointed to the bench and he thinks he can do it by making headlines with this case." She looked at Hamp. "There's no way in hell I can get Donny off. It's not just the evidence; it's the town."

"Get him a change of venue."

"Not worth the fight. The evidence against him is huge. But I won't let him rot in jail until he's middle-aged. I can't."

She was pretty, fired up and intense about this unwinnable case. The law and justice meant a lot to her, maybe more than she knew or was able to express, and her resolve was infectious. She was young, not yet flattened by reality, still hoping—maybe believing—she could pull a Perry Mason. He liked that, but at the same time it saddened him.

"I've got a really good shrink coming in. Alexander Itkin. He'll interview Donny, run a gang of tests. He'll take a bite out of that twenty-five thou, but I need to know this kid inside and out."

"Where do you want me to begin?" he asked.

"The father."

Hamp stood to go.

"Hang on a minute." Sophie gestured to him to sit again. Her dark-eyed and unblinking assessment unnerved Hamp a little. "What's your story?" She glanced at her watch. "The five-minute version."

"San Diego, born and bred. Two blocks from Ocean Beach."

From the day he turned six and his father bought him a boogey board, the beach and waves were all that interested Hamp. At eight he rode his first surfboard, got up and stood for all of two seconds on an ankle biter. From then on he was a grom through and through. Over the next couple of years he wiped out a thousand times but he didn't give up and for this the older surfers liked him. They schooled him in surf etiquette as well as the skills he needed. They laughed at him when he fucked up.

At eighteen he'd gone to college to please his parents, and after graduation with a degree in criminology, he'd been accepted to the police academy. He liked being a San Diego cop. There was plenty going on and the weather was good. He married and two months later he was the father of a daughter, Bronwyn. Six months later he was living on his own again in Ocean Beach.

"Where's your daughter now?"

"Oregon."

Lies complicated life and cluttered the mind, so Hamp had a rule against lying. There were two exceptions to his rule. As an investigator, he lied when it helped him do his job. And he never told the truth about Bronwyn.

"In school."

Sophie said nothing to signify that she didn't believe him, but her unwavering regard made him feel uncomfortably transparent. As if she could see the truth tattooed across his forehead and knew that his daughter had been missing for two years.

16

In a Denny's off the highway outside San Sebastian, Hamp ordered bacon and eggs. While he waited to be served he used his computer to scan a recent copy of the *Salinas Californian.*

Salinas sits in the middle of a wide, fertile valley surrounded by thousands of acres of farmland. Chamber of Commerce signs call it the Salad Bowl of the World. Countless times, driving north or south on 101, he had bypassed the little city, paying no attention to the sprawl of homes and shopping centers. The contents of the online newspaper affirmed his guess that it was a typical California agricultural town. Though larger and more prosperous than most, Salinas had not evolved much beyond the time when farmers drove their tractors to Grange meetings. The news in the paper was about a local union disagreement, a cancer society fashion show, and arguments regarding the city's new logo. Scanning the real estate ads, he found a column listing properties for rent and sale by Bradley Crider. He shuffled through the business cards he kept, found one that suited, and used his cell phone to call the number in the ad. Reading off the card, he identified himself to a secretary as Edward Cooper, an investor interested in commercial property. The secretary said Mr. Crider could see him at three p.m.

Crider's office was on the top floor of a glass-and-steel office building that by Salinas standards qualified as a skyscraper. Hamp circled the block a few times until an unmetered space opened. Stepping out of his truck, he was assaulted by the town's distinctive smell, a mix of car exhaust and ripe vegetation. On the tenth floor, a receptionist walked him back to an impressive corner office with floor-to-ceiling windows. Brad Crider closed his computer and stood up. Almost immediately his warm smile cooled. In ponytail, Levi's, and a blue denim shirt, Hamp didn't look like the successful investor he claimed to be.

Time for honesty.

"I'm Lorne Hampstead." He stuck out his hand and Brad shook it somewhat reluctantly. "Thanks for seeing me." He offered his business card, the real one.

"You're not Edward Cooper? I don't understand." And then he did. If he had taken a bigger step backward he would have gone through the plate-glass window. "I'm not talking to you. This is about the shooting, isn't it? I haven't got anything to say."

"I'm working for your son, not against him."

"I don't know you and I don't know him. I haven't seen him in fifteen years."

Without being invited to do so, Hamp pulled a chair up to the desk and sat in a relaxed fashion that said he was going to stay awhile. Getting settled gave him a minute to take in Brad Crider, a strikingly handsome man. In a starched shirt with an expensive tie loosely knotted, a wide gold watch on his wrist, he had a showy glamour that probably wasn't typical of Salinas. At the moment, he looked nervous and ready to run.

"Mr. Crider, I'm not here to make trouble for you." Hamp could be soothing when necessary. "I got into your office under false pretenses and I apologize for doing that, but we both know that if I'd said I was a PI, you never would have seen me." Most people were disarmed by a straight-out admission of guilt.

"I could call security right now."

"You could, but then word would get out and the next thing you know...well, I wouldn't be able to guarantee your privacy."

Crider stared out the window a moment and then dropped into his chair. "Ask your questions."

"Did you give Elena, your ex-wife—"

"You don't have to tell me who she is."

"—twenty-five thousand dollars for Donny's defense?"

"And now I suppose it's not enough. I told her, it's all I can spare right now—"

"Business isn't good?"

"I'm paying taxes on seven empty properties. What do you think?"

"Well, I have good news. I'm not here to hit you up for cash. I just have some questions about Donny—"

"I don't even know him."

"You never paid child support."

His chin jerked up. "The fuck I didn't. Every month for the last fifteen years I've sent that woman eighteen hundred dollars. A thousand for the mortgage and eight hundred for the kid."

Hamp's surprise showed.

"You don't believe me? I can prove it. I'll show you the statements online. The check goes out on the first of every month and she deposits it in her account. I told him that. He thought I was lyin' to him."

"Wait a minute, you told Donny? When did you see him?"

"He came to see me a couple of weeks ago." Brad fidgeted with the papers on his desk, checking his calendar. "Yeah, two weeks yesterday. Some girl drove him up here. I don't know why he decided..." More fidgeting.

"What did he want?"

"You tell me. He didn't seem real bright."

"You told him you'd been paying support?"

"I told him I'd been sending Elena money for years. He didn't know." Brad pulled a pen out of a cup and stabbed it in Hamp's direction. "The bitch told him I was a deadbeat. All these years, he's thought I didn't give a shit."

"How'd he take it?"

"He didn't even say good-bye. Stood up and left without saying anything, like I'd insulted him or something." Crider looked out the window, turning the pen in his hand from end to end.

"You didn't go after him."

"I hate her."

Hamp knew that with a little supportive encouragement, a bitter spouse would go off on his ex like a rabid dog.

"You've been conscientious about the money, okay. But why didn't you see Donny once in a while? He was only two hours away and you had a right to see him."

Crider shot up out of his chair. "I don't have to talk to you about this." Hamp stayed where he was and Crider sat down again. "I could tell when he was here, he's a weird kid. He tried to kill the governor. I don't know why he did it, but it has nothing to do with me."

Hamp took a breath. "Not directly. But the more Donny's attorney understands the circumstances of his life, the better chance she has of getting him a fair deal."

"A fair deal? He knew what he was doing. I read the paper. It was premeditated."

"I don't know what paper you're reading, but no one knows if he planned it or not."

"Why shouldn't he pay for his crime?"

"Is that what you want for your son, Mr. Crider? Life in a prison with hardened criminals?"

"I don't know him." Crider's smooth tan had faded. "Try to get it from my point of view, okay? I'm a happily married man with a successful business. This recession hit me hard, but we're making it through. I've got twin girls, ten years old, and a beautiful wife. I mean beautiful inside and out. Right when we first met, I told her I had a son in San Sebastian, and she wanted me to connect with him. She believes in family, and she had this idea of making him part of ours. But she didn't know Elena. My wife's a sweet and generous woman. Elena'd make dog meat out of her. I couldn't let that happen. My wife never did get why I walked away from Donny the way I did. We had some rough times around that, believe me." He stepped away from his desk and paced for a moment.

"Have you met my ex? She probably seems like a nice enough lady at first. I saw her on television the other night. She looks pretty good. But you know what I noticed? She wasn't crying. Her eyes weren't even swollen, so it wasn't like she was just getting control of herself. All the time I knew her, she never shed a tear for anyone or thing." He stopped, looking at Hamp. "So long as Elena's getting her own way, she's sweet as candy. But I'm telling you, if she was hungry and she had to, she'd cut a hunk off your flank and fry it up with onions and potatoes. She's a nightmare, that woman."

Hamp had done divorce work and met a lot of scarred spouses. Residual anger was common, so was resentment, but Brad Crider was the first one in whom he sensed fear.

"Living with her just about killed me. Nothing was ever enough for Elena, not good enough or big or fancy or expensive enough. She only ever thought about herself; nobody else ever counted for shit. It got so I was hearing her voice in my head all the time, carping and criticizing, belittling everything I did. I swear to God she enjoyed making me feel small. And I started having these thoughts..."

He stopped and sagged at the waist. Hamp imagined that he felt a draft as the resistance left his body.

"It's been fifteen years, but it's like, you know, yesterday. Seeing the kid brought it all back. My wife, before we got married, she made me promise I'd see a psychologist. I guess it helped. A little." Sweat beads shimmered at Crider's hairline. "She's a parasite. It's like the only thing that gave her pleasure was beating me down, making me feel like I was nothing."

If Elena were as bad as all that, getting out of the house and into Roman Devane's program must have seemed like a rescue to Donny.

"I used to lie in bed at night and she'd be only a few inches away and I'd get started imagining...imagining how I could kill her. I know it sounds awful to hear about it, now, but it was worse then. I'd think about choking her and the palms of my hands would get hot. It was so real it scared me. I had to get away—either that or I was going to hurt her. I'm not a violent man and never laid a hand on her, but near the end...She was sucking the life out of me. Killing me. I knew when she got through with me I'd be like one of those zombie things. Walking around dead."

"You talk to Donny about this?"

"Jesus, no."

Having once begun to tell the truth, Crider couldn't stop himself.

"Toward the end, I used to steal her stuff. I didn't have the guts to strangle her, but I knew how to make her go crazy, and that was better than doing nothing, believe me. I'd take little things, things she valued. I remember she had a pair of pearl earrings she'd saved up for. I threw them away and then I sat in the kitchen pretending to read the paper, listening to her talk to herself while she tore the bedroom apart looking for them. Elena values order, likes things to be neat and clean and in their place. She knew where she'd put those earrings, but they weren't there."

He was sweating profusely now. "When I left, Donny was about three. Not talking yet and, honestly? I thought he was a little slow. Mentally. Either that or he knew already that there was no point trying to talk to Elena. I barely knew him. I didn't want to leave him, but I had to. It was safer for everyone."

Hamp got back to SanSeb after dark. Returning from Salinas, he'd stopped in coffee shops and restaurants along the highway, shown Bronwyn's picture around and asked if anyone had seen her. Responses were always the same. Negative, with a touch of pity.

As he drove he reran his conversation with Brad Crider. He didn't doubt that he'd wanted to kill Elena and the power of this had frightened him. The memory of it still scared him. But Hamp's understanding had limits. He would never have abandoned Bronwyn, not even if her mother had been a black widow, as Elena apparently was.

He and Terri had married for one reason: she was pregnant and they agreed it was the responsible thing to do. Their parting had been amicable. No matter how much they both loved Bronwyn, a baby wasn't enough to hold a marriage together. But in the years that followed, Hamp never missed a weekend visitation, not once. He used every opportunity to be with Bronwyn. It was he who had taught her to surf and to drive a car, and they had an agreement between them that if he would listen without comment to the music she liked, she wouldn't hammer the oldies he preferred. Until Terri remarried, Hamp had paid her alimony, and he had been faithful with child support until the day Bronwyn vanished.

Sitting in the truck with his laptop propped against the steering wheel, he made notes for Sophie, listing the things he'd learned. At the bottom he wrote, *Elena triggered violence in her husband. Did she do something to trigger the same in Donny? And if so, why didn't he shoot her? Why did he target the governor instead?*

17

Sophie had a bail hearing before Superior Court Judge Hugh Arthur, a mercurial jurist widely thought to be going through a prolonged and, to observers, often entertaining midlife crisis. The year before, he'd grown his hair into a gunmetal bush that stood out as if electrified. Six months ago he'd bought a Harley. Though many attorneys griped about Judge Arthur's often irascible and eccentric courtroom demeanor, Sophie liked him. He was kind at heart and almost always saw the men and women called before his bench as human beings, not statistics.

As was often the case, His Honor was running late that morning and Sophie spent the waiting time reading about brain development in adolescent boys. The author of the article called the prefrontal lobe "the executive organizer."

It was interesting information and perhaps relevant, but as a rule, juries didn't care about science. Could she make them care? Could she make twelve randomly selected jurors understand that Donny had not thought through the consequences of his act because he *couldn't*, because his brain hadn't learned how to do that yet? Probably not. There must be thousands, maybe millions, of boys with immature brains. Most of them led ordinary teenaged lives and by the time they were in their twenties, their brains had caught up.

At twelve minutes after ten Judge Arthur swept onto the bench with his usual flourish, greeting everyone by name, asking after their families, joking with the marshal as if he had all the time in the world. He scanned the court documents the clerk had laid out for him.

"Ms. Giraudo, your client is accused of rape, a heinous and violent crime, and you want him released on bail? You want me to give him license to walk the streets of this town, entertaining whatever perverse desires come into his head? Should we tell our wives and daughters to stay at home until after Mr. Deplaine's trial? Honestly, Ms. Giraudo, what's to keep him from doing it again?"

Judge Arthur loved the sound of his own voice.

"But that's the thing, Judge. We don't know that he *did* do the crime. Like you said, he's *accused*."

As a prosecutor Sophie had taken particular pleasure in the trial and punishment of rapists, but now she was a defense attorney, and even a scumbag like Deplaine, who had virtually admitted his guilt to her, was entitled to robust counsel.

"Prior to his arrest my client was a model citizen."

Ward Deplaine had never been convicted of a crime, though he'd been a suspect in several rape cases; he had no police record and paid his parking tickets on time. He had lived in the same apartment and held the same job for almost

five years. He and his longtime girlfriend went to church together most Sundays.

"What's his job?"

"He's a programmer, Your Honor." It was all in the memo
Clary had typed and delivered to the clerk, but Judge Arthur
probably hadn't read it.

"Who's standing bail?"

"His girlfriend, Ms. Schultz."

"They live together?"

"They do, Your Honor."

"How long?"

"Almost two years."

Judge Arthur scrunched his eyebrows together. "Very well.
Electronic surveillance and he never leaves the house unless
he's with you, Ms. Giraudo, you lucky woman." He looked at
the prosecutor, a redheaded ninety-day wonder Sophie had
not met. "That okay with you?"

"The people find that acceptable." He looked slightly dazed
by the speed with which the matter was being handled. Sophie
sympathized, remembering how at sea she'd been, fresh out of
law school and expected to do justice "for the people."

Perhaps the judge was remembering too. He smiled and
said, "That's very wise of the people."

Sophie left the courthouse that morning feeling disgrun-
tled. Walking back to her office across the courthouse corner,
her mind resisted clearance. A bag of dirt like Deplaine was
allowed to live at home awaiting trial, while Donny would
spend weeks and maybe months in the San Sebastian lockup
because no one cared enough to stand his bail.

* * *

Anna was in the office sorting a stack of pink message slips.

"Is it okay I let her in?" Clary asked, looking nervous. "She's your mother, right?"

"What are you doing here, Ma?"

"Delio called your father this morning. A customer told him someone broke your window."

"I'm okay. I wasn't even here when it happened."

"Go in your office." Anna wore her work uniform, the same that she'd worn to the market every day, pressed khaki slacks and a Lacoste golf shirt, tucked in. She had a closet full of them in every color.

"I want to talk to you."

In Sophie's office a man in a white coverall was repacking his tool kit, having just replaced the broken window glass.

"I called him," Anna said when he was gone and she'd closed the door to give them privacy. "Don't look so upset, Sophie. What if it rains? You can't have cardboard over your window."

"I was going to do it after court."

It was like being thirteen all over again.

Tamlin and everyone else she knew had long ago stopped resisting their parents, but she was still at it, still trying to prove something.

"Clary showed me where you hide the vacuum. You've got a beautiful carpet there, Sophie. Don't tell me how much it cost, I don't want to know, but that glass would do serious damage to the fibers."

"Ma—"

"It must have cost you a bundle."

"That's it. Enough. Thanks for calling the glazier, but you don't have to hang around here."

"Don't be in such a hurry to get rid of me." Anna fussed, straightening the papers on Sophie's desk. "We need to have a little conversation."

Sophie knew about those.

"I've got work."

"I'm sure you do. You're a busy and important lawyer defending an attempted assassin, but I was in labor with you for over thirty hours. You can spare me a few minutes."

They went to separate corners of the couch.

"This morning, after Del called, your father and I talked about you, about this mess you've got yourself into."

"It's my job. I'm a defense attorney."

"Yes, but who defends you, I'd like to know?"

"I do, Ma. I defend me."

"Your dad and I decided that we aren't going to let you go through this alone. Personally, I think you were foolish to take the case and if you could get out of it now, I'd say do it. Do it! But I suppose that's against lawyers' ethics or something, so you're stuck with it."

"He's got no one on his side except me."

"No one throws bricks at my daughter. They do and they mess with me."

Sophie laughed.

"You think I'm here to entertain you? Whatever it is you want for this boy, I want it too. But this—" Anna gestured toward the window and then the half dozen packing boxes still stacked, unopened, in the corner. "In a mess like this, you can't be a good lawyer. And that girl in the front? Clary? She can't answer phones and keep your calendar at the same time she's doing her paralegal job. You need an office manager, someone to get you organized so you can do what you have to."

Sophie remembered telling Anna to get a job.

"After Mass a dozen people came up to me and not one of them had anything good to say about what you're doing. I told them we live in a democracy and everyone, even Donny Crider, has a right to a good lawyer."

"You don't have to defend me."

"It's my choice. You're my daughter, Sophia. Blood. So do you want my help or not? If you don't, I'll go home and that's that."

Sometimes when she was indecisive, Sophie asked herself what Tamlin would do. Her once hot-tempered friend had mellowed into someone thoughtful and philosophical, a good role model. Tamlin would hire Anna in a minute and be grateful for the help. Anna would manage all of them with schedules and memos and deadlines. She would voice her opinion about every person and case, and Sophie would react and say things she didn't mean. Anna would get her feelings hurt. She'd play the martyr. They would fight. They had been fighting for as long as she remembered.

"Of course we'll fight. But you think we're bad? You should have heard Mémé and Grandmère go at it. You and me, we're a couple of marshmallows."

"This isn't the market, Ma. It's a legal office and I'm the boss." She felt foolish saying it.

Anna smiled.

"That smile, that's what I mean. You don't take me seriously. You drive over me like a bulldozer."

"You're the boss. That's fine with me. But that doesn't mean I can't have opinions. It's a free country. We have free speech. Isn't that what you're always telling me?"

"You know that's not what I'm talking about."

"So listen to me. I can say what I want but you don't have to pay any attention. Let it be like water off a duck's back." Anna made a graceful, flicking gesture. "I may not be a lawyer, but I'm smart. And I'm more like you than you want to admit, Sophie. We both see things other people don't. I can help you." She stood up. "And if I don't, you can fire me. I'm tough. I can take it."

Sophie worked at her desk and responded to the phone messages her mother recorded in her careful print. A number were from reporters wanting interviews. She put them off until the next week, hoping that by then she would have a better idea where she was taking the case. Ben called twice on her cell, but she ignored him. From time to time she heard Anna's voice from the front office, sounding efficient. It wasn't bad having her there. Of course it had been only two hours.

At five Anna looked in. "You're still working?"

"I'll be here late."

"Watch out when you go to your car. Stay in the light."

Sophie felt her jaw tighten. "I have pepper spray in my purse."

"What about food? You're thin, Sophia."

"That'll be the day, Ma."

"The deli delivers now. I could order for you."

"Go."

"I'll lock the door so you're safe."

Hamp e-mailed his notes on Brad Crider and she read them over several times. Donny had said nothing about going to see his father, and Elena had told her that Brad never paid alimony or child support. What had she gained by claiming to be the victim of a deadbeat? And why wouldn't Donny open up to his attorney when his freedom depended on it? What was he hiding?

Near ten, as she prepared to leave the office, she heard footsteps in the hall, the knob rattled, and a business-sized envelope shot under the door. There was nothing written on the front and for a moment she didn't want to pick it up. When she did, she held it up to the light, two fingers pinching the corner. It appeared to hold a single sheet of paper. She went back into her office and laid it on her desk and looked at it. She was tempted to put it through the shredder unopened; then, realizing how cowardly that was, she picked it up and slid her fingernail under the flap. She pulled out a piece of ragged-edged paper ripped from a spiral notebook, folded in half. A picture was glued to it and a message written beneath in bold letters torn from a magazine.

KABOOM!

Above the word was a glossy magazine ad for a Toyota

4Runner, black like Sophie's own. Another picture had been taped over the hood of the vehicle, apparently torn from a skin magazine, of a woman bound, spread-eagled. The face was covered with a photo Sophie recognized: her high school graduation picture.

18

Deputy Chief of Detectives for the City of San Sebastian Cary Hering had an athletic body and a boyish wave of sandy hair, but the worry line between his eyes was as deep as an old man's. Doctors said his permanent case of bronchitis was due to tension. Hering had been one year ahead of Carmine at San Sebastian High School, where they played basketball and baseball together, and for a time Cary had been part of a crowd of boys to whom Mémé routinely fed huge meals on Sunday nights. In Cary's eyes Sophie would always be his buddy's little sister, the shrimp who made a pest of herself.

"You could sleep at Carmine's, right? Don't you even want me to call someone? Your mom? Ben's gonna be upset."

"Don't even think about it, Cary. It's not his business."

The round face of the moon lit the public parking lot with a cold white light. In planters marking the perimeter, the sprinklers went on, and the damp air smelled of rosemary. Sophie buttoned her jacket.

"If my car's okay to go, I am too."

"We'll take a closer look at the note, but I don't expect

we'll find anything. It's gross, but I think someone just wanted to scare you."

"Well, it didn't work."

As a prosecutor she had received her share of threats by mail and from time to time there had been ominous phone calls. None of them had frightened her enough to admit it. She was angry with whoever had tried to scare her and with herself for overreacting, reaching for the phone to call Cary Hering.

"We could check the truck for prints, but who knows how many folks might have touched it today or whenever. Do you ever wash this thing?"

"Maybe someone saw—"

"Sure, but where are they now? Could be your witness is a tourist driving home to Monterey." He scanned the many office windows overlooking the almost empty lot. "Stinks like a college prank, if you ask me. You've been in the paper, your picture and all. A bunch of frat rats are prob'ly laughing their asses off right now."

"Fuckin' A, Cary, I'm really sorry I called you out for nothing on a cold night."

"I'm not saying it's nothing. I'm just giving you a reality check, okay? My guys checked your car; it isn't rigged. You can drive home anytime. Want me to follow you in case, watch you get into the house?"

"I'll be fine."

"Just stay alert, Sophie, okay?" He opened the door of the Toyota. "You really landed in the stink when you sided up with Donny Crider."

"I'm his attorney, Cary. I'm *defending* him."

She sat behind the wheel, rubbing her hands around the leather-wrapped steering wheel. It felt good against her palms. Seven years she'd had this car. She'd slept in the 4Runner, driven cross-country and eaten a hundred meals in this car. She'd sat in it and cried in it and talked herself into staying one more day with Ben in it. She had driven drunk and it had brought her home safely. She loved her faithful old truck and she was pissed that someone had tried to use it against her.

"I hope the kid gets how lucky he is."

"It's not luck." She held her breath, thought *KABOOM!*, and turned the key in the ignition. The reliable engine surged and steadied. "It's my job."

"Folks aren't so rational."

She pointed at the message he still held in his hand. "Someone had some creepy fun putting that little number together."

"We're on it, okay?" He handed her his card. "This is my number, good twenty-four/seven. But can I say one more thing? Without you biting my head off? The bastard's guilty, Sophie. Plead him and get him behind bars where he belongs. You and me both know a trial would be a waste of time and money. You want to put all this behind you."

"Thanks for telling me what I want. Do I want to go home now?"

"Yeah, yeah, yeah. And from now on you park under the courthouse. They've got security cams everywhere. D'you have a garage at home?"

She shared it with two other condos in the block, but like her neighbors she preferred to park on the street and use her garage space for storage. Among the towers of packing crates, motorcycles, bikes, holiday decorations, and suitcases, one tenant had upended a couch and shoved it in a corner like a piece of upholstered statuary. Sophie's space was mostly clear, however. She wasn't a person who collected much.

She was wired. Thinking about her empty condo gave her a hit of something close to panic. Across town Ben was probably just getting home with a briefcase loaded with files. He would drop it on the couch on his way to the kitchen, where he'd put his keys and the day's collection of pocket change in a chipped SAE fraternity mug. Next stop, the refrigerator for a Corona. The phone was right there. If she called the landline he'd pick up on the first ring. She would know from the way he said her name that her voice was the one he most wanted to hear.

Ben had wanted to set down roots, have children, a couple of dogs, and a cat all running around in one of the old Craftsman houses up on Diamond Back, overlooking town. In the garage of his dreams there were four dirt bikes, four sets of skis, and tennis rackets for everyone and a couple of extras for guests. He had brought into their marriage a detailed picture of the way their life would be, but Sophie could never fit herself into it.

Ben would be a distraction and a temporary escape on a night when she needed both, but he would interpret it as much more than that. When it came to their failed marriage he was an incorrigible romantic, making Sophie think there was something to be said for acrimonious divorces where love was deformed beyond recognition. She knew Ben's every vulnerability and still cared enough to protect him from the hope he harbored.

She couldn't go home to the empty condo crowded with memories, the good times and the bad; and she never went alone to the bars in town, not even to the Beagle, which was frequented by most of the local attorneys. The liveliest place in SanSeb was the College Grill. Even on a weeknight the parking lot was full to capacity, and as usual there was live music and a noisy crowd on the outside patio that overlooked the creek. On the rare occasions when she wanted to meet someone, she drove to Monterey or even LA. She hadn't done that in a long time. That behavior was another Sophie.

She craved a place without people or memories, but she didn't want to sit at a bar, waiting for someone attractive or interesting or merely diverting to walk in. She needed to do something, to move, to yell *fuck you!* at whoever it was who had tried to scare her. Without giving it much thought, she drove under the 101 and took the back road west toward Mars Beach.

She parked the 4Runner in the empty public lot. The long curve of beach was shrouded in fog and she seemed to have the place to herself. Closer to town, there was a faint golden glow of beach bonfires, but there was no one nearby. She reached for her pepper spray in the center console but decided not to take it. Her jacket pockets were shallow and on a walk it was irritating to have to carry something in her hand.

Leaving her shoes hidden behind the driver's side front tire, she crossed the beach to the hard sand at the water's edge. Far to the left a line of ghostly gray and white breakers rolled and fell in eerie, silent succession. She walked fast. The mist felt good on her warm skin and soon she wished she'd left her jacket behind. After a few hundred yards the knot of anger in her gut released a little; she moved faster and then began to run, turning, dodging imagined blows, pumping her fists in front of her like Ali in training.

After almost a mile she reached the boulders at the end of the beach and turned around. She was tired now but her mind was clear. She buttoned her jacket, lifted the collar, and strode back to the parking lot.

As she walked she thought about the case.

Watching David Cabot at work had taught her that good trial attorneys have a gift, the ability to hold in their minds the intricate ins and outs, the web of connections among the incidents, the individuals involved, and their testimony. In the same way that the letters of the alphabet may be rearranged to make different words and sentences and eventually whole stories, a trial lawyer moved case elements around, creating new fact patterns and explanations until she saw the sense of them, and this became a theory of the crime and the defense.

In Donny's case the facts and explanations kept slipping away from her, resisting theory. Since the crime she'd spoken with him every day and in each conversation he had remained largely uncommunicative. Barring a miracle (which Sophie did not believe in despite the best efforts of the sisters at All Angels), he was going to prison.

At her car, she discovered that her shoes were gone.

"Goddamn son of a fucking bitch." The fog deadened the sound of her yell. She jumped back, away from the 4Runner, and crouched to look beneath it. Nothing and no one around. Except for the 4Runner, the lot was still empty. The car doors were locked and no windows had been broken or jimmied. She could see the bulky shape of her purse where she'd left it, crammed down by the gas pedal and almost out of sight.

A little breeze came, lifting the fog in scarves. The beach wasn't as empty as she'd thought. A quartet of kids sat on the seawall, and closer to the parking lot at a small fire, a man and a woman shared a bottle between them. Her chest tightened as if someone had grabbed her from behind and pressed a fist up under her rib cage. At the fire, the couple turned and watched her.

She got in the car and locked the doors. For a minute she couldn't move, just sat where she was, filled with rage. Then she turned the key in the ignition and gunned the gas pedal, speeding out of the parking lot and back to the freeway. Those were very good shoes, and now some drunk—probably that woman toasting by the fire—had them. To sell online? To wear? They'd cost three hundred fucking dollars. On sale.

She was halfway home when her cell phone sang its electronic version of "A Hard Day's Night."

Ben.

"What'd they find?"

The theft of her shoes had driven the threatening note from her mind.

"Who'd Hering have with him?"

"I don't know. Never saw them before."

"Jesus, I was afraid of that. He works with some real clowns."

"Well, I'm home now." Unless he was parked in front of her house—which was always a possibility—he wouldn't know that she was just leaving the Mars Beach city limits. Barefoot, with grit between her toes. "Just leave me alone, Ben."

"Don't bite my head off, Sophe. I was worried."

In his ever-optimistic dreams she would run sobbing into his arms.

"Good night, Ben."

A moment later she was shaking so hard she had to pull off the road until the tremors passed.

19

At the corner of her left eye, a pulse beat like a fist on a door. She pressed the heel of her hand against it, hard, and thought about what to do next. The prospect of going home was even less appealing than it had been two hours earlier. What an idiot she'd been to put herself in such a vulnerable position, a woman alone on an almost empty, fogged-in beach. There were people who hated and wanted to hurt her, but she hadn't even taken her pepper spray out of the glove compartment. Because it was too much trouble to hold it and walk at the same time.

Sophie remembered running along the beach, punching the bad guys, laying them flat to the left and right. Reckless. Rash. Irresponsible. It was the way the old Sophie behaved, the self she hadn't seen in a long time and believed was gone for good, outgrown and shed like a skin that no longer fit her.

She called Tamlin.

When Sophie was thirteen she invaded the homes of

strangers, she was raped by a man who drove a red Miata, and she met Tamlin— Thank God, she'd met Tamlin.

Sophie had been registered to enter All Angels High School in September, but her new friend would be attending the public high school. Sophie could not endure the thought of being separated from her and returning to the rules and restraints of parochial school. She began having headaches and her stomach ached constantly. The family doctor diagnosed tension.

"She's thirteen," Anna said. "What's she got to be tense about?"

That made the doctor laugh, which Anna did not like or understand. Later the same day Sophie heard her parents arguing in the storeroom, filled with unpacked boxes of canned goods. Joe kept saying the same thing over and over in the maddeningly calm voice that drove Sophie's mother wild.

"Let her go to high school with her friend. It won't kill you to give in for once."

Out from under the control of the nuns, Sophie began to relax as the doctor had suggested she might. Thanks in part to Tamlin's natural sociability, at SanSeb High she became part of a crowd of bright, rowdy kids, high achievers who got away with murder because their grades were good and they were smart enough to know when and with whom to push the limits. Anna's nagging continued, but her influence diminished. The girls smoked cigarettes and shared their first joint, got drunk together. Sophie had sex with several boys her mother would not have approved of, and Tamlin went with her to get birth control pills. After high school they shared a dorm suite at San Jose State and then an apartment. They worked summers waiting tables at Camp Curry in Yosemite. There were more unsuitable boys and men. After graduation, Sophie went to San Diego for law school, and Tam went home to SanSeb and married a doctor named Jimmy, who was Vietnamese like her mother. By the time Sophie returned to SanSeb to work for the county prosecutor's office, a temporary job while she awaited her bar results, Tamlin was the mother of twins, Julia and Ryan. Sophie met Ben and stayed on. When the twins started school, Tamlin got a job as assistant to the president of the school board and had been there ever since.

They lay at either end of the couch in the family room, talking as they had since they were girls, by the light of candles clustered on end tables and shelves, breathing the spicy aroma of incense. There had always been a stick burning somewhere in the house where Tamlin grew up. It had seemed a wondrously exotic custom when Sophie was thirteen.

"What were you thinking, Sophie? Mars Beach?"

"I wasn't thinking."

"That's not an answer."

"I don't know why. I just wanted—" *To do something risky. To prove I could get away with it, that I wasn't afraid.* "I don't know, Tam. Does there always have to be a reason?"

Sophie had never talked about that crazy spring when she was thirteen, never spoken to anyone about the house on Mariposa Street, about any of the houses, and after so long it seemed unlikely that she ever would. There was no easy or half way to tell the story, and once she had begun, it was a one-way street all the way to the truth Sophie didn't want to look at.

"I needed to clear my head. After that note..."

"Thank God the office door was locked. Right? It was locked, wasn't it, Sophie?"

"Yeah." Anna had made sure of that when she left.

"I think you need a dog." Tam's fingertips touched the head of the German shepherd lying on the carpet next to the couch. "How 'bout I give you Psyche? Everyone needs a dog, and at the very least, she'd give you a reason to go home at night."

"I really need a half-blind ex–police dog." She didn't want to be responsible for another life when she couldn't adequately manage her own.

"She's a good girl, but the raccoons drive her bat shit at night."

"I'm okay, really."

"Of course you are." Tamlin didn't bother to hide her smile. "Do you remember that girl, she was in tenth grade when we were seniors?"

She'd been found murdered behind the rocks at the end of Mars Beach. Remembering the circumstances of her death made Sophie angry. How terrified she must have felt. Powerless.

"What are you saying? Because something awful happened to one girl twenty years ago, all girls should be afraid to walk on the beach?"

"Alone, Sophie. On a foggy night."

"If I were a guy I could walk anywhere.

"But you're not a guy, and anyway, that's not the point, not really. You're not an unhappy kid anymore, and you don't have anything to prove."

Tamlin didn't know her nearly as well as she thought she did. She would be hurt if she knew the secrets Sophie had kept from her.

Rape was a crime and the man on Mariposa Street was guilty; still—no matter how young and vulnerable she had been—the memory of that night filled her with shame. She had walked into those closed houses in order to imagine living another life, to pretend that she was someone else, not Sophie Giraudo with Anna's rules, demands, and expectations holding her back, dragging her down like a ball and chain. She had done it for the excitement and met the man on the stairs and followed him into the hidden room. He had not forced her to gulp down a glass of vodka and tangerine juice; she'd done that on her own because she wanted to see what would happen. She had participated in making herself a victim. That was what shamed and silenced her.

For a reason she could never quite grab hold of, the more time passed, the harder it was to think of telling Tamlin. She would be horrified and sympathetic, outraged on Sophie's behalf. Even so, she would never understand that a midnight walk on Mars Beach had been Sophie's way of thumbing her nose and saying *See how brave I am?* The crazy risks she'd taken in her life, even the decision to be a defense attorney, had all been ways of yelling in that man's face *I'm not afraid. You never really hurt me.*

Sophie told Tamlin about Anna's decision to manage the office. "She just walked in and gave herself a job."

"Good! You need her." Tamlin went into the kitchen and came back with ice cream bars. Ravenous suddenly, Sophie ate hers without pausing between bites.

When she was finished, Tamlin took the stick from her. "I know I'm not supposed to say this, but I wish you weren't defending Donny Crider. What's he like anyway?"

"Who knows? You wouldn't believe anyone could be shut down so tight. You know those canisters they store radioactive waste in? They have to be sealed shut and buried?"

"And do you know what kind of dumb-ass people open those canisters?"

"I just keep picking away, asking questions. There's something in this case that I don't know yet."

"Hundreds of people saw him shoot her."

"I'm not denying that. But he did it for a reason and I have to figure out what it was."

"Like how come you walked on Mars Beach."

"It's not the same thing."

"Motive, Sophie." They sat in silence for a while. "People do things, sometimes crazy things, for reasons."

"He hasn't caught any breaks in life, and his mom is a queen bitch, let me tell you."

"He's very pretty. He's got that going for him."

In the newspaper photos Donny looked dark and surly. "How do you know what he looks like?"

"Roman's Gardens has the landscaping contract for the schools, including the admin and board offices. I used to see him sometimes. We had this part-timer in reception, a funny gay guy named Ricky. When Donny came around with Roman, Ricky'd get all flustered and invent some reason to go outside."

"What was Donny's job?"

"I don't know. All I ever saw was him and Roman walking around, checking stuff out. Quality control maybe?"

Sophie stroked Psyche's brindled coat. At some point in the last hour the pulse at the corner of her eye had stopped beating and the tension between her shoulder blades had relaxed.

"I've got to get out there and talk to Roman Devane."

"I'll ask around the office. Someone'll probably know about his program. What's it called?"

Sophie yawned. "Boys into Men."

"You sure you don't want Psyche? She's good for you. She calms you down."

"My life's too complicated for a dog. I'll be okay."

"Of course you will. You're not thirteen anymore."

"And isn't that a blessing?"

In an old teak chest Tamlin found sheets, a pillow, and a comforter. Together they made a bed on the couch.

"Jimmy's on early so he'll be in the kitchen around five. He doesn't know how to be quiet. I'll leave him a note to make you a cup of coffee."

"I have to get started early anyway."

"I'm glad you came over. I'm glad this house feels like home to you."

"*You* feel like home to me, Tam."

"As soon as we kick the twins out, you can have their rooms. We'll bust down a wall, make a suite."

They stood for a few moments, their arms around each other.

"I love you."

"Ditto, Sophe. But you don't always tell me the truth."

Sophie bridled. "I don't lie to you."

"No, but you leave things out."

20

I va was preparing breakfast for Roman and the boys, the radio playing softly in the background. On the hour she turned the volume up a little to hear the local news.

"This morning at ten," the announcer said, "friends and well-wishers of Governor Duarte will gather at St. Mary and All Angels Catholic Church on Iglesia in San Sebastian for a service of praise and thanksgiving. Those wishing to attend should come early because there is likely to be a very big crowd."

Iva didn't care about the governor one way or another, but she was thankful that she had survived the attempt on her life because it meant Donny would not be on trial for murder. She knew where St. Mary and All Angels was. The big church was almost a town landmark.

After breakfast she told Roman she'd be gone for a couple of hours.

"I'll be home in time for lunch."

"Take little Cobb with you."

"I could use a break, Roman."

"You're not the only one who needs to get away."

Roman rarely criticized her directly, but he had a tone of voice he used when he thought she was being selfish. "The big guys have been riding him pretty hard."

Milo could be especially vicious. Urged on by him, all the boys had tormented Donny when they thought Iva wasn't looking: *pretty boy, kissy-kissy*. Dragging down his pants to make him prove he wasn't a girl, smacking their lips, rubbing their crotches and moaning ecstatically. Now that Donny was gone, Milo had a new target. Cobb, as slender as an elf, with uncalloused hands and pale golden hair as soft as the silk on the butterfly weed.

The night before, he had come downstairs crying because Milo had called him some name or other. He wouldn't say what and Roman said it didn't matter anyway. He would deal with Milo when the time was right. In the meantime, Cobb could sleep in the downstairs bedroom that had recently been Donny's. Cobb cried for his mother and Iva turned away to hide her own tears.

Cobb climbed into the cab of the truck, gloomy as a gallows dog.

"If you're riding with me, you'll put on your seat belt. I don't want to get a ticket."

Roman handed her a ten-dollar bill through the driver's side window. "Stop at that ice cream place and get him a big cone or a banana split or something."

"This isn't a joyride; I have things to do today. If he wants to go home, maybe he—"

"Let me worry about Cobb. You just get him off the property for a bit. And don't get careless." Occasionally boys on outings took off on their own for no sensible reason. "Keep your eye on him."

At Dry Creek Road she came to a full stop and looked in both directions, although she could easily see some distance to left and right without doing so. Her father had taught her how to drive on ranch roads outside Yreka, emphasizing always that she could not be too careful. Her caution and adherence to the rules made Roman impatient. Even on the exhausting Arizona trips they made twice a year to visit his brother, Omar, he would not let her take the wheel.

"What's your favorite kind of ice cream?" she asked, feeling more agreeable now that they were off the property. "I like mint chocolate chip myself. Roman likes butter rum, but that stuff's way too sweet for me. Do you know, in Brazil they have avocado ice cream? Doesn't it just make you want to puke, thinking of that? Talk about a way to ruin good ice cream!"

As Iva talked into Cobb's silence, he watched the road ahead, pressing his slightly bucked teeth into his lower lip. Iva thought he looked slow-witted. She wondered about his people, the explanation for his silvery hair and large eyes slightly tilted at the corners, as if from some wandering ancestor he had inherited an exotic Eastern gene.

She heard herself reminiscing about a time when her mother was still at home. "We made this big old crock of ice cream and we had to use dry ice. Do you know what that is? Well, neither do I, not exactly. I think it's ice from some kind of gas instead of water, though how you'd do that, I can't imagine. But, oh, my heavens, that stuff took a long time to melt. I didn't know what it could do, and coming back from the store with it, I let it sit on my legs—I was wearing blue jeans but they weren't thick or anything. And when we got home, I had this big old burn on my thigh. The thing was, when I was getting burned, I never even felt it, not like it was an iron or a skillet or something. It was just really, *really* cold. I still have a scar."

Cobb looked at her and she imagined the question he was asking in his mind.

"You bet it was worth it. That was the best ice cream I ever tasted. Real cream and sugar. That's basically all ice cream is—did you know that? We added peaches in. And you have to churn it. That's like stirring?" It made her laugh, remembering. "I churned that sucker until my arm wanted to fall off."

After so many years it was hard to believe that she had once had a living, breathing, speaking mother who sat on the back steps and cut herself with a paring knife as she prepared the squishy peaches. Yellow jackets orbited her hands and the air smelled like a bar of fancy soap. She swatted the wasps and talked and laughed and then cried when her finger bled. Standing on the steps behind her, Iva watched her mother's shoulders heave as she sobbed, her head resting on her knees. Her hair fell forward, revealing the knobs of vertebrae at the back of her neck, white through the taut skin.

Iva braked to another full stop where Dry Creek T-boned Route 6A. Ahead, through the cottonwood thickets and across the creek, cars flew north on Highway 101.

"Did she cut off her finger?"

"What?"

"Did your mother cut off her finger?"

"No. I mean, I was only four or so. I don't think so."

"I seen my mom cut herself, in the bathroom. She had, like, a razor blade. She was in the bathtub and this guy dragged her out."

The boys who came to Roman's Gardens had terrible stories.

Her mother had departed in the night, the day after Iva's fourth Christmas. She remembered rows of red and green frosted cookies on a silver tray, a decorated tree, and packages wrapped in paper printed with Santa's picture. Iva sat between her mother and father at a big table with a plate of food she couldn't eat and a fork that kept falling out of her hand because it was too big for her to hold. She couldn't swallow and her father scolded her for wasting good food he worked hard to put on her plate. Iva was an ungrateful child. Her mother left the table. Doors slammed: the bedroom door, the bathroom door, the front door, and finally the car door.

"Are you glad you came to Roman's Gardens?" For some reason she needed to hear Cobb say that he was happy.

He shrugged.

Closer to town, Route 6A become Harmonmeyer Road. Traffic crawled and stalled where CalTrans was widening it to three lanes. A jackhammer banged in her ears and perspiration dampened the nape of her neck. In the hot truck, she and Cobb cooked like a pair of Sunday roasts. She rolled up the windows and turned on the air-conditioning, shivering in the blast of cold, stale air as the line of vehicles inched forward. Ahead, beyond the cars and trucks and workers in their yellow vests, she saw the square buildings of South Sebastian Plaza: Target, Office Depot, PetSmart, all the uninspiring name brands of retailing in one uninspiring location. Iva had walked through all of them so many times, she could do it blindfolded.

Half a mile after the shopping plaza she turned right on Iglesia and traffic stalled again. In front of the big church, police officers directed the traffic. In a move that would have horrified her father, she cut in front of oncoming traffic to enter the church parking lot where a stream of adults and children hurried toward the church entrance.

"Are we going to church?"

"You won't tell Roman?"

Cobb's face went blank. "I don't care."

St. Mary and All Angels had been constructed in the early fifties, when society's awareness of sin ran high and so did church attendance. The nation had been ruled by a spirit of optimistic, go-get-'em Christianity, and church designers and builders did a big business. All Angels was built for the ages in large blocks of stone and had soaring arches and lofty stained glass windows, a towering entrance. Inside, jewel-colored icons of the Virgin and Jesus stared out from niches set into the walls along the side aisles. Dappled light falling through clerestory windows cast Technicolor coins across the congregation.

A man in a suit with a red flower in the lapel smiled at Iva and said something about a warm welcome as he handed her a program and directed her into the nave. On the front of the program, Maggie Duarte's photo smiled at Iva.

The crowd pressed her forward to another man with a red flower who also smiled and, cupping her elbow in his hand, guided her into the last pew. She and Cobb stood with people on either side of them.

Behind her, she heard an angry voice and, like everyone else, turned to see what was happening. Her view of the portal was blocked by the choir filing two by two through a side door at the back of the nave, pairs of boys and girls in red and white with frilled collars followed by at least thirty men and women similarly costumed, lacking only frills. Outside, the argument went on, growing louder and more strident. The woman's voice rose in rage or pain, Iva couldn't tell which.

Triumphantly loud organ notes startled her and the choir began its cadenced march down the center aisle. At the head of the procession walked a man swinging what looked like an elaborately decorated silver birdcage from which billowed incense that burned Iva's sinuses. Next, a tall bald man holding a carved wooden cross, and then a dozen priests and ministers. The choir stirred and began to sing, and though she could not understand the words, Iva knew that they were saying *thank you, thank you, thank you.*

Behind her, the huge oak doors shut.

Iva waited to be found out, to be told to leave. But there was no announcement that Iva Devane was a heathen who didn't like Maggie Duarte, whose husband despised the woman and called her a roach and wished Donny's aim had been better. Iva tried to block this thought. Staring down at the upholstered kneeler, she focused on a long, shallow, lightning-shaped crack in the mahogany-red leather.

The woman beside her was sobbing and smiling at the same time. She nudged Iva and handed her a tissue as if she expected that at any minute she, too, would be weeping.

With so many bodies standing closely together and the air clouded with incense, it was warm in the church and Iva found it hard to breathe. Her hips and ankles ached like they were about to break. She remembered all the things Roman had told her about the governor: that she wasn't a real citizen, that she was lazy and bone ignorant no matter how many fancy schools she'd conned herself into, that she was against marriage and encouraged abortion. The list of her sins went on and on. Fearing that her expression would reveal her thoughts, Iva covered her face with her hands. The woman beside her gently patted her back.

Iva and Cobb did what everyone else did. They stood and sat and kneeled. There was more singing, and the happily sobbing woman handed Iva an open hymnal. In high school Iva had sung in the choir and piano lessons had taught her how to read music, but it was years since she did more than hum to herself as she worked in the garden. The sound of her full-throated contralto was a happy surprise, something strong and beautiful she carried within herself and had forgotten. Cobb stared at her, a look of wondering confusion on his face.

An old priest with scant flyaway white hair climbed to the pulpit and introduced himself as Father Peña, who had been at this church for more than fifty years. He had known Maggie Duarte since she was a baby, and he believed that her miraculous recovery was a sign of her goodness and God's grace and favor to all the people of California. He talked a long time and the congregation listened to every word without growing restless, except for Iva, whose back hurt, who couldn't draw a deep breath no matter how she tried.

In the whole packed church she knew she was the only person whose gratitude had nothing to do with the governor. Staring down at Maggie Duarte's picture on the service program, she realized that she did not care about her at all. It was Roman who had the political opinions. All Iva wished was that Donny hadn't gone crazy that day. It was Donny she cared about.

There was more praying and singing and even a speech from a tall man in a dark suit who said he was Robert Cervantes, the governor's husband. He thanked the citizens of San Sebastian for their loyalty and affection and prayers. At the end everyone stood and applauded, which Iva had never imagined happening in church. The choir sang and people clapped in time, and then at the end there was cheering. It was like a ball game. In her eagerness to escape, Iva staggered as she exited the pew. The woman who'd given her a tissue smiled with understanding and laid her hand on her arm to steady her.

In the garden outside the church the argument was still going on. As the crowd poured through the door and down the wide front steps, Iva caught a glimpse of the woman making the commotion and recognized Donny Crider's mother.

21

S ophie had not slept well on the sofa in Tamlin's family room, and not long after she drifted off, the smell of Jimmy's coffee woke her again. She got up as soon as he was gone and left the house as the sun was rising over the mountains in the east county. At home she showered and scrambled her last egg. Her first stop was the Starbucks drive-through, her second the jail.

She sat with Donny in the same featureless room, facing him across the same steel table. His olive skin had lost its glow, turned a jailhouse gray, and his hair, which had been thick and lustrous at their first meeting, now hung in oily clumps. A constellation of blackheads spread along his jaw-line, his eyes were bloodshot, and he had chewed his nails until they bled. The stink of despair surrounded him.

"You need a shower. Aren't you getting shower privileges?"

She pushed a cup of coffee and a scone across the table.

He looked over his shoulder at the door.

"It's okay. Eat. No one's going to stop you."

Little by little, the jail authorities were easing up on Donny. No one felt any sympathy for him, but he was so obviously not a threat that the initial extreme security seemed excessive. Though his ankles were still shackled, it was loosely done, and in the interview room his hands were free. "My investigator met your dad yesterday. He says you visited him a couple of weeks ago."

"So?"

"What happened?"

"What d'you mean?"

"What did you talk about?"

"Nothin'."

"Did you ask him why he never came to see you? Salinas is just up the road."

"I know where it is. He's got other kids now. I saw their pictures on his desk. Girls." He chewed a hangnail. "He's just a guy."

"Why'd you go up there? You must have had something you wanted."

"I was going to ask him for money. Jenna said I should do it."

"Did you?"

"No."

"Why not?"

He licked the blood off his cuticle.

"He told you he'd already paid money that month. Isn't that what happened? You found out that your father has been paying support for you since he left. Almost fifteen years ago.

How did that make you feel, Donny? Your mother lied to you. Didn't that make you mad?"

She already knew that the conversation was making him angry but it wasn't in his nature to admit it or show his emotions directly. The tells were subtle, a tightness at the corner of his mouth, a rolling muscle in his jaw. That day in the park something had pushed his anger out of hiding and into the open.

"Can we talk about something else?"

"What would you prefer?"

"Whatever."

"Okay, how 'bout this? Tell me everything you remember about the day Maggie was shot. I know we've been over this before, but I need to hear it all again."

He groaned and slumped in the chair, looking exhausted in the way Sophie had seen her father look near the end of his time at the market. A look that said he'd had enough, had reached his limit or nearly so.

"I've already told you. I don't remember nothin'. I was at the fountain and then I was in the parking lot and the cops were grabbing at me."

"Let's go back to that morning. Before you went to the park. Come on, Donny," she urged. "What time'd you get up that morning?"

Every morning at six fifteen for as long as he remembered, Elena had knocked on his bedroom door with the heel of her hand. One-two-three.

"Did she come in?"

"Couldn't."

"Why not?"

"The door was locked."

"Really?" Sophie was surprised that Elena let him have a lock on his door.

"I just put 'em on." She saw the hint of a smile. "On the windows too. Both of them."

Elena had been the kind of mother who snooped in her son's drawers and between the mattress and the springs.

"You were hiding the gun."

"I guess."

"When you woke up that morning did you know you were going to shoot the governor? Did you steal the gun so you could shoot her?"

"No."

"You had a reason, though. Tell me what it was."

"I liked it. The way it felt."

"In your hand you mean? Taking aim?"

"I just liked it."

"Did it make you feel strong?"

"I don't know."

Sophie knew it did. "Okay, so you woke up at six fifteen. What did you do then? Did you eat breakfast?"

"This is stupid."

"Maybe, but you've got to go along with me. I know what I'm doing." She hoped this was true. "I know you're tired of answering my questions, but this is the way it goes. I'm trying to figure a way to help you, to get the prosecutor to give you a sentencing deal, and I'm telling you right now, kid, it doesn't look good."

"I just wish..."

"You wish you didn't do it. Believe me, I get it. I bet you were sorry the minute you did it, weren't you? Right now, you're so full of regret you can hardly breathe sometimes."

He licked the tip of his index finger and pressed it down on a crumb. He wasn't looking at her, but she sensed him listening.

"You'd like to live that day all over. But there's not going to be a do-over, Donny. I got a call from the prosecutor yesterday." She and Ben had one of their rare strictly business conversations. Two professionals doing their jobs.

How many times do I have to say it? I'm not dealing on this, Sophie. I've got a list of charges as long as your arm, and every one of them'll stick.

Attempted first-degree murder, assault with a deadly weapon, battery, possession of a firearm without a license, discharging a firearm in a public place, reckless endangerment, mayhem.

He's going away for life or good as.

She told Donny, "At this point, there's no way I can keep you out of prison."

"I know that."

"Do you? Really? From where I'm sitting, I see a kid who thinks if he keeps stonewalling his troubles'll go away. That isn't going to happen. Don't you see, Donny? You have to talk to me. You've got to help me understand every element of the crime. You need to let me inside your head. Give me something to work with."

He nodded, at what she wasn't sure.

"I didn't eat; I didn't eat all day."

Was low blood sugar a defense for attempted murder?

"I wasn't hungry. I couldn't eat anything."

"You sound angry. Now. Talking about it."

"Here's what I did." As he leaned across the table, there was a spark in his eyes. "I got up. I peed and I went into the kitchen. She was frying something and I thought I'd throw up from the smell. That's the only way she knows to cook. Toss everything in a frying pan. I thought about grabbing the pan and throwing it out the back door or hitting her over the head with it. She told me to sit down and I told her to fuck off."

"Really? Did you always talk that way?"

He shrugged.

"And you said those words: 'fuck off'?"

"Maybe I thought 'em."

In Elena's version of the day—her birthday—there had been nothing but hearts and flowers that morning.

"You were mad because she was frying food?"

"She said something."

"Tell me."

"It doesn't matter."

"Trust me, it matters."

"I was sick of her messing with my life."

"What had she done? Specifically."

"I don't remember."

"Did it have something to do with your going up to see your father?"

"I forget."

Sophie pressed the point, but it became clear that he wasn't willing to say more. On another morning, after a good night's sleep, she would have the patience to probe further.

"So when did you leave the house?"

"Around lunchtime."

"What did you do between then and breakfast?"

"She wanted me to use the Weedwacker in the backyard."

"Then what?"

"I listened to music in my room."

"With the door locked?"

"Yup."

"So you just sat?"

He was a teenaged boy. Maybe she didn't want to know what else he did.

"I cleaned the gun."

"Was it dirty?"

"I like messin' with guns."

"How were you carrying it when you left the house?"

He mimed shoving it into his waist.

"Did you plan to use it?"

"I don't know. I don't think so."

"Why did you take it with you?"

"I guess I liked the way it felt."

Powerful.

When Sophie was fifteen a boy sent her a note during Mr. Mather's geometry class.

I got something cool. Wanna see it?

She thought he meant it as a stupid sexy joke and didn't bother answering, just rolled her eyes in his direction. After school he caught up to her at her locker. He was a tall, thin boy with wicked blue eyes and Sophie kind of liked him, especially because Anna labeled him as trouble when he came into the market and talked to her on the days she worked the deli counter.

He leaned against the lockers and whispered, "I got a gun."

Though she made an effort to appear unimpressed, the idea horrified and excited her.

"Meet at the depot behind Slopes Mill on Sunday."

"I've got church." That had been part of the deal made with Anna. If she went to public school she had to promise never to miss either Mass or Confession.

"Come after lunch," he said. "I'll let you shoot it."

Slopes Mill was on the north end of town, the ruin of a mill that had thrived on Peligro Creek one hundred years earlier. Behind it, a trail meandered for a half mile roughly parallel to the 101. It terminated at an abandoned CalTrans depot, where the boy was waiting for her.

"You better not be lying to me," she said.

He showed her six bullets.

"Big deal. Everybody's seen bullets."

Grinning, he said, "Gimme a blow job and you can shoot 'em all."

"In your dreams." Sophie tossed her head and started back up the trail, mad at herself for having walked all that way for nothing.

He came after her and grabbed her arm. She whirled on him.

"Touch me again and I'll kill you."

She meant it and apparently he knew that, because despite the obvious difference in their sizes and strength he stepped back and dropped his arms, his palms facing her, empty and innocent of threat. His laugh had a squeak in it.

"You sure got a temper. Can't you take a joke?"

"I don't think you even have a gun. I think you're a lying fuck. If I tell Carmine—"

"No, no, really, I got one." He grabbed at the pocket of his Windbreaker. "See?"

A snub-nosed pocket pistol. For several seconds she could not take her eyes off it. It was the only pistol she'd ever seen up close in real life, not a movie. He grinned and she realized it was a mistake to let her interest show. She turned away and continued toward home, conscious that the boy was behind her. With a gun in his hand.

"You want to hold it? I'll let you if—"

"I wouldn't touch your dick with a six-foot stick." She liked the rhyme and thought how Tamlin would laugh.

"I'm not sayin' that. You don't have to do anything."

"You bet I don't."

"Yeah, yeah, it's okay. I get it." He wanted her company, her approval. "Here."

When she told the story to Tamlin later in the day, her friend was more shocked than entertained.

"Why did you go out there?"

"I wanted to see it."

"A gun?" Tamlin looked disgusted. "I'll introduce you to my grandfather. He's got a closet full of them. What did you think was going to happen?"

"I don't know. I guess that's why I went."

22

Hamp was waiting in the office.

"Fair warning," she said, glowering at him. "I just came from Donny and I'm pissed. He gives me nothing, zero. Plus I didn't sleep well."

"You want me to come back?"

"Just speak calmly and quietly and don't tell me anything that'll make me unhappy."

He elaborated on his interview with Brad Crider. She'd read his report but wanted to hear details.

"If you ask me, he's a spineless creep." She was too cranky to apologize for being cranky.

"He tried to take her to court, Sophie. When Elena found out, she told him she'd lie to the judge to keep him away from Donny. She was willing to perjure herself and ruin his reputation."

"And he let her get away with it. A real prince." Her words made Hamp look uncomfortable. "What is it with you and this guy?"

162

"I agree with you, he's spineless. But that woman's a real ballbuster."

Sophie couldn't disagree with that.

"Did you ask him about standing bail?"

"He won't do it."

In frustration, she slapped her hand against the desktop.

"He says he's protecting his kids."

His *other* kids. Donny didn't count.

"If Elena was such a bitch to be married to, so bad that he still doesn't want to have anything to do with her, imagine what it must be like to be her son." She told him about the locks on Donny's door and windows.

"Plenty of kids have horrible mothers," Hamp said.

"That morning, though, there was something specific bothering him. He acted like he didn't remember what it was, but he was covering up. I want to know what it was."

At that moment, they heard raised voices from the outer office. Anna had taken time off to attend the church service for the governor, leaving Clary in charge. Her voice, sounding young and distressed, rose above the other.

The inner office door opened and Elena Crider stepped into the room like a storm system. Her hair was a mess and smeared makeup haloed her eyes. Behind her stood a young woman, smiling broadly, obviously enjoying herself. A man wearing a backpack was videotaping the scene.

Clary pushed her way to the front of the group, her round cheeks bright with indignation. "I said we don't allow cameras in the office. We don't, do we? And I told Mrs. Crider you were busy. I said she had to wait."

"You have other clients more important than my son?"

"Elena, all my clients—"

"I've just gone through the most humiliating experience of my life. In front of hundreds of people." She gestured to her two companions. "These people will vouch for me. They were witnesses. It's all on film. Tape. I want you to sue the church."

"What are you doing?" Sophie asked the woman holding her phone at arm's length in front of her. "Who are you?"

"Georgie Jobin," the young woman chirped. "*EyeSpye* magazine. This is my cameraman. Andy."

Sophie saw the red light of his camera and reached out as if to cover the lens. "Turn that thing off."

"I want you to sue St. Mary's."

"I'm so glad to meet you at last, Ms. Giraudo," Georgie said. "I'm hoping we can talk—"

"Make him stop recording or I'll call security."

Hamp made a move toward Andy.

"Easy, buddy." The light went off.

"They wouldn't let me go inside," Elena said. "I've been a member of that church since I came to this town. Father Peña baptized Donny."

Through the half-open door Sophie heard her mother's voice greeting the outer office receptionist and then the determined click of her Sunday shoes, indestructible thirty-year-old Ferragamos with sturdy two-inch heels.

She strode into the office in time to hear Elena say, "They barred me from worshipping in my own church."

"That's not true." Anna spoke to Elena directly. "You

know you were welcome. It was them"—she pointed in Georgie's direction—"the fathers were upset about. There was a church service going on, Mrs. Crider, not a carnival. We were there to thank God that our Maggie is alive after your son tried to kill her. I was on the steps outside the church, Sophie; I saw the whole dustup. If you need a statement from me, I can tell you precisely what happened. Plenty of others were there too."

Sophie looked at Hamp, hanging back, grinning, and for a fraction of a second, she wanted to laugh. Sometimes the practice of law was more like stopping a catfight than the high calling she believed it to be. She pointed at Georgie and Andy. "Both of you: out. You can wait for Elena in the outer office. Clary, you show them where. Ma and Elena, sit down."

Wary of each other, Anna and Elena took their places, side by side in two straight-backed chairs facing the desk. At the back of the room, Hamp leaned his lanky frame against the bookcase, arms folded, trying not to smile.

Sophie took a moment to collect her thoughts and remembered David Cabot's advice. *A good lawyer is a good listener.*

"You go first, Elena," she said, sitting down. "And stick to the facts."

23

Elena kept the most important fact to herself.

From the moment she handed Sophie the check for twenty-five thousand dollars, she wanted to take it back. What was the point of spending so much money when everyone knew that Donny had done the worst thing a person could do, committed the gravest sin there was and been damned to hell for all eternity? In the eyes of God it didn't matter if he had actually killed Maggie. In God's opinion intention was sufficient for damnation.

Fact number two, also kept to herself: if she could figure out a way to do it without the media tagging along, she would pack a bag and get out of San Sebastian. How much of her life was she supposed to sacrifice for a child conceived in a storeroom behind a grain and feed store, a child she'd never wanted in the first place?

In the days following the shooting, Elena's phone had rung all the time. She turned the volume down so she didn't have to listen to the messages until she wanted to.

She began cleaning the house in the morning and did not stop until evening. It was all that calmed her nerves, that and her imagination, which took her away from San Sebastian and into a world where she had plenty of money, could pack up and leave town on the train that five days a week stopped in San Sebastian for half an hour on its way to San Francisco. With the twenty-five thousand she'd given Sophie Giraudo, Elena would move to a city, change her name, and go to a community college, take a business course and learn about computers. She would become an executive and wear expensive clothes and stiletto heels, have her hair done in a salon and get a manicure every week. Dressed well and armed with an education, Elena believed she could do anything she set her mind to. She and Maggie Duarte had been born under the same star sign, and the only important difference between them was that Maggie had gotten the breaks and Elena had not.

She had mopped and dusted and run the Hoover. Down on her knees on the blue rubber kneeler, she scraped out the waxy gunk that gathered where the molding met the floorboards, a composite of dirt and lint and hair that she dug out with a dull knife.

The phone rang and she ignored it. The answering machine clicked on.

To enter Donny's bedroom, the police had taken the door off its hinges. Three officers ransacked the place, removing papers, books, and electronic equipment. What a relief it was to see the room cleared out. Immediately she had stripped his bed and tossed the sheets into the black trash barrel. The contents of his chest of drawers and everything in the closet went into the barrel as well. After dark she'd rolled it out to the curb for the collectors. With clean sheets and blankets, she remade his bed and then she scrubbed his dresser drawers with soap and water, which she knew wasn't good for the wood, but there was no other way to eliminate the odor of him. After she had scoured the closet in the same way, it still smelled of his shoes and his leather jacket and the perspiration that had dried in the armpits of his shirts.

At the end of the day she poured a jigger of gin over a pile of ice and listened to her messages.

Some of the recorded calls had come from newspapers, magazines, and television shows. Some of the voices on the line went on as if they were old friends and offered her money for exclusive interviews. Tell-alls. She wasn't fooled. She knew they wanted her shame more than her story. Wouldn't they just love to hear her confess that she had exactly three hundred and fifty dollars and twenty-eight cents left in her checking account? They would salivate like rabid dogs if they knew her refrigerator held half a quart of milk, some bread and mayo, a hunk of cheddar cheese and various despondent vegetables, two bagels, four eggs, and some cream cheese. For the media, public humiliation was the fat that made the steak sizzle.

Her resentment and worry had been manageable during the day, but when night came she couldn't sleep without the tablets she ordered online. Four of the little pink bullets knocked her out fast and kept her under until almost noon. It was not a healthy way to live; however, it would take more than pink pills to rock Elena's constitution. She came from strong German stock, and though she might have been the last child of thirteen, a bad-luck baby according to her father, she was made tough to last.

She wondered if any of her twelve brothers and sisters had seen her name in the paper or heard about Donny's wickedness on the television. She had left Garland, Nebraska, more than sixteen years before, and if her siblings saw a photo they might recognize her name but never her face, so little did she resemble the weedy teenage runaway, four months pregnant and willing to do anything, even marry a milquetoast like Brad Crider, to get away from the farm.

The message from the producer at *EyeSpye* had a respectful tone, which was in marked contrast to others.

"Mrs. Crider, believe me when I say that I'm sorry to intrude at this difficult time. This is the part of my job I really don't like. But I think when you hear what I'm offering, you'll be glad I called. I really do. Please don't erase this message, please, ma'am. You've had it up to your hairline with calls from the press, I know, but I'm offering something different. Just take a minute and hear me out."

He represented an online magazine Elena had never heard of, something called *EyeSpye* that specialized in telling in-depth video stories about people in the news.

"But we're not ghouls, ma'am. Our viewers want to know about *you*. They know you're a lot more than just Donny Crider's mother, and that's what interests them."

The deal she had been offered included an hour program

devoted to her on *EyeSpye*'s television show, which broadcast on a channel not included in Elena's cable package. He said something else about the Internet that she didn't understand.

"Millions of people all over the world watch *EyeSpye* stories online. We appeal to folks who want to get a deeper view of events, not the same old headline-grabbing stuff." A reporter would shadow her for a number of days, asking questions. Someone would be with her to film it all. She had been assured that it would be a comfortable relationship, without pressure. "All we want is for you to be yourself, Mrs. Crider."

The caller had said that *EyeSpye* would pay her twenty thousand dollars in two installments. As soon as she agreed, she would receive a check for ten thousand. She could stop worrying about money and regretting the sweeties, who were really not so sweet, not sweet at all.

24

Attending the service of thanksgiving at St. Mary and All Angels had been Elena's idea, a good one according to the producer at *EyeSpye*, who said it was just the kind of human-interest item *EyeSpye* was looking for. He told Elena that seeing her in church praying for Maggie Duarte's safe recovery would make her more sympathetic to the audience. She had made sure he understood that her desire to attend the service arose from her love for Maggie. Georgie had been particularly interested in that side of the story. She asked her to explain her feelings fully for the camera, which Elena had been happy to do.

Afterward Georgie had gone through her closet looking for an outfit that would set the right note for the service. Elena didn't need a twenty-three-year-old girl to tell her that the choices ranged from plain to worn-out.

"Let's go shopping," Georgie said. "Let's drive to Santa Barbara and get you a makeover."

Elena had money in her bank account now and a new

credit card crying out for attention. Why not splurge and lift her spirits?

In every store along State Street, saleswomen fluttered to her side in a way they never did when she shopped at South Sebastian Plaza. She bought a blue linen suit, a white silk blouse, a blue and green scarf with streaks of gold woven through it, and shoes that cost more than everything else combined. She thought as she wrote a check for all of it that no one from Garland, Nebraska, would recognize the sophisticated woman she had become.

The good feeling of yesterday had carried over to the morning, when Georgie helped her with makeup. More blush and eyebrows than Elena normally wore, but she wanted to be sure that she looked good on film. Or tape. She didn't really know what the difference was. She could not remember ever having been as excited as she was driving to the church in the EyeSpye van. She knew it was silly, but it felt as if the thanksgiving service had been arranged to honor her.

Afterward, sitting in Sophie's office, she related enough of this to make it clear that her intentions had been admirable. "Don't I have a right to thank God that Maggie is going to recover?"

Sophie said that she did, of course. "At the same time, you have to face the facts of your situation, Elena. People in town see you first as Donny's mother."

Anna Giraudo said, "No one wanted to keep you out of the church. It was the camera the fathers objected to. Father Peña doesn't even like them at weddings."

"Andy's only interested in me. He wasn't going to photograph anyone else."

"Well, if you want to see yourself on television"—Anna's tone was thick with disdain—"don't miss the news tonight."

"That's enough, Ma. You can go back to work."

Waiting for Anna to shut the inner office door, Elena looked up into the shadows of the beamed ceiling. The spiderwebs she'd noticed on her first visit were still there.

Sophie said, "You look very nice, Elena. That suit is a beautiful blue."

Elena blinked and looked down at hands that could have been her mother's: palms red and raw, fingers stubby and big knuckled, the dried-out nails pleated and broken. There had been no time for a professional manicure, and a slapped-on coat of clear polish couldn't conceal the damage done by chemical cleaning agents. She tucked her thumbs into her fists.

"I'm sorry you weren't allowed into the church. I know you care about Maggie. More than most, I think."

Elena waited for, expected, a *but.*

"I wish you'd told me about your arrangement with *EyeSpye.* We have to be so careful about the image you present to the public."

"I have nothing to hide. It wasn't me who shot Maggie. And anyway, you don't know what it's like to be poor, to struggle for every penny."

She didn't like the way Sophie looked at her.

"Come on, Elena. You can stop lying to me. You say you signed the deal with *EyeSpye* because you need the money pretty desperately. You say you struggle every month to make the house payment. But Brad Crider's paid you eighteen hundred dollars a month for the last fifteen years. What's happened to all that money? And why did you tell me he's never paid a penny?"

"You believe him?"

"I'm not asking you to explain, Elena. But you need to understand that I can't do my job if you lie to me. If you don't tell me the truth and Donny doesn't talk—"

"He never has. Dumb as a bedpost."

Watching Sophie shift in her chair as if she were uncomfortable, it occurred to Elena that for some reason her son's attorney was nervous. She sounded confident, but looks could be misleading. Heartened by what she perceived might be an advantage, Elena found her voice.

"People like Brad distort the truth to make themselves look good. You must be very gullible if you believe what he says. And what does he matter anyway? Brad's got nothing to do with the case."

"You're wrong, Elena. Everything about Donny touches the case. Donny feels like he hasn't got a friend in the world, that he can't trust anyone. Not me, not—"

"I'm his mother. He trusts me."

"Does he? He knows you lied to him about Brad. And I'm the only person who visits him. You won't even walk across town to spend fifteen minutes with him. Why should he trust you?"

"Just because you're his lawyer doesn't mean you can speak to me like that." Elena's back was so rigid it hurt.

"You're a single woman. You don't know about mothers and sons. It's a complicated relationship."

Elena had seen a television clip of Maggie Duarte addressing a hostile audience of central valley ranchers who were angry over her water policy. The madder they got, the straighter she stood. It was obvious that she wouldn't budge to pressure by bullies in cowboy hats and muddy boots.

"I won't argue," Elena said, steel in her voice. "I never told Donny the truth about his father. It has nothing to do with what he did, but if you must know why, I'm going to tell you. I started lying to him on the day Brad walked out because I knew that if I used the same words over and over, he'd get used to hearing them and when he was old enough to know what they meant, they'd just be words and couldn't hurt him."

Elena had never thought this through, never had the need to explain her behavior; surprisingly, it felt good to set the record straight. She wished Andy were in the room with his camera.

"Brad wanted to see Donny once a week. I knew that if I agreed to that, Donny would grow up thinking his father loved him. He would believe that the visits and the special treats and all the hugging meant something. And maybe for a while they would, for a few months or a couple of years maybe there would be some fondness there. But life interrupts, Ms. Giraudo. That's what life does. I knew that eventually Brad would start to cancel their weekends. He would always have an excuse and be so terribly sorry. Donny would say it was okay and he'd stand up straight and never let on that his little heart was breaking. After a while Brad would only come once a month because he'd be busy at work or with his new wife and pretty soon he'd begin forgetting things like his son's birthday. Do you see?"

Sophie nodded, irritating Elena with her neutral expression. Elena was talking about her life, her existence, but from the look on the lawyer's face she could have been reciting a shopping list. Planting her hands on the desk, Elena leaned in. "Brad's the kind of man who always leaves. But a child, a little boy, wouldn't know that, would he? You can say I lied to Donny, use that word if you must, but really, I was doing him a kindness. I'm a very good mother, Ms. Giraudo. An excellent mother. I wanted to protect my son, so I started saying it to him when he was a little sweetie—*your father doesn't love you, he never loved you, he doesn't want you*—and by the time he knew what the words meant, he was used to them. The truth couldn't hurt him."

25

After breakfast Iva cleared the table, but she didn't lay out papers, books, and pencils for her morning students as she normally did. Roman had asked her to wait until after he'd spoken to Milo.

The boy came into the room and stopped in the doorway, immediately suspicious. "What's happening? Where's the rest of the guys?"

Roman sat at the head of the table and used his foot to push out the chair on his right. "Sit."

Milo's particular variation of waifishness—part orphan with an outstretched hand, part urban sneak thief—had never appealed to Iva. Sallow skinned and squinty-eyed, he looked like he'd never eaten a balanced meal or had a good night's sleep; a childhood of deprivation showed in his eyes.

"Iva, honey, could you bring us a two-liter and some glasses? With ice, please, if it's not too much trouble?"

Milo could learn a lot from Roman, about good manners for one thing. About *please* and *thank you*. Did Iva want to fetch and carry from the time she got out of bed until she closed her eyes at night? Of course not. But she and Roman were a team and his requests were unfailingly polite. If he wanted a bottle of cola, he had his reasons, and if he wanted her to sit with him during his talk with Milo, there were good reasons for that too. She knew Roman inside and out, and she'd never had cause to doubt his wisdom.

He confessed that he could not face this talk without her moral support. It was a rare statement of dependence, but Iva knew the strongest man might falter after a week like the one just passed. Roman's gun with Donny's fingerprints on it had been found by a woman walking her dog along Peligro Creek. Since then, officers had come to the nursery three times asking questions about Donny and talking to some of the boys. Roman supported the police, but he had a deep distrust of them as well. Their attention made him jumpy and short-tempered.

She put the tray of drinks on the table and poured a soda for Milo, who watched her sullenly, his back and shoulders rounded like a tortoise's protective shell. He asked again, "Where is everyone?"

"In the orchard with Mr. Gotelli, checking the apricots." Gotelli was one of three senior nurserymen who assisted with the program and the business.

"Am I in trouble?"

"I was going through the record books a couple nights ago," Roman said in his friendly drawl. "I realized you're eighteen years old. That stunned me, Milo, and I felt real bad because you had a birthday and we didn't celebrate. Eighteen! My God, boy, that's a milestone. You should have reminded us. Eighteen means you're a man, Milo. You can vote now."

"What am I gonna vote for?"

"The thing is," Iva said gently, "Boys into Men is a program for boys."

Milo looked at Roman. A smile started at the corner of his mouth and then vanished.

"Ms. Iva's right. It's time for you to go."

"Go where?"

"You're eighteen, so you can choose for yourself. Take a bus north or south, San Francisco or LA or points in between. There's lots of farmwork over in the valley, farther east in the Imperial. You present yourself right and you could start in as a supervisor."

"I don't get it."

"I want you to go on upstairs now and pack your things, and then Ms. Iva and me'll sign you out."

"I been studying U.S. history. I know all the presidents' names. I know the times tables."

Iva's father had drilled her in multiplication until she knew the tables so well she dreamed the combinations. Sevens and eights on parade. Nines like stern fathers. Sixes were babies.

Milo looked at her. "What about the test?"

"You didn't pass," she said. "You haven't been a good student, Milo. You know that. You barely even try."

"You said I could take it again. You said a lot of guys fail the first time."

Roman pushed a white envelope across the table. "There's

five twenty-dollar bills in there. A little something to start you off."

"The money's supposed to be a present for passing." Milo looked from Roman to Iva and back to Roman, his expression narrow and calculating. "You told me that when I came here. You said I'd get a hundred bucks for a graduation present if I followed the rules and got my GED. You said I had to pass, I remember that real clear. And you'd give me a certificate so I could get a job. Am I gonna get one of those too?"

"You haven't earned it, Milo."

"You're kickin' me out but I still get the money? That's bogus, man."

"It's your behavior, toward the other boys—"

At emotional moments a vein rose and throbbed in Roman's forehead, a slightly doglegged line that ran down from his hairline almost to his eyebrow. Iva wondered if it was that telltale vessel that made Milo's ferrety half smile reappear.

"Is Cobb what got you pissed off?"

"Language, Milo."

"You don't like the way I am with Cobb? What about you, man? What about the way you are with Cobb?"

Roman stood up. "I'll get someone to drive you to the bus. You can go where you want."

"I don't want no ride. I want to stay here." Milo looked at Iva. "Tell him. You got eyes, don't you? You can see, can't you?"

"I'm done with you, Milo." Roman gave an odd small toss

of his head that Iva did not recall ever having seen before. "You'd best let that settle in your mind."

"You old creep."

She would be glad to see the back of Milo. The mood among the boys would be happier without his cruel teasing. Even so, the scene made her body ache inexplicably. She almost always understood Roman's behavior, but between him and Milo she sensed a new and puzzling dynamic, something previously hidden that she had not been meant to see.

26

A migraine. Half-blinded by shatters of white light streaming across her field of vision, Iva stumbled through lunchtime and was on her way upstairs intending to lie down for an hour when she heard a car in the driveway and the dogs' fierce barking. Looking out from the window on the landing, she recognized the woman getting out of the black 4Runner. She had seen Sophie Giraudo on television. The man with her was a stranger.

Iva's head ached so, she wanted to weep.

Roman invited them onto the porch, and snatches of their conversation drifted through the open windows as Iva prepared a tray of iced tea and lemon shortbread. Roman hadn't asked her to do this, she didn't want to do it, but she knew it was expected. Mother to a houseful of boys, partner and wife to Roman: until that afternoon these roles had given meaning and satisfaction to her life. Now, for the first time, she felt the pinch of resentment.

"We built the barn first," Roman was saying. "There's a

nice apartment at the back. We lived there while the house was being fixed up. That took a couple of years. My wife, Iva, has the patience of a saint, let me tell you that."

"Those dogs are pretty fierce looking," Sophie said. "What breed are they?"

"Cane Corso. Mastiffs. Mother and son. You don't want to mess with them."

"I'm sure I don't."

"We don't favor trespassers."

"Are they always chained?"

"At night the female, Riga, stays in the house. Laz, he's got the run of the place."

"Are they okay with the boys?"

"It's strangers they take against."

Iva wondered if Sophie and her companion heard the change in Roman's voice. She could not always trust her judgment when she had a headache, but it did seem that he was being almost threatening.

"Maintenance must be brutal," the man said. "A big place like this can't come cheap."

"We get by. Iva's some kind of genius with the budget, and the nursery turns a profit. We're mostly a wholesale shop, but we get a lot of visitors on weekends when we're open to the public. Boys into Men has private contributors, of course, growers and nurserymen all over the west who like to do their part supporting a worthy cause."

"Do you get grant money? From the city or the county?"

"I prefer to avoid government handouts. Keeps me independent."

Roman was not a fan of the federal government. Before he had a chance to wade into that subject, Iva stepped through the front door onto the porch. The screen door slammed behind her and she thought her skull would explode. Roman jumped up, took the tray, and made the introductions. "Hamp is Ms. Giraudo's private investigator, Iva."

Having seen detectives only on television, mostly dour and skeptical men in baggy suits, Iva was surprised by Hamp's faded blue jeans, his scrawny ponytail and pleasant smile.

"These cookies look great, ma'am. My mom used to make shortbread."

"Have all you want."

"Iva bakes cookies by the hundreds."

"We appreciate you taking time out to talk to us."

Hamp was like a neighbor dropping by for a lazy, catch-up conversation, but Sophie Giraudo had an impatient voice. Iva didn't believe her when she said she only had a few questions to ask.

"I was hoping you could tell me something about Donny. As you probably know, he isn't very talkative."

Iva had never known a boy who could not be drawn out by good food and kindness, but for a long while it had seemed that Donny was the exception to the rule.

"Can't hold a quiet nature against a boy," Roman said. "To be honest, most of them talk too much and what they say isn't worth listening to. Working with Donny was a pleasure. He's a good boy. I know he did a terrible thing, but it doesn't change my feelings about him."

Iva looked down, not wanting the visitors to see that Roman's words had brought tears to her eyes.

"How long was he in the program?" Sophie asked.

"Well, Donny's was a special case," Roman said, "but even so it was almost two years. There's a lot to learn." He sat forward, happy to talk about Boys into Men. "You take a boy like Donny, he's no good in school and he wants to quit or he's already quit and he's going nowhere. You know this kind of boy. We all do. These are the lost boys; our society's full of them."

"I've known a few in my time," Hamp said.

And done nothing to help them, Iva thought with a leap of satisfaction, as if she'd caught Hamp cheating. It was Roman who cared enough to step forward and offer his hand to the boys everyone else was ready to toss away like trash.

"We depend on word-of-mouth recommendations. A school counselor or a friend maybe. In Donny's case it was a neighbor who lived across the street from him. A customer of ours, a professor of anthropology over at the university. Boys into Men is a kind of trade school, I suppose, but we're serious about who gets in and who doesn't. We screen the candidates pretty good."

"It just about kills Roman when he has to turn one away."

"Do you ever get it wrong?" Hamp asked. "Misjudge a boy?"

"It's been known to happen. This out here"—Roman gestured toward the barn and greenhouses—"it isn't for every kid. The boys who stay with the program work hard, and in the end I give them a good reference when they leave."

"That means something," Iva said, thinking of how Milo

had reacted when he learned he would not get a letter from Roman.

"We've got boys who live at home and work here for minimum wage. If a boy wants to learn about the plant business, we figure out a way to make it possible. A few live in the bunkhouse and there are usually six or seven more residing here in the big house with my wife and I. We're like a family and Iva's the housemother." He patted her knee. "And the teacher."

"And you're the father figure?"

"Iva and I have not been blessed with children. That's a great sorrow to us. Both of us, we're important to these boys. I've got a file folder full of letters from them, thanking us for the time they spent in the gardens."

"You said Donny was an unusual case."

"He started out in the big group, coming in at seven a.m., going home at night and getting paid a little. Right off, he showed himself to be someone special."

"We'd never had a boy like him," Iva said.

"That's right. He came early, stayed late. I never knew a kid who worked with plants the way he did." Roman dug deep for words to explain himself. "One day, he'd been here...How long was it, Iva? About two months, maybe a little less? I told you. Remember? Donny didn't just look at a plant. He smelled it and he'd rub the leaves between his fingers to get the smell of them. This one time, I even saw him put a bit of dirt on his tongue like he could tell what nutrients were missing from it by the taste. Spooked me a little."

"The other boys would never do that," Iva said.

"He was born with a gift, let me tell you. He could make things grow."

"So you put him in the more intensive program," Sophie said, "and he lived here in the house?"

"In a manner of speaking. Most of our candidates are glad to get away from their families—if they have any—but Donny and his mom were close. He'd stay here most nights and then she'd get to needin' him and he'd go home and maybe we wouldn't see him for three or four days."

"Did it surprise you, Mrs. Devane?" Sophie asked. "When you heard about the shooting?"

Iva answered without thinking. "It almost broke my heart." A lump of grief swelled in her throat. "He was such a sweet boy. I suppose he still is. Either that or I never really knew him, except I'm sure I did."

Of all the boys, he was the only one who without being asked cleared the table after meals, the only one who stuffed his dirty overalls and socks, his smelly sheets and towels, in a pillow case and set it beside the washing machine, the only boy who volunteered to help her work the fruit and vegetable stand on Dry Creek Road during the bounty months.

The right side of Iva's face hurt, from temple to jaw. "I blame his mother."

"Iva—"

"Well, I do, Roman." With the migraine pain came a touch of giddiness and a lack of caution. "A while back she came here and demanded that Roman put Donny out of the program. Kick him out, just like that. All of a sudden he had to be at home with her. If you could have seen how unhappy he was." *Don't make me go. Let me stay. Please, Ms. Iva, I can't go back there.*

Roman said, "Iva, Donny's full-grown."

"The boy asked for so little, just a chance to work in the garden, but she was set against it. And us. You'd have thought we wanted to harm him, the way that woman carried on."

"Honey, these people need facts, not opinions. It was pretty near time for him to leave anyway."

"She could have let him stay a few more weeks—"

"When was it, Ms. Devane? This time you're talking about?" Sophie asked. "Was it around the time of the shooting?"

"A few days before." With the back of her hand, Iva blotted the tears from her cheeks. So what if these strangers knew how she felt. "She doesn't deserve him. A boy like Donny...I loved him." In the silence Iva was aware of Sophie's intense gaze and her face reddened. "I have to go inside. The boys get hungry in the afternoon so I send snacks..."

"Could we just talk for a little longer? Ms. Devane? Do you mind? Please?"

In an instant of eye contact, Iva saw that Sophie's interest was more than professional. She cared what happened to Donny.

"Ask your questions."

"I'm wondering if you'd have time to visit Donny in jail. I'm sure it would help him."

"That wouldn't be a good thing," Roman said. "We have to think about the other boys."

"I wouldn't mind..." Iva sighed. "But Roman's right. It might give the wrong impression."

Boys, always the boys. In Stockton they had come to the youth center for pancakes and scrambled eggs and basketball on Saturday mornings. Even back then Roman had his special favorites. If Roman cared for Donny, why wouldn't he visit? Why couldn't she? The other boys would never know.

The subject changed again. Now Sophie was talking about the gun and Iva wanted her to leave and never come back.

"You know that the police believe Donny stole your gun."

Roman smiled wryly. "We've had a few conversations on the subject."

"Where did you keep it?"

"I'll tell you what I told them, Ms. Giraudo. It was in the entry on top of the armoire. You couldn't see it even if you knew it was there."

"Not locked up?"

"No sense having a gun if you have to go hunting for the key when the bad guys come."

"You don't worry about the boys?"

"Of course he worries about the boys," Iva said. "How can you ask that question?"

"Easy now, sweetheart. They're just doing their job. Like I said, I kept the revolver well hid."

"Did you tell Donny it was there?"

"Now, why would I tell a boy where I keep my guns?"

"You have more than one?"

"I keep one next to the bed." He paused, holding her gaze. "As do many people."

"How do you think Donny found the one on the armoire?"

"As I told the police, I'd like to know the answer as much as anyone. I'm not even sure when it went missing. Two, three weeks ago, I reached up for it—"

"Did you have a particular reason? For reaching for it?"

"I clean my weapons regular."

"You use them, then? Frequently? Do you go to a shooting range?"

"A gun needs to be kept clean whether it's used or not."

"What did you do when you realized it wasn't on the armoire?"

"I called the police and reported it missing, of course. I didn't want the boys involved at all. It was the only thing I knew to do."

Hamp asked, "Could Donny have seen you put the gun on the armoire?"

"I suppose it's possible. I suppose it must have happened that way, else how would he have known it was there? Still, I've got to say I'm surprised. I hate to think I was in any way responsible..." A shadow of confusion clouded Roman's expression for a moment. Iva grabbed for his hand. "He was a good boy. We were both fond of him."

27

I didn't like him," Sophie said, driving back on Dry Creek Road. "He wasn't being straight with us. You saw the vein in his forehead? That didn't pop because he was calm and relaxed."

"He's emotional about the kid. Obviously he was special to both of them. You jump to conclusions, Sophie."

"And you've known me such a long time."

"Devane's pretty stuck on himself. Maybe that hit you wrong."

"You didn't pick up any false vibes?"

"I'm not saying that."

"What are you saying, then?"

"How could either of those people have anything to do with the shooting? From what I could tell, they're the only people Donny has who care about him."

"Okay, I'll give you that. But what about the gun stuff? Did you see the look on her face when I brought it up?"

"Cut her some slack. She was in pain."

"Yeah. I think she had a headache. She kept rubbing the side of her face."

Sophie had observed something else. At the mention of the gun, Iva crossed her arms over her chest and tucked her feet, one twisted about the ankle of the other, deep under the wicker chair. "She wanted to disappear."

Hamp stared at the passing scene a moment. "I'll try to find a way to talk to her. Away from him. But, Sophie, what difference does it make? Donny's an opportunist. He saw the gun somewhere in the house and he took it. He's a kid, a boy. Boys do things like that."

"Maybe. But I still don't like Devane and I don't think he's telling us everything. He might have gotten careless or the boys always knew where the gun was kept. However it happened, he's covering his ass now because if it ever comes out—"

"Boys into Men would be finished."

"When you talk to her, see what you can learn about that scene she described, when Elena told them Donny had to come home. Maybe that's what he was mad about."

"That and learning she'd lied to him about his father."

"And he was ticked off because she ordered him home. He stole the gun and put locks on his bedroom. If he had to be home, he'd at least have some privacy. I think just having the gun made him feel stronger." It was only a theory but it made more sense than anything else Sophie had come up with to explain Donny's actions.

Up ahead, a tall, thin boy in a T-shirt and blue jeans with a backpack looped over one shoulder slouched down the middle of Dry Creek Road. Sophie braked and he moved toward the left shoulder to let the 4Runner pass. On the back of his tee was a silkscreened circle. Above it was written *Roman's Gardens* and below the circle, *Boys into Men.*

Sophie rolled down the window.

"Need a ride?"

He ignored her.

"You're from Roman's Gardens, right? I see it on the back of your T-shirt." The 4Runner coasted beside the boy. "We just came from there."

His eyes looked straight ahead.

"It's at least three miles into town. Hop in the back. The door's not locked."

He squinted at Sophie and then at Hamp beside her in the front, sizing them up. He opened the car door and got in.

"So what's your name? I'm Hamp and this is Sophie."

"Milo."

Watching him in the rearview mirror, Sophie said, "I'm Donny Crider's lawyer. You know him?"

He looked out the window.

Hamp said, "Maybe you could tell us what you know about Donny."

"Were you guys friends?"

"I don't know nothin' about him."

"Did you live in the house or the bunkhouse?"

"Why're you askin' me this shit?" He scrambled for his backpack and grabbed at the door handle. "Let me out."

Sophie held a business card back over her shoulder. He didn't take it, but in the rearview mirror, their eyes met.

"You'd like to help Donny, wouldn't you? He's not a bad kid, is he?"

"He shot that lady governor."

"Why do you think he did it?"

Milo's reflection expressed confusion.

"Did he ever talk to you about shooting someone? Did he talk about the governor?"

"Donny never talked period."

She fluttered the business card to get his attention. "If you think of something that might help..." After a hesitation, he took it. "You can reach me at that number." He shoved the card in his jeans pocket and after that they rode in silence until Milo asked to be let off at a bus stop.

"Why don't you stick around town?" Hamp handed him a twenty-dollar bill. "Come see us tomorrow."

"The address is on the card."

Sophie read Milo's thoughts, his classification of them as weirdos, maybe perverts bent toward boys.

"Do you have a place to stay? Where are you going?"

"Crazy." He smirked and grabbed the twenty. "Wanna come along?"

Sophie dropped Hamp off at his rental suite.

"I'm headed out to the beach for a while," he told her. "I'll check in later."

In the office Anna handed her a fistful of messages as usual. "Ben called to tell you they arrested one of the Bleeker brothers—Junior—on account of something that Cardigan boy told them. He wanted to know if you can have dinner tonight. I told him you probably could; you never go out on dates."

"Ma, you can't say things like that."

"I'm just fooling with you, Sophie. What's happened to your sense of humor?"

"Okay. Ha-ha. What else have you got for me?"

"The psychiatrist, he called. He's still in Chicago and sends his regrets."

"Shit."

Six months earlier in Chicago's Arlington community, a boy had taken a gun out of his backpack during second-period U.S. history and started firing. Alexander Itkin, an authority on teenage boys and violence, was testifying for the defense.

"He's sorry for the inconvenience and says when he knows his schedule for sure, he'll call."

"Did he say when that might be?"

Anna shook her head.

"I need him to help me make sense of this."

"Donny Crider shot Maggie. What's to make sense of?"

"I'm not smiling, Ma."

"I'm not joking, Sophia."

Anna followed her into her office.

"Can't it wait?" As she dropped her purse on a chair, her cell rang and she dug it out. "Tamlin's been texting me all day. *Call me. Call me.* Like I've got time?"

Anna waved the pink message slips. "There's two here from her. And a bunch from Mrs. Crider."

Sophie groaned.

"Your brother says you have to get over to the high school, ASAP. He's got someone in his office he says you're going to want to talk to." Anna glanced at her watch. "You've got about forty-five minutes before school lets out."

"What's it about?"

"Wouldn't I tell you if I knew?"

Sophie blew Anna a kiss and headed out of the office, ignoring her advice to stay hydrated, take time to eat. In the car, risking a fine she couldn't afford, she phoned Tamlin and made a date to meet her that evening. She left a message for Elena Crider saying she'd try to stop by later. Somewhere in the cracks of time, she had to see Donny again, and she needed downtime to think about Roman and Iva Devane, what was off about them. Meanwhile, she couldn't get the smart-ass voice of that weaselly kid out of her mind. *Crazy, wanna come along?*

28

She pulled into the guest lot at the high school and parked under an acacia tree in yellow powder-puff bloom, guaranteed to make her sneeze if she breathed too deeply. She hurried across the lawn and up the front steps. When she was a freshman, liberated from the nuns at All Angels Academy, SanSeb High had served the whole county, almost three thousand students crowded into a facility meant for half that number. As long as Sophie and the other kids whose grades and deportment were satisfactory didn't push the limits too far or hard, their overworked teachers left them alone. How great it had felt to be ignored.

Carmine's counseling office was on the second floor in a recent addition to the building. At his open door she paused a moment, observing him behind his desk with his fingers splayed on either side of a pile of papers, arms hyperextended, his head lowered as he studied whatever was written there. In a buttoned-down oxford cloth shirt and loosely knotted tie, wearing a gray cardigan sweater not unlike the ones their father had worn for work, he was not quite her brother, more like Mr. Lovelle, who had counseled seniors when she was in high school, similarly fusty and slightly seedy. When had her handsome and athletic brother become this overworked middle-aged man? Did he look forward to work in the morning? Did that gray sweater fit him comfortably or did he wish it were a football jersey, a police uniform, a rich man's bespoke suit?

A girl, brunette with large black-outlined eyes and unblemished caramel-colored skin, sat to one side of his desk. She wore black denim jeans, a black T-shirt with a metallic tribal design, and a khaki fatigue jacket. The thought of spending a day in her open-toed, three-inch platform heels made Sophie's feet and calves ache.

Carmine introduced her as Jenna Feliz.

"Jenna and Donny Crider were friends." He stood in the doorway. "I'll be outside in the hall. Maintaining calm among the savages." He added more softly, "I could get in trouble for this, so just remember she's a kid, okay? No third degree."

In the closed room Sophie smelled the girl, a rich floral bouquet mixed with the chemical fragrances of hair spray and a heavy application of deodorant. All this effort to smell sweet but look tough. For some reason, it made Sophie sad. She took a minute to compose herself, standing at the window looking down on the student parking lot. Trucks, SUVs, a black Lexus, not a beater in sight. Apparently student jalopies were things of the past. It was only twenty years since Sophie was Jenna's age, but it felt like a century.

"Thanks for talking to me, Jenna. Like my brother said, I'm Donny's attorney and I'm trying to learn more about him so I can make sure he gets a fair trial." Carmine's chair looked more comfortable than any other in the room, but recalling how friendly Hamp had been when they talked to Roman and Iva, she brought a folding chair from across the room and positioned it at an angle facing Jenna. On second thought, this seemed confrontational. She pulled it off to the side.

"Thanks for talking to me, Jenna. I really need your help." She would woo this girl into cooperation, girl to girl. If Carmine were listening in, he'd wonder what sociable clone had replaced his straight-shooting sister. "I need to know Donny better. Would you be able to help me? Answer a few questions?"

"I guess." Jenna looked down at her hands, and her long hair, crookedly parted in the middle, concealed her face. "My cousin's in the choir." Using her index finger, she tucked it behind her ear. "He could've killed her." Her look challenged Sophie to deny it.

"But he didn't. It's important to remember that." Sophie smiled, hoping that her words didn't sound like a reprimand. "You drove him up to see his father in Salinas."

"Am I in trouble for that?"

"No, but I wondered why."

"Why not? I told him he should confront him, like, demand something. Money. Donny wanted to go places, but that takes money. I went online and found his father's name, found out he had a bunch of property so he was probably rich. I mean, why not ask for some of it? He owed him, right?"

"But he didn't get it."

Jenna pushed her hair out of her eyes. "I don't think he

even asked. He wouldn't talk to me on the way home. Like whatever happened it was my fault."

"Was he angry at you?"

"I don't think so. He got that way sometimes. Just quiet in a heavy kind of way."

A weighty silence.

"Was he your boyfriend?"

"No." She said the word as if it had two syllables, to indicate that Sophie's question had been, like, totally dumb.

"You were friend-friends, then. For a long time?"

"Sophomore year we were lab partners in biology."

"How'd that happen?"

"Everybody else paired up except us, so the teacher put us together. Donny knew I needed a good grade for college. He helped me out."

Hamp would have asked where she was going to college and what she planned to study, but Sophie was interested in Donny.

"Was he smart?"

"Sometimes. Especially in science."

"He's not much of a talker, is he?"

Jenna rolled her eyes. "Get him going about plants and he doesn't shut up."

"Such a good-looking guy, I guess he didn't need to talk much."

"He didn't think he was good-looking."

It was an odd insight for a teenage girl. "How do you know that?"

"You could just tell he didn't think about stuff like how

he looked." Jenna looked at the wall clock and reached down for her backpack. "I gotta go."

"You could tell that. How?"

"It doesn't matter, does it?"

"Everything about Donny matters, Jenna."

For a minute she pleated the strap of her backpack. "He told me one time that he felt like he was invisible."

"What did he mean by that?"

"How would I know? I thought it was weird."

Sophie asked herself if, on the day he shot Maggie, Donny had come to a moment of decision. He could stay invisible or be seen. She remembered Elena saying that he'd shot the governor to get attention.

"Did he ever talk about doing something to get attention?"

"That's not why he shot her."

She sounded absolutely certain. "Then why?"

"He wasn't like that."

"What did you two talk about?"

"Nothing."

"Come on, Jenna. Help me out, will you?"

"School. Stuff in the future, I guess. Sometimes. Plants mostly."

What a strange boy he must have seemed to this semitough girl. Handsome, quiet, smart in science and willing to help her. A boy who felt invisible.

"Plants and all were the only thing he ever got excited about, you know? He told me there was this guy, like his hero kind of? He went to China and discovered all these new kinds of flowers and bushes and stuff. He brought the seeds back and pretty soon there's all these Chinese plants in everyone's garden. We used to walk around and he'd, like, point to stuff and say, 'That's an Australian blah-blah,' or 'That's an Amazon lily.' He liked to say the Latin names." Jenna looked at Sophie and then, quickly, away. Donny's eccentricity made her an oddball by contagion. "He had dreams. He wanted to be like the guy who went to China. Have you ever heard of that?"

"A plantsman." Sophie wondered if Elena knew anything about her son's dream. "He sounds like a special person."

"He tried to kill the governor."

"Do you think he felt invisible when he was with you?"

"How should I know?"

Sophie thought of Hamp, of being friendly and not pushing too hard, but she was impatient. This girl knew things. Sophie was sure of it.

"What about Mr. Devane? Did Donny ever talk about him?"

"You mean Roman? Omigod." She rolled her eyes. "He thought he was great. He sure didn't feel invisible around him. He was always telling me how smart he was and how he was helping him so much. Teaching him. I told him he could study plant stuff in college but first he had to graduate high school. You can't do anything without a diploma, right? He said the guy's wife was helping him get one, but I guess that's not going to happen now."

"Actually, he took the test, Jenna. And he passed."

"You mean he could go to college? Then why did he... you know?"

"That's the big mystery."

"I don't know anything about it. And besides, we got so we didn't talk all that much. He mostly lived out there, at Roman's."

"He was happy there."

"There was this, like, place they called the clubhouse? With a big TV and a pool table. And they played basketball." Jenna looked at Sophie from the corner of her eye. "He was glad to get away from *her*."

The voices of students in the hall had grown louder. Glancing at the wall clock, Sophie saw that the final bell would ring soon.

"Him and his mom didn't get along so good."

"Isn't it normal—"

"He hated her."

"Did he tell you that?"

"I could tell."

"How?"

"A feeling?"

"Did you ever meet her?"

"One time. He only took me over there to make her mad."

"Mad how?"

"Like, jealous? She had it out for me, I could tell."

"Did Donny know she didn't like you?"

"I told you. That's how come he wanted me to meet her. To make her mad. It was like a dig, you know? It wasn't like I was anyone special." She was caught unaware by her memory, and the teenage façade of belligerent apathy dropped, revealing a tender heart. Jenna had cared for Donny and perhaps daydreamed of being more than friends.

"You were friends and then you weren't. What came between you?"

"Nothing."

"There had to be something, Jenna. A turning point?"

"You mean like a fight? Donny didn't fight. He never had a fight with anyone. He just changed is all." She hugged her backpack, resting her chin on its bulk. The veil of hair covered her face. "He told me he was going to get a cell phone and call me, but he never did."

"Can you describe the change in him, Jenna?"

She shook her head.

"Did you ask him—"

She stood up. "The bell's gonna ring."

"Would you say he was depressed?"

"I don't know. Maybe. Sad and mad, mad and sad, all mixed together. But he was happy too. He liked what he was doing." Jenna pulled one strap of the backpack over her shoulder. "He just didn't like me anymore."

29

Hamp kept the picture of Bronwyn stuck in the visor of his 1995 Jeep Cherokee. When he looked at it he saw a brown-haired girl with her mother's Aztec cheekbones standing beside his O'Neill long board, which was, at the time, the most valuable thing he owned. She was fifteen.

I like the scary feeling, Daddy.

He didn't remember how old she was when she told him that. Maybe seven or eight, a fierce little grom in a blue bikini who wouldn't wear sunscreen and never burned, not even after an August day at the beach.

On the Cayucos pier, Hamp leaned against the wooden railing. Under his forearms, the old wood was swollen with damp and sticky with salt. As the ocean rose and fell, the old pier shuddered slightly under his feet. He focused his binoculars on the surfers astraddle their boards, waiting in the line behind the breaking waves. Sometimes he heard them calling to each other as they jockeyed for position. The wind was coming from the east now and the waves broke in shoulder-high swells, decent rides. There was a time when Hamp could spend the day floating, paddling, riding generous waves like these. He missed those days, but he didn't dwell on them.

On the horizon, the clouds were piling up, keeping their distance until the wind changed again and they could sail in. He guessed they might bring a spring storm to the Central Coast, a phenomenon less common than when he was a boy. Back in the day, his grandfather had kept a dozen acres of fruit trees over the mountains in Modesto. He and his old buddies called April storms the "cherry rains." They came when the crop was ready to harvest. A bad storm would ruin the year's fruit.

He focused his binoculars until he could see each surfer. From day to day, hour to hour, his disposition seesawed between the extremes of *today will be the day* and *give up, she's in a landfill somewhere*. When the surfers were in wet suits he could not always tell if he was looking at a boy or girl until they scrambled to their feet. That was when he'd recognize Bronwyn's smooth, quick moves. There was nothing tentative about his girl. When the time and the wave were right, she was up in one silken motion, sure and beautiful to behold. The guys noticed. Some didn't like that she waited until she wanted the wave and it wanted her. There was a lot of sexism in surfing and a girl had to prove herself every time she paddled out to the line. A natural like Bronwyn was a threat to some. They broke the rules and dropped in on her rides. When she was learning the short board and getting dumped all the time, they taunted her without mercy, but she took it all with the defiant little sneer she had. They didn't like that either. Her boldness worried Hamp. He made sure she understood that no matter how much fun a mixed group was having while the sun was up, no matter how harmless the teasing seemed, it always got dangerous on a beach after sunset.

A few months back the body of a girl had been found at Trestles. Because of the description in the paper—a girl in her late teens, a healthy Caucasian with brown hair—he'd gone down to look at the body. Hamp had been a cop and seen a few stiffs in his time, but when the officer opened the drawer and he got a whiff of the cold chemical air, it wasn't easy to look at the body. The girl had a tiny heart tattooed on her neck, just below the ear. Bronwyn thought tattoos were gross.

Afterward the officer on duty said the Jane Doe had been raped and strangled. Hamp hadn't been able to drive for fifteen minutes after that. He told himself that as sad as Jane Doe's story was, the girl was a statistic. He couldn't let himself think of her as someone's daughter.

His favorite memory of Bronwyn had nothing to do with the water. He liked to remember her the way she'd been on the weekend he drove her up to UC Santa Cruz and helped move her into the dorm. All the way up the 101 she was full of uncharacteristic self-doubt, pounding him with questions he couldn't answer.

"What if I don't make the team? What if my roommate doesn't like me? What if I don't like her? What if I can't find my classes? How'm I gonna get to the beach?"

"You'll be on the team and there's a surf club. You'll always be able to bum a ride." He would get her a car in a year or two if she made the dean's list. Maybe an Element with plenty of room to stow her gear. "You're a good student, Bronny. But you have to study. This isn't like high school."

"What if they don't like me?"

"Why wouldn't they like you?"

They both knew the answer to that. Bronwyn, who spoke her mind and didn't suffer fools, would never win the prize for Miss Congeniality. Her defensiveness and inclination to be abrupt reminded him of Sophie.

"And you'll make the team, for sure. Only listen to the coach, okay? Good as you are, you can always learn more." They'd been going over the same territory since she opened her UC acceptance letter.

Both Hamp and his ex-wife, Terri, would have preferred that their daughter stay in San Diego where they could keep an eye on her. She wasn't a bad kid or even particularly wild, but she got off on excitement and sometimes ignored her good sense. San Diego was stale bread to her and she couldn't wait to get away. Swami's, Windansea, Seaside: she'd been surfing them her whole life. In Santa Cruz she would prove herself at Natural Bridges and the legendary Steamer's.

Bronwyn had been in Santa Cruz two and half months when she stopped showing up for class. There were no more e-mails home, no texts or phone calls. When the coach called to say she'd stopped surfing with the club, Hamp had flown north and made a pest of himself on campus, speaking to her teachers, her roommate and friends, other surfers. Hamp and her coach had walked the beaches and talked to everyone with a board or wearing a wet suit.

He came back to San Diego with nothing.

Somewhere along the line a cop had told him, "You've got to wait, man. There's nothing else now."

Bronwyn's mother lived in a big house in Rancho Santa Fe, five miles from the nearest beach. Terri and Mel, a rich plumber, had been married for twelve years and had three sons under ten who played baseball and soccer. Terri made sure they never went near the water. It had been a good, though claustrophobic, environment for Bronwyn to grow up in. Stable.

Since Bronwyn's disappearance, Terri had been texting or phoning Hamp every day, leaving angry or pleading, occasionally manic, messages on his machine. In these she never called Bronwyn by name. She was always *my baby* or *my little girl*.

Two years ago he stood in Terri's living room—hadn't even taken off his coat—and told her he was leaving the job and going on the road.

"You won't see me again until I find her."

"I don't *want* to see you. I want to see my little girl."

Mel and the boys hung back during the conversation, knowing better than to get involved.

"You did this to her." Terri had a high, sharp voice. Even when she spoke softly, he could hear the scream waiting in it. "If she's dead, it's you who killed her."

The youngest boy started to cry, and Mel shushed him.

Hamp wanted to walk out of the house but didn't because

although what Terri said wasn't exactly true, it wasn't exactly false either. His encouragement hadn't changed Bronwyn's destiny, only facilitated it. She had been born to surf and taken to the waves like a flying fish. If he thought Terri would listen, that his words could lessen her pain, he would have said that whether Bronwyn lived in Denver or Fargo, she would still have found her way to the waves eventually.

He knew Terri was frightened—so was he. Fear could make people cruel. She beat him up because he was there, a stand-in for God or fate or luck. Maybe all three. He let her say what she had to.

"Surfing's an addiction and you fucking hooked her, your own daughter. You stuck the needle in her arm."

Her hands were clenched, her shoulders as rigid as a T-square, and for a second Hamp thought she was going to punch him. Without warning, the stiffening went out of her, her knees bent, and she was as limp as a dying flower. Hamp caught and held her to him. They stood with their arms around each other while Mel and the three boys looked on.

Surfing was a dangerous sport; Hamp knew that better than most. The sun gave you cancer. Bodies were ripped and torn on reefs and rocks. There were sharks in the water and jellyfish that stung. Occasionally you wandered onto a sandbox someone thought belonged to him alone and things got nasty. Waves and boards and rocks battered and hammered and broke ribs and necks and heads. Hamp had been concussed at least six times that he knew for sure. After the last wave bounced his head off a rock that shouldn't have been there, the doctor told him not to surf anymore. His brain had taken all the punishment it could stand. There was no way of telling whether it had already suffered too much. If that was the case, Hamp would know pretty soon. He was only forty-eight years old, but he might be running out of time.

In some places along the coast, he had a rep. He was the crazy father, the sad old gray. Guys laughed at him behind his back. Hamp didn't care; there wasn't time to care what people thought of him. He had to find Bronwyn before he forgot what he was looking for.

30

I nactivity did not agree with Elena, and yet there she was, sitting like a stooge with her hands on her lap, nothing to do but watch television and wait for something to happen.

She had cleaned until her hands were raw and the pine smell in the house almost asphyxiated her. Donny's room was as if he had never lived there. On the scoured hardwood floor there was a decorative rug his feet had never touched. She'd bought it on the shopping binge in Santa Barbara. At the time the rug had seemed like a bargain, twenty-five percent off, only seven hundred and thirty dollars.

Until that disastrous excursion, Elena had always been cautious with money, never forgetting her hard-luck child-hood. She blamed Georgie Jobin for the lavish spending spree that had depleted her bank account by thousands, knowing that on her own she never would have been so undisciplined. Clothes and shoes, new towels and sheets, the rug and that lurid purple satin comforter she absolutely did not need. Or even want.

There was food in her refrigerator now and the mortgage

had been paid for the month; nevertheless, it was a challenge to get out of bed in the morning. She forced herself to take a shower and get properly dressed, knowing that if Georgie and Andy showed up unannounced and found her in her pajamas at noon, they would be delighted to record the day for posterity. She wouldn't give them the satisfaction.

Since her humiliation at St. Mary and All Saints, Elena had retreated further from the world and spent her days indoors, walking from room to room, never venturing onto the front porch during daylight hours. Though most of the media had lost interest in her, there were still a few die-hard reporters lurking about. The backyard was secure and private, but without Donny's controlling hand, spring had taken over. The weeds grew tall and thick and she was afraid to walk there, imagining herself bitten by a snake and left to die. Snakebite, an electrical short, or a bit of meat caught in her windpipe—that was all it would take. A slip on that damned throw rug.

She had never feared for her safety when Donny lived in the house. He had the filthy habits of all adolescent boys, but if she fell down the back stairs, he would at least give her a hand up or call 911. She wondered if he got phone privileges at the jail, and if so, why hadn't he called her. He must realize how awful it was for her to be alone.

In the beginning, she had cursed her telephone for ringing, but now it was mostly silent. Even Sophie Giraudo didn't return her calls. The yellow light on the answering machine had stopped blinking. She had cleared all but one message, a surprising one from her sister Myra, which she saved.

"Honey, I just saw what happened. I've been in Mexico and we don't have a television down there so I'm way behind times, yeah? Omigod, I couldn't believe it. Honest to God, how horrible. They didn't say about your husband so I guess you're alone which must make it even worse. You should think about coming back here to Iowa. Marshalltown's nice and you wouldn't have to tell anyone who you are. Or if you want me to come out to California, I will. Remember how I used to take care of you? Well, I got to be a nurse. You maybe didn't know, but that's what I always wanted and I met a doctor. Hy's his name; he's a bit older'n me. No kids, thank God. Remember how it was with Ma, poor thing? Well, that wasn't for me. Anyway, Hy's retired now and we live in Marshalltown. Did I say that already? He had his practice here, but we go to our place in Mexico for the winter. That's why I'm so behind the time."

Myra talked more now than she ever had when they were young. In those days Elena didn't remember her saying anything but *do this, do that, I'll slap you if you tell on me*.

"Can I be honest? You looked dog tired on the TV, Elena. I'm a nurse so I notice things. Not that I'm criticizing. What you're going through? Who wouldn't be wore out? The boy's handsome, though, like Brad, yeah? Did you two ever get married? You should've written something, Elena. To your family, after all. Joanna and me keep in touch. Not a lot, but I got the word when Papa died. God rest his soul."

It was almost twenty years since Elena left home. She had figured that her father must be dead by now. Nevertheless and although she had no fondness for him, it came as a shock.

She could not recall when he had ever called her by name and now he never would. She hoped he hurt at the end. She hoped he called out for help and nobody came.

"I could stay at a hotel. I wouldn't want to impose on you and I'm sure there's somewhere nice in that little town. I never heard of San Sebastian, but then I'm not too familiar with California. I wouldn't mind paying a visit and I could maybe take your mind off things, yeah? I've got a lot of gossip I bet you'd like to hear. Joanna's still on the farm, her and Jacob. Brother and sister, close as I don't know what and I don't want to know!"

Myra's laugh was familiar. Her flat Nebraska voice filled the house and was the only sound Elena heard except for the television, which she had started turning on when she got up in the morning and kept on until bedtime.

"Let me say, honey, if I come out there, I can take care of myself. I won't be a financial burden. I'm just saying that I know trials and all can be expensive. Hy's had a couple of malpractice suits so we know what leeches lawyers are. I'm not a moocher. Freeloader. Whatever. I'm worried about you is all. You always were my little sweetie."

31

Sophie sat in the 4Runner for a moment with her notebook on her lap, watching the high school kids leaving school as she typed out the substance of her conversation with Jenna. In spite of what he'd done, as she came to know Donny through people like Jenna and the Devanes, to see him through their eyes, she felt a growing sympathy.

His mother had left innumerable phone messages, but Sophie had not returned them, not trusting herself to listen with patience to Elena's complaints and demands. Elena. A pretty name, but ruined forever by association. Sophie would never be able to hear it without imagining a spider eating its young to keep herself alive.

She parked the truck in the courthouse lot and walked across the corner of the park to her office. The temperature had dropped while she was at the high school and the sky was full of dark, wind-driven clouds. An empty potato chip bag rustled over her instep and blew off behind her. Across the park and through the trees she saw the mission bell tower and realized she hadn't heard it ring since Maggie was shot.

She stopped at the office long enough to confer with Clary and dictate a couple of letters. In the twilight she drove north along Highway 1 to meet Tamlin in Cambria. To her left, the ocean lay like a sheet of rippled steel under heavy, charcoal-colored skies. The coastal downs rose to her right, their lush spring green almost black in the gloom. As she turned down the hill into the village, still thinking about Donny and of how much she disliked his mother, an idea came to her. Maybe Maggie had never been Donny's real target.

Sophie dropped her purse on the floor of the Land's End Bar and Grill, famous for its spectacular sunsets and not much else. She signaled the cocktail waitress. "Tell me why I'm here, Tam."

"Don't get snotty." Tamlin pushed a basket of chips and salsa across the table. "You're going to thank me for this. I have some information for you."

"You couldn't tell me in SanSeb?"

"God, you're grumpy."

"It's not you, Tammy. It's the case."

"In that case, you're going to love what I've got."

"Couldn't I love you closer to home?"

The waitress brought Sophie a Ketel One on the rocks. The simpler the order, the less chance the Land's End bartender would find a way to ruin it. She took a long drink and exhaled as the tightness across her shoulders relaxed.

"Remember the other night I said I'd try to find out about Roman Devane and Boys into Men? Well, I asked around and what I got was either blank stares or raves about the gardening. I wasn't going to ask the boss because, like I've told you, he's strictly by the book, and if it isn't about school board stuff, he doesn't want to have the conversation."

The boss in question was the president of the San Sebastian school board, Phillip Ren, currently in his second term in office. "Finally, I decided I would just ask him straight-out. I mean, he's a nice guy and he's seriously committed to kids. He'd never fire me because his office would fall apart. So I asked and he made this sour face and said he didn't know anything about Devane or the organization. Predictable. But I've worked with him long enough, I knew he wasn't being completely honest, so I pushed a little bit." Tamlin sat back, sipping what appeared to be a Coke and looking pleased with herself as she dragged out the suspense. "Ren asked me why I wanted to know and I told him. About you defending Donny, how you think he's a good kid but there's something in his story that isn't right? He said Donny was lucky to have such a conscientious attorney. I told him you felt there might be something strange about the setup out there at the gardens."

"I never said that. You can't just go putting words in my mouth, Tam." Sophie had revealed no attorney-client confidences to her friend, but it was a measure of how deeply Donny had tunneled under her skin that she had talked about him to Tamlin at all. "I spoke to you in confidence."

"Give me some credit, Sophie, I was very discreet. And Ren was just as vague and indirect as I was. But finally, *finally*, he did give me a name."

"What do you mean, 'a name'?"

Tam laid a piece of paper on the table between them.

Sophie looked at the name written on the paper. "Judy Gray? Who's Judy Gray? And where's Missouri Point?"

"Up the 1, north of San Simeon."

"There's nothing up there until Big Sur."

"It's a wide spot in the road. If you go off the highway a few hundred yards, there's a general store and a farm where someone makes specialty cheese. And a glassblower, I think. It's that kind of place. Old hippies."

"Judy Gray's an old hippie?"

"I don't know what she is, but that's where Dr. Ren says she lives."

"And I'm interested in her because...?"

"Ren wouldn't say, so I called her."

"Oh, my God, Tamlin, you're going to get me disbarred." Sophie swallowed the last of her drink and signaled for another.

"Don't get loaded, okay? You're going to want to be on it tonight."

At first Judy Gray had refused to talk to Tamlin. "But I told her it was a matter of life and death and that got her attention. I mentioned Dr. Ren's name. And Boys into Men." Tamlin grinned widely, obviously pleased with her investigative skills. "That was all it took. Are you ready for this? Her son was at Roman's Gardens. He was part of Boys into Men."

It was dark by the time they reached the Missouri Point turnoff. Heavy mist had transformed the buildings in the community to featureless shadows. Tamlin drove, creeping along the narrow road, slowing to a crawl wherever a sign appeared. At regular intervals the windshield wipers cleared an arc of visibility, a narrow strip of shining pavement. Sophie was wound as tight as a tin toy with a key jammed in its back. Though she had no idea what she was going to ask or what Judy Gray might tell her, she felt an anticipatory buzz. Mémé would call it a potentiality.

Missouri Point wasn't a town—it was barely a settlement, half a dozen houses sited at quarter- or half-acre intervals along a narrow stretch of road that ended at an unpaved turnaround. Beyond a barbed-wire fence, a fog that was almost rain dipped and swirled and soaked the hollows of the coastal downs. To the right a lit porch and a large hand-painted sign planted in a square of ragged lawn announced that they had reached their destination: JUDY'S BAKERY: HANDMADE ARTISAN BREADS. They picked their way along a path of redwood bark to the front door and onto a small porch. Tamlin rang the brass ship's bell affixed to the side of the house, and the door opened immediately, as if Judy Gray had been standing on the other side waiting for them.

"Which one of you is Tamlin?" she asked, fidgeting with a pair of glasses hanging from a beaded necklace.

"I called you, Mrs. Gray."

"I'm blind as a bat without these." She put on her rimless glasses and peered at Tamlin and then Sophie. "That makes you the lawyer. Come in."

The room was part cluttered living room, mostly kitchen.

Sophie said, "It smells wonderful in here."

"Does it? Everyone loves the smell of baking bread, but

I'm immune. Sorry for the mess. Sit anywhere." Judy perched on the arm of an overstuffed chair with several brightly colored afghans piled on the back. She wore an ankle-length dirndl skirt and a bulky sweater. On the wet April night, her feet were bare.

"After I hung up I got to thinking about this and I wish you hadn't come all the way out here tonight. The fog's a bitch."

"I'm so grateful that you're willing to talk to me." Sophie would have come in a hurricane.

"Yeah, well, that's what I mean. It's not like I have anything specific…" She addressed herself to Tamlin again. "How did you get my number anyway? Did you say Dr. Ren? The school board guy?"

"He didn't give me your number and he doesn't know we're here."

"It's been a long time…He was principal of University High when Justy…When it all happened. I was still married then. Justy and I moved out here after his father left." She took off her glasses and squeezed the bridge of her nose between her thumb and index finger. "Ren wasn't supposed to say anything. I think he broke the law. I think—"

"Justy's your son?" Sophie asked, wanting to keep the conversation on track.

"He's not here. He works up in Monterey." From a table beside the armchair she handed Sophie the picture of a grinning kid with braces on his teeth. "We never should have let him leave school. My husband should have put his foot down. But he said let him do it. He'd learn his lesson. Real laissez-faire, that guy. I told him some lessons could ruin your life but he didn't give a shit." Her chin lifted a little, as if daring Sophie to say she'd done the wrong thing. "I got so sick of the arguing, you know?"

"Was Justy one of the boys who lived in the big house? With Roman and Iva?"

"Have you met them? Roman and Ms. Iva? Does he still have that phony cowboy accent? They seem like the kind of people your sixteen-year-old son would be safe with, don't they? Our pastor said he'd seen the program work miracles with boys who were…"

Resting her hand on her chest, Judy stopped for a breath. "I may as well tell you. Justy'd been in trouble since he was in junior high. Nothing big, but it kinda gets your attention when you get a call from the cops saying he's been caught vandalizing the school or being drunk and disorderly or shoplifting. My ex said he was a typical boy and what were we raising, anyway? Some kind of sheep who'd follow all the rules, a conformist?"

She didn't seem able to control the breathless spill of words.

"I didn't care, I just wanted a decent kid, but then he was caught selling joints to middle schoolers. Babies. When I heard that, it had to be the worst day of my life. Second worst. The principal made him sound like public enemy number one, right? But he wasn't; he was a good boy. To me he was anyway. I don't think my ex gave a flying fuck." She looked at Sophie, then Tamlin and back at Sophie as if daring them to criticize her. "I never gave up on Justy. I never could see anything bad in him."

"What happened at the gardens, Judy?"

"Everything was great and Roman Devane was God Almighty, and then one day—no warning—Justy hitched a ride home and wouldn't go back. He never would talk about how come. We lived on Viola then, down the road from the old cannery. He said that he didn't like the other boys and Roman Devane was…creepy."

"He said that? He used that word?"

"Actually, he called him a creepophile. I asked him what he meant but he wouldn't tell me. But, you know, the first time I met the man, I thought there was something off about him. My husband said I was paranoid. What do I know? I'm just the mother. And in the beginning, Justy was so excited to be in the program. He'd been interviewed and he'd filled out an application and been accepted."

Judy stared into the middle distance for a moment. "You know how in school they give kids awards and the parents get a bumper sticker saying their kid's a good student? I think Justy's the only kid in America who never got one of those. He never won a spelling bee and he was the last kid picked for sports. Being accepted into Boys into Men was huge for him." She paused, trying not to cry. "He was so innocent. It breaks my heart to think of him with that pervert."

She took off her glasses and wiped the lenses with the hem of her skirt.

"Devane has this place at the back of the barn. He called it 'the clubhouse' and there's a sign on the door that says NO GIRLS ALLOWED. Like a joke, right? Only Justy told me it was for real and even Ms. Iva couldn't go in. Justy thought it was the greatest place he'd ever been. There was a flat-screen television, pool table, games, and—I don't know. Whatever boys like, Roman Devane had it."

If Tamlin had been sitting closer, Sophie would have grabbed her hand and held on tight.

"I never should have let him leave school. It was my fault it happened. I should have stood up to my husband. But you get so tired when it's fighting, fighting all the time. All you want is a little peace and quiet." She slid onto the chair cushion and sat with her feet tucked under her, arms wrapped across her midriff. "I don't really want to talk about this. I try not to think about it. That boy who shot the governor, was he part of the Boys into Men thing?"

"He was."

"He's still guilty."

"I'm not denying that, but I know him and he's a little like your Justy."

"Justy'd never shoot anyone."

"No, of course not." Sophie spoke carefully. "And I don't believe Donny Crider would have either except that some things happened that pushed him over the edge. Judy, I worked with a lot of juveniles when I was a prosecutor. Really bad kids. I can tell you that Donny isn't one of those."

An image came to Sophie of Judy Gray kneading bread. In the same way Elena had pounded and knuckled and beat on Donny, forcing him to conform to her wishes. Twisted though Roman Devane might be, he had made Donny feel valued, maybe for the first time in his life. Then Elena dragged him away. First she had intentionally separated him from his father and then she had taken him away from Roman and the work he loved.

"I don't want my son's name dragged around in the dirt," Judy said.

"It won't be. I promise you that."

"And you'll never speak to Justy?"

Sophie had to be honest. "It would help our case if I could." She had no concrete proof that Roman was a pedophile. Judy Gray's story was useless without proof. "He'd never have to testify in court."

"No, absolutely not."

"If you don't care about Donny—"

"Why should I care about him? I have one son, only one, and he's precious to me. He's got a second chance and I won't let you jeopardize it."

"Judy, that's not my intention—"

"I don't care about your intentions. Intentions mean shit. I know what will *happen*."

"You're protecting—"

Judy was up off her chair, standing at the door. Outside the fog had turned to rain. "You have to go now. I'm finished. I'm done. I don't want to think about what goes on out at that place. It's history and Justy wants to forget. I want to forget. He's got a good job now and he's in community college. He has a life. So you can just leave. Get out." She shoved Sophie onto the porch. "He's my son. It's my job to protect my son."

* * *

Through the car windshield they stared at the rain-blurred house and saw the porchlight go out. In the darkness the only sound was the hard rain on the roof of the car.

"All those boys—" Sophie couldn't finish the sentence.

"She should have reported Devane."

"She was protecting her son."

"Maybe."

"You don't think she was?"

"Do I think she's lying? No," Tamlin said. "She wants to protect him, but she's also ashamed. She let him go out to the gardens. She let him drop out of school."

"She loves him, Tamlin."

"She can still be ashamed. For him, with him, ashamed of herself."

"If it were your Ryan, you'd go screaming to the cops."

"But only if I thought he could take what came after, the public side of it. You know a story like this can't be kept a secret."

"Donny loves Roman," Sophie said. "The best part of his life was spent at the gardens."

"He'll never admit what happened," Tamlin started the car. "If you want proof, you'll have to find it somewhere else."

32

The condo was cold and unwelcoming when Sophie returned to it that night, wishing she had somewhere else to go but knowing that anywhere she went she'd feel a chill when she thought of Donny and Roman Devane. And no wonder the apartment was cold; the living room blinds were drawn back and the slider onto the deck was open.

She stood a moment, looking at the rain-soaked rectangle of carpet in front of the window, unable to make sense of what she was seeing. Was it possible that she had left the door open when she went to work that morning? All at once, her hands were shaking and she tucked them up under her arms to still them. Before work, she had drunk her first cup of coffee on the deck as she did most mornings, weather permitting. She had refilled the hummingbird feeder with red sugar water and the finch stocking with niger seed. When she came back inside she pulled the door shut and automatically flipped the lock up. Locking the slider was an automatic action, like putting the cap on the toothpaste.

Ben was always after Sophie to buy a gun. Tamlin wanted

her to have a dog. If she had either now, she would not be standing in the middle of the dining room, reluctant to walk down the hall to her bedroom. Feeling slightly ridiculous, she grabbed a knife from the kitchen and stepped into the hall connecting the living room with two bedrooms and a guest bathroom. The first door on the left hid the untidy spare room. She nudged it open with the toe of her shoe, reached around, and flicked the overhead light switch. The small space was crowded with bags for Goodwill, packing and file boxes, stacked books waiting to be put in the bookcase she had yet to buy, a dresser, and, along one wall, a guest bed. Across the narrow hall, the bathroom was empty, of course. By now she was sure there was no one hiding in her home. She would have felt a presence if there had been anyone lurking. Even so, she hesitated on her bedroom threshold. The hall light illuminated her bed and a dresser. The switch by the door turned on track lights. She forced a deep breath and let it out slowly. The room looked as it always did: untidy. She'd left her bed unmade, the sheets and comforter thrown back. But the pillows were wrong. They were stacked, one on the other, and crowning them were her three-hundred-dollar shoes.

She called Tamlin and then Hamp, and in less than thirty minutes they—as well as Psyche—were standing in her living room.

"I told you to call the cops. Where are they?" Tamlin wore blue-and-white-striped pajama bottoms under her coat. "You had a break-in and you didn't call 911?"

Once Cary Hering saw the shoes, Sophie would have to explain about Mars Beach.

Hamp took a quick look around the apartment, finding nothing out of the ordinary except the shoes, which he lifted off the pillow with his fingertips and put in a plastic bag he laid on the kitchen counter.

"In case you decide to bring the cops into this, there could be fingerprints."

He pulled out one of the chairs at the dining table and, taking Sophie by the arm, urged her to sit across from him.

"So tell me. What's this all about?"

Reluctantly, she told him about the threatening note pushed under her office door a few days before his arrival. She confessed that she had not gone directly home that night but instead gone to Mars Beach, where her shoes were stolen.

"Why would you do that? Walk on a lonely beach late at night?"

"I didn't walk. Mostly I ran." It seemed an important distinction.

"The same night you'd gotten a death threat?"

"It wasn't a death—"

"I was a cop, Sophie. I know a death threat."

"Cary said it was a prank."

"You never believed that," Tamlin said. "You knew he was just trying to calm you down."

"Obviously someone followed you out there from town. You could have been killed. Why would you do anything so dangerous?"

"It happened. And I don't like being threatened."

229

"You'd hate being dead even more. Whoever did this is a scary son of a bitch. There was no sign of tampering to the lock on the slider. Did you leave it open?"

"I'm not an idiot, Hamp."

Psyche, standing at Tamlin's side and alerted by the intensity of their voices, tracked the conversation from speaker to speaker.

"It was the Bleekers. The note and this— It's their scumbag style." Hamp had never heard of the Bleekers, so between them Sophie and Tamlin gave him a description of the brothers.

"That's it?" he asked. "Three brothers? How old are they?"

"I don't know. Junior's the oldest; he's maybe thirty."

"What's his real name?" Hamp asked as he pulled a notebook out of his back pocket.

"Phineas."

"Any of them done time?"

"Not as far as I know."

"Well, maybe they're responsible, maybe not. Either way, you shouldn't be alone."

"Stay at our place, Sophie. I'll put Julia in the family room."

"I'm not going to let them run me out of my own home."

Tamlin snorted. "Look around you, Sophie. This isn't a home. This is where you sleep and take a shower."

"I could stay," Hamp said. "I've got to get out of that place on the southside, anyway. The bikers wake me up every night after hours."

"Psyche—"

"I don't need a damn dog!" As if this explosion took the last of her energy, the resistance went out of Sophie. She looked at her friends and the dog and realized that she was tired of turning every disagreement into a battle.

Hamp.

A one-eyed dog.

Both of them could stay.

"But we don't call the cops."

Hamp collected his things from the motel and Tamlin went home without Psyche, who did not seem to mind being left behind and appeared to know what was expected of her. She followed Sophie into her bedroom and lay outside the bathroom door while she showered. By the time Hamp returned with his bag, Sophie had changed into clean sweats and her hair was almost dry.

"One bag? That's it?"

"A rolling stone."

"What about your board?"

"I don't have one," he said. "Not with me."

A surfer without a board. Sophie kept her questions to herself.

"I made up the bed in the spare room. It's got a good mattress." In the kitchen she showed him how to make coffee. "Whatever you want, help yourself."

Not that there was much. She was conscious of how empty the cupboards and refrigerator were, how austere and stripped down her home must look through his eyes. Tamlin was right. It wasn't much of a home.

He retrieved a Pinch bottle of Scotch from his over-nighter and held it up. "You a drinking woman, Sophie?"

"Sure am. Glasses are left of the sink."

She lay on the couch and Hamp sat in the Danish recliner near the windows. The curtains were drawn, but she felt the wet darkness pressing against the glass.

"Why do the Bleekers hate you so much?"

"I got Will Cardigan off by shifting the jury's attention to them. Remember?"

"Was the kid guilty?"

"Of being young and stupid and having bad taste in friends."

"Are they dangerous?"

"They aren't stupid and they know what they can get away with."

"So probably not?"

Sophie rocked her hand from side to side.

"Have you actually met them, talked to them?"

She hadn't, but when Sophie was a prosecutor, she had filed a stalking complaint on behalf of Melody, Gaylon Bleeker's ex-girlfriend.

"She'd come home after work and find the couch in the kitchen. Stupid stuff. Of course, she got all the locks changed, but a sheriff's deputy told me there wasn't a lock in the world the Bleekers couldn't open. Melody wanted Gaylon arrested, but the sheriff wouldn't touch it. That's why she came to us."

She had the locks changed again and after a few days the entries resumed.

"Gaylon was entering, using her toilet, leaving a present. Cooking pizza in her microwave and packing the leftovers in her fridge. She complained, but the sheriff never took it seriously. He and Gaylon and the others are old friends."

"Friends?"

"Oh, yeah. The Bleekers are a big family. They've been in the county as long as the Giraudos and Marsays. They know everyone."

"I'd feel better if you were a little more worried."

"Girls and chop shops and drugs are more their style than making serious trouble for me. It'd be too risky for them to get involved with the city cops."

"Then do yourself a favor. Don't leave the city limits."

The silence between them was companionable. Even Psyche relaxed and stretched out on her side next to the couch, snoring slightly.

Hamp said, "Tell me what happened tonight. You and Tamlin." On the drive back to Cambria, where she'd left the 4Runner at the bar, Sophie had called Hamp and left a brief message on his phone. "You said you learned something about Roman."

When she told him that Roman Devane was a pedophile who preyed on adolescent boys, Hamp didn't seem surprised.

He pulled several pages of printout from his canvas briefcase. "I got this off the Internet, background stuff about Devane. Before he and Iva moved to San Sebastian they were in Arizona, staying in a town called Merryville, about twenty miles south of Tucson. There's an amusement park there called Santa's Summertime Village. Roman's brother, Omar, runs it."

In Santa's Summertime Village there were carnival-style rides with names like Santa's Swinging Sleigh and the Flying Toy Shop. There was a year-round skating rink, a campground, a couple of restaurants, and a gift shop. It was a good moneymaker.

"And there are kids all over the place." A brackish taste filled Sophie's mouth. "I think I might be sick."

"Before Merryville, he and Iva lived in Stockton and he ran a program called Breakfast and Basketball for boys ages eight to sixteen."

More kids.

Sophie laid out everything they knew, like a game of solitaire. What they could prove, what they couldn't, and what was guesswork only. No matter how she matched the suits and ran the numbers, she couldn't clear a single ace. "It's all coincidence and supposition unless we can prove Roman's bent. And even then it doesn't explain the shooting."

She went to the kitchen and brought back the bottle.

"But here's an idea I got when I was driving." Before she met Tamlin in the bar, she had stopped at a beach overlook where she wrote several pages of notes to keep the theory fresh in her mind. "Have you ever heard of 'displacement' theory?

"A guy's mad at his boss so he goes home and beats up his wife?" He paused, thinking. "Donny's mad at his mother so he shoots the governor?"

"Elena's astral sister."

"Christ, you think he believed that?"

"Maybe. Probably not, but on some level he might have mingled the two of them in his mind. It wouldn't be the strangest thing I've ever heard. And she does kind of look like Maggie sometimes."

"But horrible as Elena is, she's his mother. She makes him feel like shit but she's all he's ever had."

"Still, there's this anger growing in him."

"And the anger never goes away, but what can he do? He's successfully repressing it until?"

Hamp looked at Sophie, wanting her to fill in the blanks.

"He finds out his dad's not a bad guy after all, that his mother's been lying to him his whole life. And then she drags him away from the only place he's ever been happy. Roman's Gardens."

Hamp finished his drink and reached for the bottle.

"Iva told us he begged to stay at the gardens. He was willing to work for nothing to avoid going home. And Jenna told me he had big ambitions that the Devanes encouraged. Being at the gardens must have been pretty intoxicating for a kid who never had the spotlight shine on him before. The sex part was probably something he thought he had to endure, a kind of quid pro quo. And I'll bet Roman said he loved him and Donny hung on to that."

"Women stay with their abusers," Hamp said. "When I was a cop I saw that a few thousand times."

"There's an extra twist to their relationship. Elena needed Donny." Sophie leaned into the conversation. "Elena could only tolerate sharing him up to a point. Then she realized she was on the point of losing him completely. He had his GED and a good trade, he could take off for the hills anytime. This boy had dreams. He had ambition. She had to get him back. Without him she feels diminished, maybe unbearably so. Elena doesn't have boundaries like most people. Not between her and Maggie. Not with Donny either."

"Then why'd she let him go to the gardens in the first place?"

"She probably figured it didn't matter how he got his diploma, just so he got it." Sophie was sure Elena never had a clue that her son would love the work he did at the gardens. "I bet she was screaming jealous."

"It hangs together," Hamp said. "But it's a stretch."

"A stretch is okay if it doesn't snap." If she didn't end up standing in the courtroom with her pants around her ankles.

"Why didn't he shoot Elena if he hates her so much?"

"Matricide is a heavy old crime, Hamp, one of the strongest taboos in human society. In this country, it accounts for less than one percent of homicides. Maggie was the perfect substitute. Elena loved her. She was obsessed with her. For Donny, hurting Maggie meant hurting his mother, a pain she'd have to live with. It was the worst thing he could do."

"So he meant to do it? There was premeditation?"

"Donny says he doesn't know why he did it and I think he's telling the truth. Whatever his motive, it wasn't conscious. Of course, at this point I can't prove that. I can't prove anything."

"What about the gun?"

"He liked the feel of carrying. Strong and powerful."

Sophie thought about the sentencing memo she would eventually write for Donny. With the right judge, Dr. Itkin's psychological assessment (which she was almost sure would be the same as hers in essence) would carry persuasive weight. And if she could prove that Donny was also the victim of a sexual predator, the right judge might—*might*—be inclined to leniency. Donny would do time but not the thirty years Ben wanted for him.

"You feel so strong about this kid, Sophie. Are you like this with all your cases, because if you are—"

"I'm going to crash and burn." The truth made her laugh for the first time that night. "Believe me, I didn't want the case at first. I didn't like Elena and I thought Donny was a sullen brat. I don't like him now, particularly. But I think I *get* him. I know what it's like to be scared and overwhelmed, acting crazy."

Hamp looked at her and then his gaze shifted and she felt a distance between them that hadn't been there a moment before. It was not the first time she had known him to leave a conversation in this way.

"What are you thinking about?"

He considered the question for so long that she thought he might not answer. "Kids," he finally said. "My own."

"You miss her."

"I do indeed."

"Oregon's a long drive but not hard."

"It's so easy for them to get fucked-up. I mean, how do any of them make it?"

"Or you could fly her down here." Sophie's intuition was

alert, sensing a complicated story, untold. "She's welcome to stay here."

Another long silence and then a sigh. "I don't know where she is. She's been gone two years."

A little at a time, between the silences, he told Sophie about his daughter. They drank a lot, but Bronwyn's story and then the history of Hamp's injuries had a sobering effect.

"So you don't surf anymore. That's why you don't have a board with you."

"I think my brain's okay, but every time I forget a name or walk into a room and can't remember why—"

"Everyone does that, Hamp."

"Yeah, I know. But that doesn't stop me wondering. I have to find her while I can."

Sophie didn't have any response to that. The silence was necessary, not awkward, but after a while she needed to get away from the bright light of the condo and the intense atmosphere their conversation had created. "I'm going to walk this no-account dog."

"It's still raining."

"I don't mind getting a little wet."

"I'll go with you."

33

While Hamp hooked up the dog's leash, Sophie found plastic bags and a couple of old umbrellas. They stepped into a steady downpour, the kind that filled reservoirs and overflowed the gutters.

"We better walk in the road," Hamp said. "Up or down?"

"Up. There's a wild area at the top of the hill."

Sophie's condo was part of a loosely gated community where an effort had been made to retain the natural look of the rolling Central Coast hills. The occasional sallow street-light led them up a gently sloping grade lined with complexes like Sophie's, clusters of condominiums surrounded by native trees and plants. At the top of the hill the street ended in a cul-de-sac. Beyond a rustic fence, the wilderness area was a swathe of darkness. Fifty yards away, a covered picnic pavilion offered shelter. Sophie and Hamp sat on one of the tables. Off lead, Psyche wandered in and out of the shadows, untroubled by the rain, checking back with them every few minutes.

It was dark and wet, but it was a relief being away from the house. Hamp's story had been powerful, its pain underscored by a deep sense of responsibility. Listening, she had wanted to hide her face so he wouldn't see how much his story had affected her. Now, curtained from the world by falling rain, hidden by the darkness and with her voice muffled by the drumming on the pavilion's tin roof, she was compelled to honesty.

"Bronwyn could be me. I've done some dumb-ass things in my life. When she told you that she liked being scared, I get that, the thrill." Sophie barely recognized her timid voice groping for the right words, the path into her story. "When I was thirteen, I went into strangers' houses. I didn't exactly break in, but as good as."

She told him how she hated All Angels Academy, the move from the apartment over the market to the new house and Anna's sudden obsession with every crack and crevice of her teenaged daughter's life.

"I hated her and school was just an extension of her. I would have given anything to be someone else. I was really only happy when I was out at night, by myself."

Down the hill, the condos were shrouded in darkness, but here and there she saw a porch light or the rectangular glow of a lit window. At the bottom of the hill and beyond, the city's street- and traffic lights blurred and flickered through the rain.

She told him about sitting in a lawn chair, drinking sodas from someone's outdoor cooler. "Looking back, I can understand that it was plain old puberty having its way with me. But it was the weather too. The nights were incredibly hot.

Lying in bed, I couldn't keep still. I'd end up with the sheet twisted around me like a straitjacket. I had to get out."

Hearing herself, she knew she was circling, moving in on a dangerous target. She didn't have to continue. *Leave it there.*

"I almost didn't go the last time. Other times it was like I *had* to go, but that time it was more curiosity than anything." She spoke softly and felt Hamp shift beside her, bend closer to hear. "There was this family on Mariposa Street."

She told him everything she remembered: a scene from the subtitled movie, horses galloping and music with a bossa nova beat; the sharp clean click of the hidden door when it closed behind the man; the man's boxer shorts with a Disney pattern; the white scar just above his right knee.

"He raped me."

She bent forward, wanting to vomit, to get it out that way.

"I drank a screwdriver. With tangerine juice. I could have said I didn't want it. Except..."

She wanted to drink it.

"Who else knows about this, Sophie?"

"Only you."

"He should have gone to jail for what he did."

"He said he'd tell my mother I was stealing. I believed he'd call the police. I was afraid."

What Sophie understood now was that the man could have accused her of anything and Anna would have believed her. But Sophie at thirteen was in full rebellion and did not understand—or even care—about her mother's love and loyalty.

I'm not you. I'm me and I can do whatever I please.

"Do you ever think about finding him?"

"I try not to think about him at all." Like Judy Gray. If she didn't think about it, it never happened.

"It took courage to tell me."

She understood that he was honored by her trust.

Sophie wanted to respond appropriately, to create a tidy denouement to her confession, but she had no words for it. She began feeling embarrassed by her candor.

"We should go back."

They didn't bother leashing the shepherd, who herded them gently down the hill. As Tamlin had said she would, Sophie felt safe with the dog. And with Hamp too. The circumstances of one's life could change so quickly, and usually the change was bad, or so it had seemed until that night. She did not feel lighter by having told him. She did not feel relieved. But something was different.

Outside the condo, Hamp stopped under the protection of the overhanging roof.

"I want you to know, I won't ever mention this again. Not to you, not to anyone. If you want, it can be like you never told me."

"That would be good," she said. "And Bronwyn, the same."

"There's just one thing, Sophie. And I'll say it now so it'll be out there. If you ever want to confront the guy with what he did, I'll find him for you."

She started to say it would never happen, but what did she know?

"I'm just saying, Sophie, it might be the next step."

34

After Sophie let Milo out of the 4Runner earlier in the day, he stood on the shoulder of the road and watched the car out of sight, thinking of the way the light flashed in her blue glass earrings when she turned her head to look at him in the backseat. She hardly watched the road at all when she was driving. That was like his mother.

Milo didn't like lady lawyers. The judge in juvenile court had glared at him as if her eyes were power drills and he was a piece of rotten plywood. She said she was giving him his second and only chance and he believed her. If he had not been scared he would not have filled out the application form and mailed it to Roman's Gardens. He did not expect to be chosen for Boys into Men, nor did he want to work in a nursery. He just wanted to stay out of juvie.

When Roman sent him away, Milo went to his room and crammed everything that fit into his pack. The rest he left behind. As he passed through the kitchen Ms. Iva wanted to give him a bag of sandwiches. Her pitying expression had frightened him because it made him forget how angry he was. He ran out the door, calling her an old whore.

He felt bad about that.

He had begun to cry when he was almost at the end of the driveway, at the place where it turned and he could no longer see the house and barn behind him. He ducked into the black shade of the cottonwoods that grew along that section of Dry Creek Road and lay curled on his side. An ant explored his cheek and he couldn't be bothered swatting it off. He cried and fell asleep, and then he woke and started walking, not knowing where in the empty world he was going.

Everything he'd done that day he'd done without thinking. Vaguely, he recognized that he could not continue in this manner indefinitely, moving from impulse to impulse. It was fine for now to sit on the bus bench, but he was getting hungry, the sky was filling with ominous clouds, and he didn't know where he would sleep that night.

He couldn't go home because he had no home. His mother was in Tehachapi. His father was whoever, wherever. As far as he knew he had no family, although there was a sister somewhere and when he was eight or nine he and his mother had ridden the bus to King City, where he had a dim recollection of an aunt, a pleasant house, and a big yard with lots of kids and dogs. He thought about taking the bus to King City, but he didn't remember his aunt's name and it had all happened a long time ago.

He thought about the lawyer and tried to imagine what it was like for Donny now. Was he afraid?

A bus stopped and the door wheezed open. The driver

looked down at him expectantly. Milo considered riding until he saw something hopeful, a sign telling him what to do next. His mother believed in signs, and everything in her dreams meant something important. If she were in his situation she would probably go looking for a fortune-teller or buy a newspaper and read her horoscope.

The driver closed the door and drove on.

In his pocket Milo had more money than he'd ever seen at one time, five twenty-dollar bills from Roman and another from the man in the lawyer's car. He had little idea what he could get for that amount. Not much, he guessed. And what should he do when the money ran out? From time to time his mother had put him in foster care, telling him that he was better off with strangers until she got on her feet again. What Milo knew of the world, he had learned from the boys in foster care, who bragged about life on the streets, making their exploits sound romantic and adventurous. Milo knew there were men who'd pay him for a blow job or the other thing, the thing that hurt. He wouldn't do that.

A man sat down on the bench beside him and folded his hands on his lap. He had pale skin and eyes and smelled like cigarettes. At first Milo didn't pay attention to him, but after some time went by and another bus stopped and opened its door and the man didn't get up and go into it, Milo began to wonder why he was sitting there. Beneath the cigarette smell Milo became aware of the odor of the man's body, unwashed, though his clothes looked clean. He wore athletic shoes that were as white as the plant Roman called Snow in Summer. He didn't know how he could tell which men would pay.

Another bus stopped. This time the man rose from the bench and disappeared inside it.

Milo closed his eyes and pretended that when he opened them he'd see Roman's truck coming. What if he said he was sorry for being mean? Milo would tell him to go blow himself. That's what he wanted to believe.

In the beginning Milo knew Roman only as Mr. Devane, and he was all business. On the first day he'd taken Milo for what he called an orientation tour, walking all over the gardens with that big dog right beside. Milo had been afraid of Laz at first, but he got used to him. Mr. Devane said he admired a boy who knew how to handle himself around dogs. They must have walked two or three miles from one end of the property to the other and Milo's head was dizzy from all the things Mr. Devane talked about. There was too much to learn. Milo would never remember about the temperature-regulated greenhouses, the seedlings and the one-gallon, two-gallon, five-gallon pots, plus all the kinds of fertilizer and the special soil, this much nitrogen and so much potassium and bone meal and calcium, and the chemistry of composting and so much more about inventory, running the office, keeping the books.

At the end of the orientation Mr. Devane—Roman by then—said it was natural to feel overwhelmed at first. He promised they would take it slowly and that gradually Milo would learn. His confidence made Milo hopeful in a shy way. *You'll like it here, Milo. I chose you because I think you're a special kid. You'll be happy in the gardens.*

Although Roman was fair to everyone, Milo soon learned

that he always had a special boy. Before Milo there was Chico. After Milo came Donny and now Cobb. Every two or three weeks, Roman took the house boys or sometimes his special boy alone to an abandoned gravel pit near the creek at the southern end of the property. There he taught them to load a revolver and shoot soda cans off fence posts. Soon Roman would teach Cobb to hold the grip with two hands and pull the trigger back slowly, exhaling as he did so. At first his shots would go wide and wild, but then he'd get the hang of it. It was the most fun Milo had ever had, pulling the trigger, hearing the ping and seeing the can kick up into the air. Roman admired a young man who was handy with firearms.

At a McDonald's he bought two big hamburgers and then, carried away by the thought of all the twenties in his pocket, he added two large fries and a chocolate milk shake to his order. He took his food to a corner of the restaurant and laid it out in front of him like spoils.

He gobbled the first hamburger. The bun stuck to the roof of his mouth and he scarcely tasted it. The next one he ate more slowly. Salty fries drenched in ketchup, he couldn't get enough of them. He went back to the counter for another order and a soda because the shake was more like a dessert than a drink.

He ate everything and afterward he was sleepy. It was getting dark but Milo couldn't tell if it was late or if the clouds made it seem that way. The cost of the meal had shown him that, as he feared, one hundred and twenty dollars would not go far. He needed a job but he didn't think any boss would hire him without his GED, a certificate, or a letter of recommendation to prove how much he knew about gardening. He remembered learning that San Sebastian was on the edge of wine country. Wine meant grapes and grapes meant plants. Roman had said that many boys from the program had gotten good jobs in the wineries around Paso Robles. Maybe he would head in that direction.

Between now and the morning lay the night and probably rain. He must find a safe place to sleep, somewhere with a roof.

At a convenience store he bought a couple of candy bars, a juice box, and a packet of sugar-coated donuts. When he stepped outside there were no cars on the road. He imagined that everyone except him must be at home having dinner or watching television. He turned back in the direction of Roman's Gardens. In the apricot orchard that ran along Dry Creek Road there was a shed where Roman stored the dismantled fruit stand and the drying racks he'd haul out later in the spring. The boys would stand in the sun and cut the cots in half, laying them out side by side on racks like hundreds of little orange bowls. Though the shed floor was a cement slab and the walls were full of knotholes and the boards had shrunk, leaving spaces between, the shed was clean enough for Milo. He could still smell the sweet, sulfurous fragrance of the drying cots.

In the dark on a cloudy night, it was scary-lonesome in the doorless shed. Branches of the apricot trees scratched at the roof when the wind gusted. Milo put on his jacket, and using his backpack as a pillow, he closed his eyes and tried to pretend he wasn't afraid of the night or of the morning either. The hoot of an owl, the ticka-ticka-tick of mice feet through the litter on the cement floor: every time he dozed off, some new sound woke him with a start. He was drifting off when he heard padding steps outside and saw the shadow of an animal in the door of the shed. Milo smelled hot coyote breath as it stepped toward him. He scooted backward to the corner of the shed and drew his knees up to his nose, making himself small. He wanted to yell but when he opened his mouth no sound came out.

In the darkness, two eyes, a pair of pointed ears.

Free to roam the property at night, Laz had found his way to Milo. He wrapped his arms around the dog's muscular shoulders and they lay together on the cold cement littered with leaves and dried-out apricot pits that rustled like something moving toward them when a gust of wind came through the doorway. Spooned against Laz's back, Milo was baffled by the complexity of his feelings. Because he hated Roman for his perversions and never truly cared about the plants, he should be glad to get away; but if they asked him to come back, he would. He cried into the dog's soft, thick neck for a long time. The tears spilled from him almost lavishly until there were no more. He was empty, parched and clean and lighter than air, and finally he could sleep.

Laz left at dawn when Milo was snoring softly, dreaming a dream that in its specifics made no sense at all. But when he awoke the memory of it was as vivid as his mother always said hers were. He went over it as he ate the packet of powdery doughnuts. Like the layout for one of Roman's gardens, the points of the dream lined up like stakes driven in the ground with string attached, a long line of them, dead straight; and if he followed the stake line, he would get where he wanted to go.

35

The next morning Sophie presented Donny with a hot egg and bacon sandwich and a large cup of cocoa with two inches of whipped cream. He accepted the food with almost no affect. She hadn't expected him to stand up and cheer; still, his lack of enthusiasm disturbed her. Every day he seemed to withdraw further from her.

The sandwich smelled delicious and she felt like taking it back from him. With her mind on the case—when was it not?—she had forgotten food for herself. She could not remember when she'd last sat down to a real meal. Or eight hours of peaceful sleep.

Despite the late night and way too much Scotch, she had awakened early and clear-eyed that morning. She had made a carafe of coffee and returned to bed with her laptop to research therapy techniques for victims of sexual molestation. She hadn't read anything that surprised her. She already knew that questioning Donny on the subject was going to require delicacy and patience, neither of which was listed as strengths on her résumé. But perhaps she had learned something the night before about listening and trust.

Hamp had told his story and in return she had told him hers, inspired by a sense of connection between Bronwyn and herself. Rain and Pinch had helped build the bridge, but more than anything it was that connection and the equality of her story and Hamp's, a similar weightiness of remorse and shame, that had made it possible for her to be completely open.

But in the interview room that morning Donny seemed more emotionally numb than usual and she doubted herself. Better not to think too much or she would lose heart. Better to begin talking and follow her instinct. She told him about visiting her father, the need for a reliable arborist, how her father fussed over his olive trees with the patience of a parent.

"Was it like that for you at Roman's Gardens?"

From across the table, she felt his sadness as he struggled to find words. After he had managed two or three sentences, he stopped and looked at Sophie as if to determine whether what he was saying was right or interesting or if he'd said too much and should now be quiet. *Of course*, Sophie thought. Living with Elena, he had learned early that nothing he had to say was of any interest or importance.

In fits and starts, guided by her interest and with growing energy, he talked about the gardens, pausing every few sentences to gauge her reaction. He digressed to tell her about the many varieties of impatiens never seen in American gardens and that in Africa and Asia they grew in bushes six feet tall.

"How'd you learn all this?"

"Online. Sometimes I went to the library and looked in books. Roman helped me."

"You were close."

The change in him was immediate. He shrank back in the chair and looked away, giving all his attention to the far corner of the room, where walls and ceiling met. She imagined that to avoid this line of questioning he would do whatever he could, even make himself small enough to hide in the intersection.

"I've learned a lot about you, Donny, and I know that you have secrets. Things you don't want to tell anyone." She chose her words carefully. If she went wrong he wouldn't give her a second chance. "I have secrets too. I wasn't always a lawyer. There are things I did in my past that I wish I hadn't. Things I'm ashamed of and don't want anyone to know."

The interview room was quiet but for a soft swishing sound like sandpaper smoothing rough wood. Beneath the table, out of sight, Donny was rubbing his hands up and down on his pant legs.

"You don't want to talk about your relationship with Roman, I understand. But the only way to get over this is to go right through it." She wondered if her words meant anything to him. "Tell me about Roman. I can't help you if you don't trust me."

"You always ask about him."

Sophie didn't think this was true, but it mattered that it seemed that way to Donny.

"Last night I met a woman who told me about her son

who used to be in Boys into Men. He lived in the house like you." She was stepping along the narrow edge now. "But he left because of something Roman did. To him."

No response.

"This boy told his mother that Roman was a creepophile."

Donny stopped rubbing his hands.

"What did he mean?"

He yawned and scratched his head; and then, moving in slow motion, he tipped his almost empty cup and let the last drops of cocoa drip out onto the table. With his right index finger, he smeared the cocoa into one circle and then another and another. Sophie watched, fascinated, as he drew flowers.

"Did he molest you, Donny? You don't have to say it out loud. Just nod your head if he did."

He enlarged his drawing to the dimensions of a place mat set before him.

"He was kind to you. Tell me about that. Start there."

The chocolate dried in swirls and circles, stems and leaves and round petals. A garden of sorts.

"You're afraid, but I'm asking you to be brave now. Please, Donny. For your own sake, tell me what happened with Roman."

One by one he put his fingers in his mouth, sucking the chocolate off them. He licked his lips, crossing his eyes to watch his tongue. She wanted to grab him before it was too late and he'd gone too far away,

"Stay with me, Donny. Tell me. What did he do to you?"

He sniffed his fingers, pressing them against his nostrils.

"Nuh-uh."

In his empty eyes she saw that he would rather be shut away from sunlight forever, rather be separated from green and living things for the rest of his life than betray Roman Devane.

Sophie had known since high school that she wanted to be an attorney, and until now she had never seriously doubted her ability to do the job. This case had pushed her to the limits.

Donny was guilty of the crime charged. Nothing could change that. Neither could the circumstances of his life be changed. He'd been as good as abandoned by his father, abused by Roman Devane, twisted and lied to by a mother whom Sophie had labeled a pathological narcissist. In the eyes of the law these things meant nothing. The facts were everything. He had shot Maggie Duarte.

She lay on the couch in her office and tried not to think, but she might as well have tried to stop blinking or swallowing. The hangover she should have had when she woke up had descended upon her, thudding in her head, wizening her skin. She couldn't get up, couldn't move off the couch. She'd been stuck for half an hour, stewing in misery, when the door opened and Anna stepped in, closing it firmly behind her.

"What are you doing, Sophia?"

"I don't want to talk to you, Ma."

"You're scheduled for court." Anna put a cup of espresso and an anise biscotti on the coffee table beside the couch. "You look like a train wreck. Are you drinking too much?"

"I can't do it, Ma."

"The biscotti's fresh."

"Stop trying to make me eat."

"You need to put some fuel in your tank, Sophia. Especially if you tied one on last night. Did you?"

"It's none of your business, Ma."

"When you have a child, that child is your business forever. After I die? I will still be watching out for you."

Sophie had heard it all before.

"I'm going to the chief judge and tell him I can't defend Donny. I don't have it. The skill, the insight—"

"Go home and take a shower."

"I already had one."

"Take another."

"You don't know—"

"You're due in court at one. Judge Palmieri again. An evidentiary hearing for Wally Bledsoe."

"Jesus Christ."

"No, but the *puzzo* thinks he is. Don't worry, you're ready for it. Just read the file—it's there on the desk. I highlighted the main points."

"Ma—"

"And like you asked me to, I did a Google search on that word *displacement*. I couldn't read all there was, but I printed a lot of it out. Also on your desk."

"I shouldn't have taken this case."

"I'm not listening, Sophia. You're talking like a failure and I don't speak that language. I didn't raise you to be a whiner or a failure."

"This isn't about you."

"I know what you're capable of. Better than you do, I think."

Sophie wanted to do something dramatic like toss the biscotti across the room or sweep the espresso off the table with the back of her hand. But then she remembered her beautiful, expensive, unpaid-for carpet and restrained herself.

"If you don't take care of yourself—"

"For once in your life will you please, for godsake, shut up? Stop trying to run the world and my life. You're not an attorney. You don't have any idea what I'm up against. I can't have you in my office. You're making me crazy."

"You're making yourself crazy. You don't sleep nights and you don't eat right. Go home, have a shower, then come back here. Your uncle will send over lunch. Minestrone."

"Stop talking about food. You don't—"

"I don't understand? You're right. When you start whining, I hear noise. That's all it is. Noise. God made this day the same as any other, Sophia. Twenty-four hours. You'll get through it." Leaving the office, she added, "And don't say 'shut up' to your mother."

36

Milo hitched a ride along Dry Creek Road in the back of a farmer's truck filled with rain-soaked bags of manure guarded by a pit bull straining at the end of a metal chain. He banged on the roof of the cab and the old man driving let him off near the bus stop. For twenty minutes Milo heel-toed along the road in the rain, focusing his gaze on the mud and litter on the shoulder. He could not be sure where Sophie had let him out of the 4Runner, but wherever that was, he had dropped her business card almost immediately. That had been less than twenty-four hours ago. He worked his way back and forth in the area of the bus bench, going so slowly that he sometimes lost his balance. Had exhaust from cars blown it off the shoulder? A narrow muddy ditch lay between the verge and a barbed-wire fence. On either side of it, the weeds grew dense and tall: bindweed, dock, and everywhere, tiny pink flowering spurge, which Roman had told him was a sure sign of spring.

No card meant no name, no phone number, no string tied to stakes. No plan.

Milo was not by nature either patient or determined, and he soon abandoned his search in favor of futility, a familiar feeling, and sat on the bench in the bus shed. After a moment, he lay down with his hands behind his head and closed his eyes, but rest was out of the question. His brain hurt from trying to remember the lawyer's name.

A bus stopped in front of the bench. The door opened and the driver yelled something. Milo sat up, gave him the finger, and walked on toward McDonald's. Inside it was hot and dry and smelled of mud and fried food. He ordered a huge meal costing almost twenty dollars. Afterward he felt as if he had stuffed himself with hopelessness. For something to do, he began walking toward town.

He'd been at the gardens for nearly two years and visited San Sebastian a couple of dozen times. Once he had helped Ms. Iva shop at Office Depot and Ace Hardware; the other times he'd gone in the back of the truck with several other boys to the landscaping jobs Roman's Gardens was contracted to maintain. Milo hadn't paid much attention to the town. He couldn't say where the bus depot was or the train station or the post office. He hoped to get lucky and see the lawyer or the guy who was with her.

The sidewalk began where Route 6A entered the SanSeb city limits and became Harmonmeyer Road. From time to time he huddled in doorways or under an awning to escape the weather. He passed several low office buildings and some apartment houses. Outside a corner strip mall he was surprised to see a phone booth, battered and ready for the landfill. It had no door, but when he looked within he saw that there was a telephone book, or what remained of one, hanging from a cord. He wasn't sure how to spell *lawyer*, but he thought it would start with *law*. He might recognize her name if he saw it. Many of the yellow pages had been torn out, others were folded back on themselves, but he found the section heading he wanted. *Lawyer. See Attorneys at Law.*

He ran his finger down the listed names. The print was small, the lines blurred, and even when he blinked and opened his eyes wide, he couldn't see enough.

A few weeks earlier, Ms. Iva had asked him to read aloud from the history book about President Kennedy and the Cuban missile crisis. Milo had stumbled over his words as if he were a second grader. The guys at the table in the dining room had laughed at him, except Donny, who hardly made a sound under any circumstances. It was one of the things Milo didn't like about him, his creepy silence and the way he always seemed to be listening harder than anyone else. Freaky. Ms. Iva said Milo needed to be fitted for glasses. Like they were a shirt or a pair of pants. She said she would speak to Roman about it, but Milo guessed she hadn't done so, because nothing more was said about glasses. He needed to get a job where he didn't have to read.

On Maine Street he found a bench outside a bakery. He sat there for a long time, protected from the rain. There wasn't much traffic. Once he thought he saw Roman's truck. A pair of boys around his age went by, laughing and kicking up water, skateboards tucked under their arms. Milo wasn't hungry but he went into the bakery and bought a bag of day-old doughnuts. He sat on the bench and ate until he felt sick.

At the gardens he had shared an upstairs room with another boy until, when he'd been there about six weeks, Roman asked Ms. Iva to move him to the downstairs room at the back of the house, the room that Cobb occupied now and after Milo, Donny. At first Milo didn't like the downstairs bedroom despite the wide bed and tiny private bathroom. To help him adjust to the room, Roman came in at night and sat on the end of his bed. He asked Milo about the things he would like to do when he was grown and the person he aspired to be. Milo was shy about talking at first, but in time it became the best thing about living in the house, better even than Ms. Iva's chicken and not going to a regular school anymore. Milo began to wait for Roman to come into his room at night, anticipating the give-and-take of their conversation.

One night Roman asked Milo if he'd like to go out to the clubhouse and shoot a few hoops. It was after bedtime, but Roman said he was restless and Milo would be doing him a kindness if he kept him company. Milo did not want to take a shower after they played, but Roman teased him, called him Stinkypits, and poked him in the ribs until Milo laughed so hard, his side hurt. He stripped down and so did Roman and they stood under the hot water together. Everywhere Milo looked, there was Roman. Tufts of gray hair grew on his chest and shoulders and around his droopy penis, and it seemed wrong to stand in the shower with a man he now saw was old enough to be his grandfather. Roman snapped him on the butt with a towel and Milo snapped him back and it was sort of fun. While Milo toweled down, Roman made them snacks.

Did Milo like strawberry ice cream or chocolate? Why not have both? With whipped cream.

Later that night, lying in the big bed in the downstairs bedroom, Milo thought about the basketball, the laughing in the shower, and the huge sundae. Together, they made a memory of something special created for him alone, and the more he thought about it, the less strange it seemed. The next time Roman asked him if he wanted to shoot some hoops, he went into the shower without reluctance.

37

Iva's Saturday had begun the same as any day, fixing breakfast for Roman and the boys, cleaning upstairs, running
loads of laundry. On a clear weekend when Roman's Gardens
was open to retail customers and the yard was crowded with
cars, Iva was always called upon to manage the cash register.
But this was a chilly Saturday scattered with rainfall, so there
was little business, nothing Roman and the boys could not
handle on their own.

In his cell Donny would know nothing of the weather:
storm or a ten-day heat wave would all be the same to him.
That thought made her especially sad.

The wind lifted and rattled the loose shingles on the roof.
The dogs were uneasy on their chains, huddled in the barn
door, barking at anything that moved.

"We should bring them inside," Iva said when Roman
came in for his morning coffee. "At least put them in the
barn."

"Rain doesn't hurt a dog."

"I wish it'd stop."

"It's a frog strangler, all right."

It was a silly turn of phrase and she should have laughed. Instead she felt like crying.

After lunch Roman said he was going into town and she gave him a shopping list, but he returned without the items she'd requested. Without speaking to her, he went directly upstairs, and later she found him in his office, perched on the edge of his chair, running newsletters and sheets of paper through the shredder.

"I can do that," she said, laying her hand on his shoulder. "You have other things to do."

"I'm fine."

"Did you get the boys to mend the tear in greenhouse three?"

In a storm the tear would widen until the cover ripped away entirely, exposing the tropical seedlings to wind and drowning rain. A whole season of care and tending would be lost.

Iva was not surprised that Roman had forgotten, for since Donny's arrest, his mind had not been on his work, and sometimes she had to say his name three times to get his attention. Even then, he gave it to her reluctantly. Of the hundreds of boys Roman had trained and mentored over the years, Donny had been the most special, and seeing them together, Iva had felt the old longing for a child of her own, a son who would belong to both of them.

"Roman, why don't you visit the boy? In the jail. It would mean so much to him."

"Leave it be, Iva."

"His mother doesn't care about him. We're all he has…"

"I saw Milo." He sighed the words. "He was sitting on one of those wrought-iron benches on Maine Street."

It was a bad sign when a boy from the program hung around town. A boy like Milo didn't even have to look for trouble. It would find him, almost certainly.

"We should have tried to help him," she said, hearing a note of reprimand in her voice. "You could have called some of the growers and gotten him a job."

Roman hunched forward, cupping his face in his hands. Gently, she pulled them away. It happened sometimes that he fell into an irrational mood of negativity and self-doubt, and when he did, it was her responsibility to lift him out of it.

"Let me help you, Roman."

"I don't want it to be this way." His voice caught. "I want it to be different."

"Milo?"

"He's nothing."

She held his hands and fixed him with her firmest, most determined expression. Conviction and optimism would flow from her into him. "All over this state there are boys who owe you everything. You've been a light in so many lives, I can't even count how many boys you've helped. Maybe thousands, Roman. Think of that."

Building a better world, one boy at a time.

True, not all boys were responsive to Roman's encouragement. Sometimes it seemed that those for whom he cared the most could not wait to get away from him once they had their letter of recommendation, their GED, and their hundred dollars. Though he never spoke of it, she believed it hurt him that they did not even send cards at the holidays; and there were times when she felt a pity for him such as she might feel for someone suffering from an incurable illness and forced to carry on as if nothing were the matter.

"You know what I'd like to do?" he said. "Let's you and me pack a bag and get on a bus going across the border. We could just keep going south until we found a nice piece of land. Maybe in Costa Rica? They say it's nice down there."

She'd heard all this before. After they left Stockton years ago, he had wanted to go to Australia. They had driven to Arizona and stayed in Merryville with Roman's brother, where for a few months he and Omar had talked of nothing else. Australia, Australia, Australia. In the end nothing had come of it.

"Honestly, Roman," she said, kneeling beside his chair, "we're happy here, aren't we? And what about Laz and Riga? How could we leave our beautiful babies behind?"

Roman's opaque expression was unreadable.

"He looked like an orphan."

"Who?"

"You're right, I shouldn't have been so hard on him."

Milo. Donny. Cobb. Her husband loved these boys.

"You do your best, Roman. That's the important thing." She looked away from the tears in his eyes, resisting tears of her own. This was the lowest she had ever seen him. Not only was he depressed; he was afraid, and this disturbed her more than anything.

"We could go to Canada," he said. "We could drive across the border with the dogs and not come back. It's a big country, bigger than America. I could get lost there."

38

Ben caught up with Sophie as she walked to her office after the Bledsoe hearing.

"You've been avoiding me. You don't answer my calls."

"Use your clout for something useful, Ben. Call the city and tell them to clean up the park. Look at this place; it's a dump."

"You're going to take the Crider thing to a jury."

"Did you hear what I said?" Her hangover had subsided to a dull ache. "Do you ever listen to me?"

"Yeah, yeah, you're right. I'll call someone."

She knew he wouldn't. "Who told you I was going to trial?"

"Rumor."

"Well, rumor knows more than I do."

Back when she was fresh out of law school and honing her skills as a prosecutor, she and Ben had offices across the hall from each other. In those days she had admired his doggedness and they had made a good team. He had the cunning and determination and she the intuition, the ability to connect with a jury.

Ben followed her up the stairs and into the office. He hugged Anna. "How you doin', Ma?"

"When I see you, Benjamin, I'm happy." She patted his cheek.

Sophie groaned audibly.

When they were alone, he said, "How would you like to go to Mammoth for a couple of days? April snow. I can get Lloyd's condo."

"I'm busy, Ben."

"He's got that big fireplace. You could read, nap. I'd grill steaks. You need some fun in your life, Sophe."

"Fun for whom?"

"Jesus, you've got a mean streak." As he spoke, he spread his arms across the back of the chair and crossed his legs at an angle. The aggressively male body language made her laugh. Men could be so obvious.

"Who else makes you laugh?" he asked.

"Bart Simpson, Paula Poundstone, Jon Stewart—"

"Me too! That's something else we have in common."

"Ben, my client has pled not guilty to attempted murder. Unless you offer up a lesser charge, you're right. I'm thinking we'll go all the way with this."

"You haven't got a case."

"Don't be so sure." She liked the way his eyes opened wider. "It's not as black-and-white as it seems."

"Plead him guilty and we'll work something out."

"Time served and probation." She knew he'd never agree to it but she wanted to see how strongly he *disagreed*. "Until he's twenty-five."

He looked at her in disbelief.

"He's a boy, Ben."

"Nobody cares how old he is. Shit, Sophe, if I wanted to I could probably charge him under the Patriot Act. Have you thought about that? I could call him a terrorist and he goes to max security and no one sees his sorry ass again." He gave her a moment to think. "I'm offering you a good deal. You should take it. Everyone saw him do it; you've got nothing to bargain with."

"There's nothing and nothing, Ben." She grinned at him.

"What's that mean? You're bullshitting."

"Am I?"

He flicked his tongue against his lower front teeth. "The problem with you, Sophie, is that just when I think I've got you figured, you do an end run."

"And how is that my problem?"

"Right now, I think you're playing me. But there's a chance you aren't. You might actually take the case to trial. It'd be a stupid thing to do and a fucking waste of money, but that wouldn't stop you if you thought you could win."

In court with a mountain of evidence against Donny, there was still a one-thousand-to-one chance jurors would find in his favor. She thought of the boy she'd left a few hours earlier, having watched him regress into a childlike state at the mention of Roman Devane. If she could show a jury that damaged boy, there would not be a dry eye.

Maybe she *would* take his case to trial.

39

Donny had been in the program almost six months when Roman asked if he'd like to accompany him to San Diego. There were growers down there with whom he wanted to establish a connection. Donny had never been farther south than Disneyland and was eager to go.

Between Santa Barbara and Ventura the highway paralleled the Amtrak line and they'd passed a sidelined train carrying steers. The smell of the animals crowded together in the metal-sided railway car reached the truck.

"It's inhumane, enough to make a man a vegetarian." Roman upped the truck windows and turned on the AC. "Just look the other way, Donny. You don't want to remember something like that." Roman reached across the cab of the truck and grabbed Donny's shoulder, giving it a rough, friendly shake.

They reached LA at the morning rush hour. Although he knew that the stop and start irritated Roman, Donny enjoyed the slow drive in the big truck, looking down on the drivers. Some were talking on the phone or smoking; a few looked half-asleep. *So many people going to work in offices and schools, all people like me*, he thought. In a way that was new to him, hopeful and expansive and completely inexpressible, he felt that his life was opening.

"Thanks for bringing me with you, Mr. Devane."

"You call me Roman. Mr. Devane is my dad."

Eventually the traffic cleared and the highway turned west and then south and there was the Pacific Ocean out the right window, looking warmer and bluer than it did at Mars Beach. How great it was to be doing eighty down the freeway with Roman, his elbow on the open window, the hot-wind smell of asphalt and exhaust and salt air in his face and Johnny Cash on the CD player. He saw ahead to what his life would be like when he was a man with a job and places to go.

In Vista, a town forty miles north of San Diego, they visited two big wholesalers who supplied retail nursery chains. The first specialized in ornamental grasses and wasn't interesting to Donny except in the general way that all plant life engaged him. The second nursery was managed by someone called Elmore, a gangly little man in a big hat with a flap at the back to protect his neck from the sun. The nursery was big but not unmanageable and appealed to Donny's ambitions. Twenty acres and more than a thousand species of plant, many Donny had never encountered before. He was especially interested in varieties of impatiens and asked about them.

"Oh, we got the usual," Elmore said. "*Walleriana*, some New Guinea hybrids. Pretty boring stuff, but the colors is good and there's always a market for 'em."

Roman said, "Don't tell Donny they're boring. He prob'ly knows more about impatiens than either of us."

In the course of the next twenty minutes Elmore listened as Donny talked about a project he was working on, adapting the cultivation of an unusual variety of impatiens, the *balfourii*, to Southern California conditions.

"It might do good on the coast where it's overcast a lot." Donny had heard a confidence in his voice that he barely recognized, and the expansive feeling of earlier in the day returned. Elmore said something corny about being impatient for the new impatiens and Donny's laugh was as hearty as the men's.

Back in the car, Roman said, "I'm proud of you, son."

Donny looked away, embarrassed by the stinging in his eyes.

"You're going to be a real plantsman."

They ate dinner at a Claim Jumper restaurant and Roman went into an EconoLodge to get rooms for the night. He came out looking distressed.

"We've got a problem here, Donny. For some reason they're full up. Only got one room left. One bed." He rolled his eyes as if to say, *How crazy is that?* "I'm beat and I bet you are too; it's been a long day, but it's okay with me if you want to head home. We could be there in six hours, maybe a little less. If you're, you know, uncomfortable. About the bed thing."

Donny wasn't sure what Roman meant. Did he want to stay at the EconoLodge or drive home? What was Donny supposed to say? They wouldn't get home before two a.m. and Ms. Iva rang the wake-up bell at six and after that there'd be a full day in the orchard or greenhouse or potting shed. He didn't say so, but Donny thought Roman should try another motel. They couldn't all be so full, but he was sure Roman must have thought of that already and discarded the alternative for some reason. So far it had been a perfect day and he didn't want anything to spoil it. Donny was having the best time of his life.

"You're the boss, Mr. Devane." *Roman*.

"Tell you the truth, I'm practically asleep on my feet."

"Okay," Donny said, and they swung their overnight bags out of the truck and went inside.

Donny stood in the little room, the first motel he'd ever been in, and he wasn't impressed by either the size or the décor, mostly tan and brown and yellow-orange as garishly bright as a *Rudbeckia*. If he spread his arms out, he could almost touch the opposite walls, and the bed, which Roman had said was king-sized, didn't look any larger than the one in which his mother slept.

Would they both sleep in it or should Donny offer to spend the night on the straight-backed chair shoved into a corner? He'd seen one of the Three Stooges put a blanket and pillows in a bathtub, but that was meant to be funny.

Roman unzipped his bag and laid his toothbrush and razor on the little counter in the bathroom, calling out to Donny, "There's shampoo if you want to wash your hair. I don't know about you, but I was sweatin' like a hog out there in Vista."

He poked his head around the corner of the door. "Mind if I shower first?"

Donny turned on the television and sat on the edge of the bed watching an episode of *Law and Order*, and after a few minutes Roman came out of the bathroom wearing a towel around his waist and using another to dry his hair. The hair on his chest was almost white, but he was as strong as a young man. They had worked together many times doing heavy jobs, lifting trees in big tubs and hauling away brush.

"Your turn, Donny-boy. It's a good shower and as much hot water as you want. That's what I like about motels. For once I don't have to think about the water bill."

After his shower Donny brushed his teeth and dried his hair with the only towel that was still dry. Afterward, he pulled on his jockeys and wrapped the small towel around himself. He'd been half-naked around Roman before, but that was in the clubhouse, where the boys often showered after work. Being alone with him in a strange place was different, not bad but strange. He pulled on the T-shirt he'd worn that day. It was damp from lying on the bathroom floor where he'd dropped it and smelled of sweat. He hadn't thought to bring another.

Roman was sitting up in the bed, channel surfing. He had pulled the blackout curtains across the window and turned down the blanket for Donny.

"You can sleep on top of the covers if you don't want to touch my hairy old legs." A joke. "But you'll freeze your nuts off if you do. They must run the air from the office somewhere. It's like a meat locker in here."

Donny propped himself against the pillows, stiff legged and as jumpy as a grasshopper, ashamed of himself for feeling this way when Roman had been so generous all day, treating him as almost an equal at Elmore's nursery. He didn't even know why he was nervous. They watched a comedy show about two young men just out of college, sharing an apartment. They had girlfriends and jobs and neither of them could cook a decent meal, which led to some hilarious circumstances that got Roman and Donny laughing hard. When it was over, Roman tossed off a couple of pillows and lay back, tugging the blanket up around his shoulders.

Donny asked, "You want me to turn off the TV?"

"Suit yourself. Tomorrow's going to be another long day."

To turn the TV on or off. To sleep on the bed or under the covers. Take a shower or don't. Donny was uneasy with so many choices. He watched another program, a comedy news show he couldn't make much sense of, but he was half-asleep and glad for the company of a third person in the cold room. He thought of getting back into his clothes but that would have been too weird, so after a few minutes of indecision, he got under the covers.

He was asleep, turned on his side, when Roman reached over him for the remote and turned off the television. The sudden silence woke Donny completely. He didn't move.

"Whatcha thinking about?" Roman lay a little closer to him than he had.

"I was asleep."

He felt Roman's hand on his back and flinched. Roman chuckled softly. "I'm not going to hurt you, boy. When me and my bro, Omar, were kids we slept in the same bed. It was either that or the floor, like here."

Donny liked the way Roman spoke, the musical rhythm of his western accent.

"When I couldn't sleep at night, Omar'd give me a massage. He was older'n me by four years and he worried I wouldn't get enough sleep to do good in school, you know?" He ran his hand up Donny's spine and around, under his shoulder blade and down again. Once. Twice. Again and again and again. His hand was warm like an iron smoothing Donny's skin. His mother had never touched him so gently.

She had hardly touched him at all, except when she called him into the bedroom to help her sleep. *Spoons*, she'd say, reaching behind and tugging his hips against her. *Cheek*, she'd say and draw his arm around her, his hand to her face. As a small boy he'd fallen asleep that way and awakened the next morning deep in the smell of her. As he grew older, he dreaded this possibility and learned to stay awake until he could safely return to his own bed.

For a burly man, Roman had a deep gentleness in him, and there was no offense in his hand cupping Donny's buttocks in their tighty whiteys. It was strange, yes, but the alarm that went off in Donny's sleepy mind was not imperative. *No. Don't. Stop.* Waking in the morning, he could not be sure if he had dreamed it all.

In this way it had begun between them, more like a kindness than anything else. That first night Roman's hands had seemed natural on his body and, in a way, generous. The bad stuff came later, after Donny had moved to the downstairs room, and he didn't know how to stop it. It wasn't anything he would have chosen; still, he understood that everything in life had to be paid for, and like anything else, being special to Roman came with a price tag.

Donny opened his eyes and saw the acoustic-tile ceiling above him. The last thing he remembered was Sophie talking about something he couldn't remember, and then he spilled his cocoa. After that he remembered only the noise, a blinding roaring in his ears. It had happened the same way once before when he saw the governor up on the stage. He couldn't remember what he'd done in the park, but he would never forget the noise.

His fingers were sticky and smelled sour, but he didn't know why.

Since the day in the park the noise was always present, a constant rumbling, a gentle bass note. When he heard it the first time, he thought it was the sound of a revving motorcycle.

It was in his head; he got that now.

Kravitz came to take him to the basement to exercise. Donny said he didn't want to go and the guard went away saying he could suit himself, it was no skin off his back. The door at the end of the hall banged shut. At that moment Donny had an image of himself as the only prisoner in a block of cells, tens of tens of them arranged in a long line like railroad cars at a siding, waiting for something to happen.

40

After work Sophie detoured under the freeway to the college area where her cousin, one of Delio's sons, owned a pizza joint. He made her a large pesto with tomato, bacon, and anchovies on a thin crust, all the while lecturing her on Donny's obvious guilt.

She felt a frisson of anxiety as the electronically controlled guard gate lifted at the entrance to her apartment complex. She wasn't going home to quiet and privacy. Hamp would be there and the dog. She would have to talk. Despite his promise, he might want to say something about what she'd confided the night before.

Coming into the kitchen from the condo's garage, she announced, "I brought pizza." Psyche met her, tail wagging. It was cupboard love but nice anyway. "Ask politely and I'll give you my crusts." Hamp started talking to her from down the hall. The heat was on and there was music. She quickly realized she'd been worried about nothing. The feeling in her home was easy. Somehow, she and Hamp had become friends.

As they ate dinner and finished off a six-pack of Sebastiani Sisters, a local beer, she told him about her conversation with Ben.

"I don't blame him for not dealing," Hamp said. "He thinks he's got a home run."

"If he won't bargain, I might chance a jury. It's a long shot, but if I got the right lineup of witnesses..." She ate an anchovy off her pizza. "We need that kid. Milo."

"No sign of him. I drove around, checked out the bus station and the train; no one remembers a boy fitting his description. I think he's in the wind."

"Trust me, he's not going anywhere."

Sophie had met others like Milo and recognized the mix of greed and fear that ran his personality. Boys like Milo went for their freedom as soon as they could—at ten or twelve or sixteen. They claimed they wanted to be *on their own*, but really they wanted a license to do whatever took their fancy while someone else provided room and board, no questions asked. When the time came and they were actually free, unmoored boys like Milo didn't know what to do with themselves. They were terrified by having to take personal responsibility for anything and often so frightened they couldn't even make a first move in that direction. Milo would hang around SanSeb just long enough to get into trouble. After that the system would take over his life and he could relax and start to complain again about the rules and regulations that were taking away his freedom.

"Suppose I do find him; what happens then?"

"He tells me the truth about Roman."

Hamp held up his beer before downing the last of it. "Good luck with that."

Sophie's cell phone chimed, signaling a text message. She fished the phone out of her purse and read the screen.

"Oh, my God. It's Donny. He tried to kill himself."

41

A police guard posted outside Donny's room at San Sebastian General Hospital wouldn't let Sophie go in until she proved she was the patient's attorney. She called Ben and he came to the hospital to vouch for her. He handed her a cup of coffee and said that according to the officer on duty at the jail, Donny had been "like a zombie" after Sophie left him. He refused exercise and lay on his cot, staring at the ceiling.

"Whatever you said to him, Sophie, it must've been bad. After lights-out he started slamming his head into the wall. They found him flat on the floor, blood everywhere."

"Has anyone talked to his mother? Is she coming?"

"Don't ask me. He's your client."

Donny lay on his back in the hospital bed, covered by a thin green blanket. Though he was cuffed to the roll bars on either side of the bed, his hands opened and closed constantly, as if he were grabbing hold of something. His head and left eye were heavily bandaged and a bruise the color of a ripe mango spread along his jawline from under his ear.

Beside his bed, electronic monitors flashed incomprehensible numbers, and graph lines ran across a screen like red and blue mountain ranges, constantly rebuilding themselves.

"I hear the surfer dude's living with you now."

"Don't start, Ben."

"And I know about the note."

At least he didn't know about the shoes. She, Tamlin, and Hamp had managed to keep the story to themselves.

"It was the Bleekers," she said.

"Can you prove it?"

She gave him a dirty look. "You know it's their style."

"Maybe, but there's plenty of other people mad at you. The whole town. I never wanted you to defend this kid. I told you not to. I knew the label folks'd hang on you. Didn't I say so? And God help you if you did, by some miracle, get him off, everybody'd be gunning for you. And him. This little drama he cooked up isn't going to win him any sympathy."

"I can't choose my clients like it's a popularity contest."

"You don't have to tell me that, Sophie. This is me you're talking to, not the newspaper. I'm on one side, you're on the other, that's the way the system works. But I don't think you get what happened when Donny Crider shot Maggie. He didn't just wound *her*. You complained about the way the park looks? Blame your goddamn fucking client."

"The park's a symbol now? Since when do you care about that kind of stuff?"

"Since Donny Crider shot Maggie. Since SanSeb turned into another bloody American city like Dallas or Birmingham or Boston."

At that exact moment, as Ben walked away from her in a rare show of disgust, Sophie remembered something in one of those articles her mother had so diligently cut from legal journals, stapled together, and put under cover in her rolltop desk with a note attached: *READ THESE.*

She pulled a chair into Donny's room and scrounged a couple of pillows and a blanket. She did this on her own. The hospital staff seemed to be ignoring her, which she supposed was because of Donny. With her feet hooked under the bed rail, she was reasonably comfortable and sat for some time just watching him breathe, thinking about him, the park, and the city. As she dozed a little she had a clouded sense of voices in the hall, a nurse or aide checking on Donny from time to time. She found the vast machinery of the hospital working around her oddly soothing and she fell asleep.

In the morning she woke with a sore back and a crick in her neck. Someone had put a cup of coffee on the table near her. She was getting ready to go home for a shower and change of clothes when Elena stepped into the room wearing a clear plastic raincoat that reached almost to her ankles, clutching a dripping pleated plastic scarf.

"It's still coming down out there." With her hair dragged back into a ponytail, her face looked huge: all forehead, wide cheeks, and pointed chin. In Elena's broad, bony face and big-hipped body, Sophie saw the raw farm girl she must have been. No one would mistake her for Maggie Duarte's sister.

"I didn't think you'd come."

"Life is full of little surprises." Elena glared in the direction of the guard seated on a plastic chair by the door, thumbing his phone. "That one wasn't going to let me in."

"Nothing's changed, Elena. Donny's still a prisoner."

"I don't need you to tell me that."

"It's a pity he's so sedated. He'll never know you visited."

"How did he do it?"

"I'm not clear on the details, but apparently he slammed his head against the floor or the wall until he passed out."

"You can do that?"

"I guess so. If you want to die."

Elena winced.

They stood at his bedside, watching him sleep.

"I've been trying to reach you, Sophie. I'm going away for a while. My sister invited me to stay with her in Marshalltown. In Iowa." She opened her hands and studied the palms. Sophie imagined that she was measuring the length of her lifeline.

"You can't leave him."

"I don't pay you to accuse me."

"I'm not accusing you. I'm just saying you can't abandon him. Whatever problems you've got, now's the time to suck it up and put him first. He needs you."

"My son is a killer."

"He didn't kill Maggie."

"Don't nitpick."

"No matter what he did, you're still his mother."

"You blame me."

It was true and not true at the same time.

"After he went out to the gardens, Donny wasn't the same

boy I raised." Elena chewed her words. "He stayed away, left me on my own to care for all those wretched children. Never thought about my needs. After all I'd done for him, he was ready to cast me aside."

"I talked to Jenna. She said he often went home."

"Oh, sure, when he wanted to, when it suited him. At his convenience. He left me alone and now I'm going to do the same to him. You think I'm heartless. But let me tell you, that man? Roman Devane? He hypnotizes those boys. He's a con man and someone ought to close down that so-called program of his. I knew what was going on over there and I told him so."

"Wait a minute. You knew?"

"He's getting rich off those boys working for him all day, seven days a week. Donny wanted to be over there on Sundays, can you imagine? We used to go to Mass and then to brunch. It was our special time, but he preferred to play in the dirt. You're a lawyer—you should know what I'm talking about. Boys into Men is a scam! Probably breaking every labor law there is. I told him straight-out that I'd report him to the police if he didn't send Donny packing."

Elena knew nothing, but Roman had no way of knowing that when she threatened him. And if she complained to the police and they investigated his program, who knew what boys like Milo might say when Cary Hering questioned them?

Later, Sophie walked home through the park, stopping beside the fountain where Donny had stood. The rain had let up but the sky was heavy and dark. There was no wind now, but earlier it had damaged trees all over town. In the park, the gardens, grass, and paths were strewn with the bark and branches of eucalyptus trees. Every purple blossom had been ripped from the jacarandas. They lay in sodden ruffles around the ankles of the trees. May's Jacaranda Festival would be a disappointment this year. Perhaps it would be canceled altogether.

Poor park, Sophie thought. *Poor town.*

Poor Donny.

She called Anna's cell phone.

"I'm at the office," her mother said. "Your filing system is a mess. It took me twenty minutes to find that Wally Bledsoe file yesterday."

"I need you to do something for me, Ma. I want you to get through to Maggie in Sacramento. Would she talk to you?"

"I don't know. Maybe."

Family lore had it that without the financial help of families like the Giraudos, Maggie would have had a hard time paying for her education despite generous scholarships. Sophie wasn't sure how much of this was a tall tale, but now was the time to find out.

"What do you want me to tell her?"

"See if you can arrange for me to talk to her. I'll drive up. Tell her it's about Donny. And SanSeb."

42

Inside the Mission Church of San Sebastian it was cold and smelled of stone and damp clay. Near five in the afternoon, Milo had the church to himself. On both sides, down the length of the narrow, windowless nave, electric candles in niches flickered realistically, casting shape-shifting shadows up the whitewashed plaster walls. The altar was a simple table ornamented with a bowl of drooping roses. Behind it and extending over the domed sanctuary ceiling and nave were bright, crudely painted images of birds and angels and winged fish flying amid the curling stems of fantastically flowered vines.

Milo had never seen anything like it. He sat at the back on one of the bare oak pews and stared until he got a crick in his neck.

Behind him there was a door with a sign on it. CLERGY AND STAFF ONLY. He wasn't sure what *clergy* meant, but he knew it wasn't a synonym for "Walk right in, Milo, and make yourself comfortable." Trespassing didn't bother him, especially when it might lead him to dry shelter for the night.

The door swung into a short unlit hall with a door at the end and one to the side. From behind the farthest of these he heard voices and then laughter and the sound of another door, one he couldn't see, closing. A phone rang and he listened as an answering machine clicked on. He slid his back down the wall and crouched on his haunches, waiting to see what would happen next.

"You've reached the Mission Church of Saint Sebastian," the recording said. "We're sorry, but the office is closed at this time." The message went on and on, listing the schedule of Masses and numbers to call in case of an emergency. Milo listened through the full length of it and waited. Hearing no conversation, he guessed that the office on the other side of the door was closed for the night.

The second door opened into a large storage closet, a clutter of folding chairs and tables and plastic bins labeled with marking pen. One small window faced the mission courtyard. A few feet away, a priest in a gray cassock, holding an umbrella, walked by. He had a ring of keys looped around his wrist and he was twirling it by circling his forearm. Milo guessed that the priest was locking up the mission for the night.

In one corner of the closet there was a blue plastic bin containing a few cardboard boxes broken down for recycling. He pulled these out and laid them on the floor in the shadows against the wall farthest from the door. If the priest looked in the storage closet he might not see Milo. He hunted among the shelves and cabinets for anything that would keep him warm. Finding nothing, he sat with his knees up around his chin, shivering as it grew darker and colder in the room. He tried to ignore how hungry he was. He weighed the benefits of being discovered. The colder he was, the less it seemed like a bad thing. Church people would never kick him out into the rain. He'd probably be given food and a place to sleep. He rested his chin on his knees and waited for the door to open.

It didn't, and he started to wonder about the office at the end of the hall and the things people might keep in their desk drawers, a candy bar at least. Maybe half a sandwich. There might be a sweater or a coat left on the back of a chair. A carpet would be warmer than this cement floor and cardboard. He stepped out of the storeroom into the pitch-black hall, laid the palm of his left hand against the wall, and moved forward until he reached the door and found the knob.

He stepped into a large office with many windows. One set faced the shadowed courtyard, its paths and borders dimly illuminated through the rain. Across the room, more windows revealed a small walled patio. An occasional arc of car lights told Milo there must be a street beyond the wall. The office had four desks arranged two and two, facing each other, and over a long worktable pushed against the windowless wall hung a crucifix. Flanking it were paintings of old men under whose scrutiny Milo felt as he had when he was caught with his hand in his third-grade teacher's purse. In one corner there was a coat tree, bare except for a scarf. Lifting it from its hook, Milo was engulfed in a cloud of sweet, musky scent. He imagined the woman who sometimes wore it to keep the draft off her shoulders and the back of her neck, a round, soft woman with plump arms and hair that smelled like hard candy. The scarf was warm and long enough to go around his shoulders twice, and its touch and smell brought tears to Milo's eyes.

Some desk drawers and all the file cabinets were locked. Those he could, he opened, but he found nothing to eat. In the wastebaskets there were sandwich wrappers and empty chip packages. One wrapper had a smear of mayonnaise on it. He put the paper in his mouth and sucked it. As he did, futility washed over him and he went weak under the burden of his life.

He discovered a small heater tucked into the well of one desk and spent the night curled on the carpet before its heat with the fragrant scarf wrapped around his head and shoulders. He dreamed of Ms. Iva's macaroni and cheese and hunger woke him before daylight.

It was still raining and the heater must have been on a timer because it had shut off sometime earlier. Milo wasn't sure what day of the week it was, but he did not want to risk being caught by a secretary coming in to work. He went back to the closet and returned the flattened cardboard to the blue bin, thinking it wise to cover his tracks in case he had to return to the mission that night. He kept the scarf, however, wrapping and tying it around his chest under his still-damp coat. He left by the front door. The next person into the office would wonder why it was unlocked and someone would be blamed for carelessness.

In drizzling rain, running from the shelter of one storefront awning to the next, he went several blocks along Mission Street and then back in the opposite direction along Maine looking for an open coffeehouse. When he found one, the place was empty except for a girl with purple streaks in her hair, filling the display case with pastries. He was light-headed with hunger, but he knew without asking that the bear claws and shiny doughnuts in frilly paper baskets were more expensive than he could afford. He ordered a cup of coffee with chocolate in it and whipped cream and grabbed the last sandwich in a basket marked *Day Old*. He handed the girl at the counter a ten-dollar bill expecting change. She asked him for another dollar.

He sat outside under the metal roof and disciplined himself to slowly chew each mouthful of sandwich. After a while he had another cup of coffee. He asked the barista if it would cost less without whipped cream and she laughed as if he'd made a joke. Later, she came out with another drink, which she said was on the house. On impulse he asked her if she knew who Donny Crider was.

"Not personally, thank God."

"Do you know the lawyer he's got?"

"Everyone does. Her brother was my counselor senior year." The girl stood hipshot beside him, her little tummy sticking out. "Sophie Giraudo. I saw her on TV. She's sort of famous, I guess. What d'you want a lawyer for? Are you in some kind of trouble?"

He quickly said he wasn't.

"She must be crazy, defending that whack job."

"I know him."

"Hey, no kidding." She sat down. "What's he like?"

Milo wondered if people driving by would think that she was his girlfriend.

"I saw his picture," she said. "He's hot looking but he's gotta be weird, right?"

"Yeah. Weird."

The other boys in Roman Devane's program didn't care any more about plants than Milo did, but Donny had been different. Though he hardly talked to anyone, Donny's lips moved when he was planting or pruning, which was definitely weird. Plus he learned the Latin names for everything, made lists of them, and muttered them under his breath as if he took pleasure in the peculiar sound of the words.

"You from around here?" the barista asked. "I used to live in Santa Barbara, but there's nothing down there except gays and old ladies playin' bridge. Bo-ring."

"You know where her office is at?"

"How come you want a lawyer?" she asked again.

Milo's plan was none of her business, but he kept his opinion to himself and spoke vaguely of having information about the case. He liked the way the barista looked at him when he said that. And it was true that he knew things about Donny and Roman that the lawyer would pay to hear. On television such exchanges were routine between lawyers and informants. It would not do to be too forthcoming, though. In Milo's experience, eagerness always meant weakness.

The girl said, "She probably works near the courthouse. There's lots of lawyers there."

The barista gave him directions and Milo set off in the

way she had directed him. Eventually he found the building with Sophie Giraudo's name on a plaque by the entrance. Now here he was, standing in her office, his muddy shoes leaving footprints on her carpet. She looked like she was glad to see him.

43

Anna made a Target run for dry clothes and stopped at the market on the way back. When Milo had changed she gave him a sandwich.

Sophie asked if she'd had any luck getting through to the governor.

"I'll do it, but don't waste her time, Sophia. Don't humiliate me."

Anna's ego-shredding comments sometimes left Sophie speechless. Before she spoke, she took a long breath and put a smile on her face. "And see if you can reach Hamp, will you? I need to talk to him."

"About what?"

"Just get him for me."

Milo ate without looking at Sophie, taking huge bites of sandwich, filling his cheeks like a squirrel. She wondered if he was actually that hungry or if he ate to fill some other emptiness. When he finished she handed him a paper towel and watched as he wiped his hands and small, rodent-like face.

"Why'd you come to my office, Milo?"

He squirmed in his new sweatpants and shirt. "You gave me your card."

"As I remember, you weren't much interested. You dropped it in the dirt."

He didn't deny it.

Sophie didn't trust him, but seeing how vulnerable he was, part boy, part man, facing a life without resources in a frighteningly complex world, she felt some sympathy. Ben used to say that her attraction to underdogs would be her undoing. But not this time. She thought of Roman Devane taking advantage of Milo's weakness and she was awash with disgust and a determination to make the man pay. How many other boys had he abused? In a way, she didn't want to know.

"What's your last name?"

"Why?"

"I like to know peoples' first and last names both."

This appeared to be a novel idea to Milo. "Gagnon."

"Do you have family? Someone you'd like to call?"

He shook his head.

He was alone in the world and she was his lifeline. Unlike Donny, who was incapable of telling her what Roman had done, Milo had no sense of shame or guilt or loss, or if he did they were buried so deep in his subconscious that he did not know they existed.

"I gave you my card because I think you can help me."

"This is about him."

"Yes."

"I don't mean Donny."

"I know you don't."

"Okay."

"Were you one of Roman's special boys?"

"What d'you mean?"

Sophie told herself to be patient.

"Did you and Roman have a sexual relationship?"

He drew back from the blunt question. "He likes the younger ones."

"But when you were younger. What about then?"

"I didn't do nothin' wrong."

"You're not in trouble, Milo."

He picked his teeth with his fingernail, and, as if he had either forgotten that she was there or didn't care, he reached inside his new sweatpants to adjust himself.

"Where will you go when you leave my office, Milo? Do you have plans?" She paused before adding, "Do you have any money?"

"A little."

"Did Roman give you a job reference?"

His jaw tightened and she guessed that he and Roman had not parted well.

"He kicked me out. No letter, no nothin'."

"Why did he do that?"

"How should I know?"

He crossed his arms over his chest and looked toward the windows.

"You need a job, but you have no reference. Is that why you came to my office? Do you want me to find you a job?"

He looked at her as if she were speaking in tongues.

"You want money."

"I know stuff," he said. "I could tell you stuff about Roman."

"I believe I already know a lot about Roman."

"Not like me, I bet."

"Do you know what a pedophile is, Milo?"

He looked away.

"It's what the police call a man who's sexually attracted to children."

"He's not gay. He's got a wife."

"Pedophiles aren't gay. Pedophiles are abusers. It's not against the law to be gay, Milo. But it's a crime to coerce children into having sex."

"I'm eighteen."

"In the eyes of the law, you're a child until you're eighteen. When you and Roman had your relationship—"

"I never said we did."

"You were legally a minor."

As she spoke he reached his right arm across his chest and shoulder and his hand around the back of his neck. The other he tucked up into his armpit. "What's that mean?"

"You were underage and didn't want to have sex with Roman, but he put you in a situation where you didn't have any choice."

Sophie did not know if she was saying the right things. A therapist skilled with victimized children would be more subtle, but she didn't think subtlety would work with Milo. Confronted by the truth, he wasn't going to become hysterical or catatonic or revert as Donny had done. He wouldn't run away either, not so long as he needed money. Revenge and money were what he'd come to Sophie for.

"You can testify in court against Roman and he'll go to prison. He'll never hurt another boy. He'll be locked up for a long time."

"How much'll you give me?"

"I won't give you money."

His face turned an angry red.

"Think about it. If I pay you to give testimony, it's like I'm bribing you. People would say you made up your answers just to get money from me. They'd say you were lying."

"He fucked with lots of guys. Donny and there's a little kid there now—"

"Tell me your story, Milo. If you're honest with me, things'll work out for you."

Even to Sophie's ears, the offer rang feeble, but it was all she had. She wouldn't bend the law for him or make promises to assure his testimony. If he agreed to be a witness for the defense, he would have a place to live and food to eat until the case was resolved. Afterward, Sophie would find him a job. Beyond that, he was on his own.

"I won't let you down, Milo."

She watched him think about her words, watched his face go slack and his shoulders drop. A boy who felt entitled, a boy with fight in him, might have tried to bargain for a better deal, but Milo expected to be cheated.

She put her cell phone on recording mode and said, as if they had come to an agreement, "Just answer my questions as honestly as you can."

An hour later, Anna took Milo home with her, leaving Sophie alone in the office. She locked the front door, poured a drink, and lay down on the couch. Her thoughts, like Hamp's the other night, were on the vulnerability of children. Donny and Milo. Roman's new favorite, whoever he was. And herself, at thirteen.

Hamp was in the kitchen making some kind of tomato sauce. The kitchen smelled of onions.

"You're cooking? Now?"

"Sweet tomato sauce."

"It's after ten."

"It's been a while since I had a real kitchen. Do you mind?"

"Knock yourself out." She stuck her finger in the sauce and tasted it. "Not very Italian."

"Good?"

"I guess. Yeah. Where were you all afternoon? You didn't answer your cell. Milo came in."

He handed her a beer.

"He told me everything. And it's just as bad as we thought."

"Now you've got the facts, what're you going to do with them?"

"Jesus, Hamp, what do you think?"

He raised an eyebrow.

"Sorry. Getting dragged through slime puts me in a bad mood." She went back to her bedroom to shower and change.

It wasn't just listening to Milo's sick history. She'd spent too long in her office, sipping Scotch, remembering things she'd prefer to forget. Telling Hamp her story had cleared her vision a little, but the keys were still in the bottom of the drawer, a reminder she didn't need but was not yet ready to part with. With or without the keys, she would never forget what happened to her on Mariposa Street; nor would she forget how it felt to be powerless. She might be a nicer person if she tossed the keys and let herself forget. On the other hand, the bristliness that made her hard to get along with was a good quality in an attorney. Anger sharpened her skill set.

Back in the kitchen, Hamp asked, "Feeling better?"

She shrugged. "I'm sorry I snapped at you. I just hate this case sometimes."

He tossed a handful of walnuts and raisins in the tomato sauce. "I was with Iva Devane today."

While cruising the shopping center on the southside, still looking for Milo, he'd seen Iva pushing a full shopping cart across the supermarket lot to her truck.

"It was raining on and off and she must have had five hundred dollars' worth of food getting soaked. I helped her put it into the backseat of the truck."

"What a gent."

Hamp ignored the sarcasm. "We both got pretty wet, so I asked if she'd like a cup of coffee to warm up a little. I didn't expect her to say yes. She's shy."

"Or afraid she'll say too much."

They'd gone to an almost empty Starbucks next to the market and sat at a table by the window.

"She'd been to the jail to see Donny and they said he was

in the hospital. The OD told her he'd fallen and hit his head. I reassured her that's all it was. She kept telling me he's a good boy."

Warming their hands around their coffee cups, they had watched the wind- and rain-swept lot.

Iva asked him, "Are you like a policeman?"

"Not anymore."

"But now, I could tell you something and it'd be private? You wouldn't have to tell anyone? We'd be like two ordinary people having a conversation?"

"I wanted to hear what she had to say," he told Sophie. "But I had to get her feeling safe first. She looked like she'd been abandoned at the side of the road." Forlorn in her wet coat, her hair dripping on her shoulders. He had reassured Iva that her confidence was safe with him.

Sophie wondered where his patient kindness came from. If she were not still fighting an old battle, protecting an old wound, would she be a nicer, kinder person?

Iva said, "I can't prove it, but I don't think he ever meant to kill the governor."

Hamp could see that she wanted to tell him something but was afraid. He gently pressed her to go on.

"Roman taught him how to shoot," Iva said. "It was something he did with the boys he thought needed it, for a confidence builder, you might say. He told me Donny could hit a bull's-eye every time."

Sophie took a moment to digest this. "That's part of Boys into Men? Target practice?"

"Seems so."

"All the boys?"

"Iva said it was mostly his favorites."

"Roman's lucky one of his favorites didn't haul off and shoot him."

The lager bottle had left a damp ring on the countertop. Absently, Sophie swirled the moisture with her finger, making a flower.

"Do you think she knows what her husband is?"

He watched the sauce bubble, his lower lip caught in his teeth. "She'd have to, wouldn't she?"

"Maybe she doesn't let herself know." Sophie pulled her cell phone from her purse. "But I know. It's all here in Milo's words."

At that moment, the phone in her hand rang. Anna's ringtone. A barking dog.

44

I va forgot to ring the dinner bell until almost five twenty.

"That's not like you," Roman said as he washed his hands in the sink. "Where's your mind today?"

"I don't know," she said truthfully. Her thoughts darted from subject to subject, lighting on none for long. A constant, numbing this and that. "It must be the rain. So unseasonable. It's making me strange."

After that he didn't say much, but she felt him watching her as she put food on the table. She got the sense of a migraine beginning—in the spring and fall they often afflicted her in clusters of three or four—a particular feeling as if something were squeezing the back of her eyeballs. She took a pill to forestall the headache but couldn't tell if it had done the job.

On the way home from town she had stopped at Colonel Sanders and bought buckets of chicken. The boys cheered when she laid two mounded platters on the table. Watchful and somber, Roman shoveled food into his mouth with the thoughtless regularity of a machine. There was none of the usual across-the-table quizzing and sparring with the boys. Seeing that Roman had his mind on other things, they devoured their dinner like young savages, scarcely breathing between bites, forgetting to say *please* and *thank you*. Cobb looked up at Iva when she refilled his glass with soda, his cheeks shining with grease. The blue vacancy of his stare stopped her for a moment.

After dinner she watched from the kitchen window as Roman followed behind the gang of boys running across the yard to the clubhouse, all splashing in the puddles and bickering noisily over which movie they'd watch first. Riga stayed with her but Laz danced around their racing-chasing hijinks. Roman was so deep in thought, he didn't seem to notice any of it. At the corner of the barn he stopped and turned to look at the house. For a moment Iva thought he might come back, and she didn't want him to.

She cleaned the kitchen and then climbed the stairs to the office, where the bills were stacked beside the computer. It was twenty to eight. The medication had dulled the pain enough so she could get some work done, and this was good because Iva needed to keep her mind occupied with neutral matters, but on-screen the numbers doubled before her eyes. Inputting payments, she made several mistakes, and while she tried to undo them, she lost her connection to the bank.

She closed her eyes and Donny's image appeared before her as he'd been when they tended the garden together by moonlight, picking the velvety caterpillars off the tomato vines. In the midst of remembering, her affection for him was the truest thing she knew. She stared at her image reflected in the blue screen.

What if all those people at St. Mary and All Angels Church the other day were right and there is a God? And what if God were trying to tell her something, using the cursor to blink a message to her? She stared at it until her eyes burned, willing the message to reveal itself in a way she could understand.

In the bedroom she folded laundry. Dozens of boy-sized T-shirts and sweatshirts and blue jeans and coveralls. Socks she'd never get the dirt stains out of. She looked the other way when she folded their underwear. Boys.

Sitting with Hamp in Starbucks she'd been awkward and shy because all she knew in the world was boys and plants. The only men she had ever been close to were her father and Roman, and even they were essentially mysterious. It seemed, as she stood in the bedroom, that she had never really known anyone. Except Donny. In the silence of the garden there had been communication between them that went deeper than words. And she had failed him. Precisely how or when, she could not say, but certainty filled and sickened her.

Later she slept a little until she was awakened by the whispers of the boys coming upstairs after their movies. Roman cautioned them to be quiet when they came in late, so they took off their shoes and left them on the back porch, but there was always scuffing and whispering and snorts of stifled laughter. Asking boys not to make noise was like asking Riga not to scratch. On the little round rug beside the bed the dog woofled softly as if she knew Iva was thinking of her.

When Roman did not follow the boys upstairs, Iva told herself that he was in the kitchen snacking on leftover chicken. She fell asleep again, thinking that she would clear her mind and make a fresh start in the morning. She would not dwell on Donny or the past, and her mind would be as it always had been: steady and complacent.

Donny. Milo. Cobb. They stood at the foot of the bed and looked at her. They told her to wake up. *Open your eyes, Iva Devane. See. See.*

She sat up.

Why was Roman taking so long downstairs?

See. See.

She could not ignore the command any more than she could ignore her throbbing head. The more she struggled, the more solidly the truth took shape before her. This was the horrendous truth that she had both known and not known, seen and been blind to. It was the answer to all the questions she had never dared to ask.

Barefoot, in her long white nightgown, she stood at the top of the stairs looking down at the dark entry. Riga sat beside her. The rain had stopped but wind rattled in the shingles like rats chasing each other across the roof. A draft hurried her down the stairs. She stepped into the living room and looked across it, through the arch into the alcove where Roman and the boys watched football on Sundays. In the far corner was the bedroom that had been Milo's, then Donny's, and was now Cobb's. A dim light outlined the crookedly hung door.

Riga shoved her damp nose against Iva's hot hand, a

touch so reassuring that it summoned the tears she had been holding back. They slipped down her cheeks as she walked to the door and pressed her ear against it.

Cajoling.

Resistance.

Remonstrance.

Sobs.

She ripped the door open and stared in at Roman with his jeans around his ankles and the boy sitting on the edge of the bed between his legs.

"Get out, Iva!"

She turned, not obediently but by choice. She didn't want to see.

She turned away because she could not stand to breathe the air in that room, because her headache was gone and her vision had cleared. She stumbled against Riva, and when Roman lurched toward her, the dog growled.

Roman didn't cross Riga's path.

"Listen to me, Iva. You don't understand—"

As she ran upstairs, Cobb was screaming.

45

S he slammed the bedroom door. Before she could turn the lock, he pushed his way in and grabbed her shoulders.

"What's gotten into you?"

Behind him the boys had gathered on the landing, whispering among themselves.

"Look how you've upset the boys."

Not true. They weren't upset. They were enjoying the scene. High drama and just deserts.

"I saw you."

"You saw what? You're distraught."

"*I saw you.*"

He told the boys to go back to their rooms. "Ms. Iva and me're having a little tiff, that's all."

All these years, all the boys must have known or guessed what went on in the downstairs bedroom. They probably talked about it after the lights were out and made fun of her for being blind or plain stupid.

Roman shut the door behind him. "Now. It's time for you to stop this nonsense."

"You had your pants around your knees and he was…"
She didn't know how to describe what she'd seen without
using words that made her cringe with shame and embarrass-
ment.

"Golly sakes, Iva. What're you talking about? 'He was'
what?"

He knew he could ask her that, straight-out, and she
would not be able to say the words. What kind of woman was
she that she had let a monster know her so well? That she
would love him?

"He was crying. I stood at the door and I heard him."

"Well, certainly he was crying. He's been crying for weeks.
The boy doesn't want to be here, Iva. You know that as well
as me. I've about had it with his whining."

"Don't change the subject."

Her tone startled him. He ran his hands up through his
thick hair. She'd seen the same gesture a thousand times in
response to some aggravation or another. The doglegged vein
throbbing from his hairline to his eyebrow.

"I saw what I saw."

Anger rippled through her voice. He seemed to plant
himself before her.

"Enough, Iva, enough. Who's going to believe you when
you can't even say what you saw? I'm a respected man in
this community. You can't accuse me and expect to get away
with it."

"I saw your backside. Bare." Surprised by the words, her
cheeks burned. "And Cobb was between…His face…on
your front side."

310

"Oh, my God in heaven, Jesus Christ, I can't believe what I'm hearing. What are you *on*, woman?" He dropped onto the bed, covering his face with his large, square hands. "I can't believe you'd even think such a thing was possible. What am I to you? A monster? After all the years we've had, all the good we've done together, is that what you think I am?"

He knew how much she needed to believe that her life had not been wasted.

"I don't know what's happened to you, Iva. I think it's this Donny thing." Again he raked his fingers through his hair. "It's got you thinking—I'm not saying you're crazy, I'm not saying that at all—but you're not thinking clearly. You need some time away, honey. A few weeks in Merryville with Omar and his family. Some time...I know you don't mean to hurt me, but that's what you've done."

Seeing him weep, a spore of doubt took hold in a corner of Iva's mind. In a world where sexual behavior was as varied and unrestrained as the plants in her garden, she had remained an innocent. Was it possible that she was mistaken in what she'd seen? She closed her eyes and knew she was not. She had heard her husband's moan of pleasure; she had seen the boy's knees, scuffed and dimpled.

"How long have you been doing this?"

"Never. I swear to God, Iva. Never."

A liar, a cheat, a predator, a pedophile. She was innocent, but she knew the word.

"Donny?"

His eyes met hers, open and candid. "On my soul, never."

Yes.

"Milo had that little room. Did you make him do it too?"

"Make him? Do you think I force them? They love me, Iva. They are grateful."

"You have to leave." She knew she should call the police. The phone was across the room, but her feet wouldn't move in that direction. It would mean that all the years were nothing, lies upon lies. The words for a phone call might come in an hour or a day, it might be possible, but not now or yet.

She could not be in the same room with him or look at his face. She went into the bathroom and locked the door. She ran the water in the tub and sink and sat on the toilet cover with her hands over her ears so she didn't have to hear him plead for understanding. The house shook when he slammed the back door. She turned off the water and raised the blind on the bathroom window, saw him walk to the truck. Sweet Laz was there, loyal and eager. When Roman opened the door, the dog leapt up on the seat. Roman gestured for him to get out but he wouldn't budge. He loved a ride more than anything. Roman yelled, and reaching into the cab, he jerked the dog out by his collar and threw him onto his back. She heard his ki-yis. Roman hoisted himself into the truck and the headlights came on, spotlighting Laz, standing in watch position. The engine roared and the dog sat and watched without moving as Roman swung the truck around the yard and drove away.

46

Shortly after six the next morning, Sophie left home dressed in sweatpants and a baggy sweater, a thermos of black coffee tucked between the front seats of the 4Runner, an overnight bag behind the driver's seat, and a change of clothes hanging on the hook. Revved and ready to go, she drove north to Paso Robles through wine country and then into the hills, picking up Interstate 5 near Buttonwillow. Up the long valley she kept the 4Runner on cruise control. Seventy-five. Slow for that stretch of highway.

A little before noon she pulled into the Holiday Inn Express she'd called the night before to make sure she'd have a clean room to shower and change in before her meeting with the governor. After doing battle with her independent-minded hair and dressing professionally as befit the occasion, she crossed a bridge over the American River and followed the directions to the Reed-Patterson Clinic, a small private hospital.

After the shooting, Maggie Duarte had been carried by helicopter from SanSeb General to Cedars-Sinai in LA.

313

After a week there, she was flown to Sacramento and from the airport taken by ambulance to Reed-Patterson, just north of the city.

Sophie was met at the entrance by two members of the governor's CHP security team. They were polite but decidedly cool toward her. She wondered if they knew she was Donny's lawyer. She felt that everyone must. It was an identity she could not escape. The male of the team asked to examine her briefcase and purse; the female escorted her into an untidy office crowded with computers and video screens and wand checked her. Afterward she accompanied Sophie in the elevator to the top floor of the clinic and handed her over to another security officer, who walked her down a hall whose walls were hung with expensive-looking fine art.

Robert Cervantes, Maggie's husband, was waiting for her at the last door, and when he didn't offer her his hand, it was obvious that he wasn't glad to see her.

"If you upset her, you're out. Is that clear?"

"Yes, of course." She felt her hands grow damp. "I wouldn't do anything...It's an honor..."

"And don't waste her time."

He opened the door and walked ahead of her into a large corner room full of light. The storm had passed, and through the floor-to-ceiling windows the air was so transparently clear that Sophie glimpsed the far-off graph line of the Sierra Nevada.

The big room served multiple purposes. It was a living room, with chairs, couches, a coffee table, and an immense television, also an office consisting of file cabinets and a long table covered with phones, computers, a printer, and piles of paper. A partially opened door revealed a small kitchen. Other doors, closed, probably connected to bedrooms and perhaps more offices. Though she couldn't hear voices or phones, Sophie sensed that there were other people on the fifth floor, that the business of the state was being carried on in this unorthodox environment.

Maggie Duarte sat in a wheelchair near a window. A woman in blue scrubs stood beside her, speaking quietly as she removed a blood pressure cuff from her arm. The wheelchair had been designed to the proportions of a linebacker. In it Maggie looked even smaller than she was.

Her still strong and assertive voice came as a surprise.

"Come in, come in. Robert, bring a chair for Sophie and stop looking so snarly, for godsake. Sophie, you've already met my grim husband; normally he's a very cheerful man."

Sophie found that difficult to believe. Dark olive-colored circles cupped Cervantes's eyes, giving him the appearance of a man who had neither slept nor smiled in some time.

"Things haven't been normal for a while now, Mags."

"And this is my nurse, Karen. As you can see, she's taking my blood pressure. She and Robert think you're going to up-set me. Are you?" Maggie's smile was still wide and toothy, but up close the stress showed in the taut line of her neck. She held out her hand. Encircled by plastic identification bands of various colors, her wrist was fragile, and her hand shook slightly.

"Before you talk about your client, sit down and tell me,

how are your mother and father? And your dear grandmother? What a dynamo. She's still alive, I hope."

"Yes, ma'am, she is. Mémé sends you her love. She hopes
you'll make time for a visit next time you're in SanSeb."

If you ever come back.

"She was so kind to me as a child. Always feeding me good
things, and when I studied French in high school I would sit
in your kitchen and converse with her sometimes."

"I think I remember that," Sophie said.

"You were very small, running in and out and making a lot
of noise, as I recall. Your mother was all business and a little
intimidating, to tell you the truth, but your grandmother, she
was special."

Maggie looked over Sophie's shoulder at her husband.
"Will you stop hovering, Robert? I'm perfectly fine." To Sophie: "And I am. When you get back to SanSeb, I want you
to make sure people know that I can't feel a damn thing in
my legs yet—*yet!*—but the rest of me is as tough as ever."

"That's good to know. There are so many rumors."

"I know, but then 'Governor Getting Better' doesn't sell
papers."

"Will you be able to—"

"Work again? Absolutely. I am already. The lieutenant
governor is on a very short leash, believe me. He's a lovely
man, but I'm too smart to trust him. Eventually I'll be back
in the office. It won't be long."

"I'm so glad. We all are."

"What about your client? I suppose he'll be disappointed
when he realizes how completely he failed?" Maggie lifted her

chin a little in challenge. "Does he have pals who'll try to finish the job?"

"Donny isn't political." It was one of the sentences she
had practiced in the car, driving up Interstate 5.

"That's what my security people tell me. Apparently he's
very bland and uninteresting."

"He's a tragic case, Governor. That's why I'm here."

"I guessed as much."

"May I tell you his history?"

"How long is this going to take?" Sophie had forgotten
that Maggie's husband was still in the room.

"Get yourself some coffee, Robert. Let me talk to Sophie
alone."

"Five minutes."

"Ridiculous. Fifteen."

"Maggie—"

"I'm fine, Robert. Please." She watched him out the door
and then closed her eyes.

Gathering her strength? Fed up with her hovering husband? Just focusing her attention? Sophie couldn't tell what
Maggie felt, but she knew Cervantes would enforce the time.
She had only fifteen minutes and she wasn't going to waste
them exercising her powers of intuition. She began Donny's
story by telling how Elena had driven his father away with
lies and threats when he was a toddler.

"I know all about that woman!" Maggie said. "We've got
a whole file on Elena Crider. Since I served in the House.
She sends me cards and notes and long letters all about her
life. Her little sweeties. The church. She writes about her

son. Never mentions him by name. She always tells me how handsome he is, though. My office ran a security check on her. Ardent fans can be the most dangerous. But no one ever worried about the good-looking kid."

"She thinks you're astral sisters."

"Oh, yes, astrology. Pages of that. I hear from a lot of nuts, Sophie. If I reacted to every one—"

"Elena might be harmless to you, but she was toxic to Donny's father. Donny, too, except he couldn't divorce her."

"Are you suggesting that instead of shooting his mother, he shot me? How bizarre." Pressing her fingers against her eyelids, Maggie rocked her head from side to side. "I've studied psychology, Sophie. I know what you're going to tell me. It's sad; of course it is. But I'm sure that every murderer, attempted or successful, has some kind of crazy mother or father and a pathetic story to go with them. It doesn't make any difference."

"Please, Governor, just hear the rest."

Though the intense concentration obviously tired her, Maggie listened carefully, learning about Roman's Gardens and Boys into Men, Donny's ambition and his talent. Sometimes she requested a clarification or elaboration. When Sophie talked about Roman's relationship with his boys, the governor grew very still.

"How do you know this is true? The boy, Milo, he might be lying."

"Iva Devane, Roman's wife, called me last night."

Iva had been crying and was hard to understand.

"She saw her husband with one of the boys. She corroborates Milo's story."

"Is he in custody?

"Not as yet."

Maggie crossed herself. "Those poor boys; those poor children. Oh, my God. Tell me, what do you want me to do, Sophie? All of this, it's dreadful. No, it's worse than dreadful. As you know, I don't believe in the death penalty, but I'd like to hang that man by his balls in a public square anyway. Leave him there for people to throw things at." After a pause she added, "If you quote me, I'll deny I said that."

"Under the circumstances, knowing this, would you come down to SanSeb and testify for him at sentencing?"

"What?"

Sophie hadn't meant to put her request so baldly, but there it was.

"You're going through with a trial?"

"I don't want to, ma'am, but the prosecutor has left me no alternative. Donny's charged with attempted murder with premeditation, and the prosecutor won't negotiate. The thing is, Donny never planned to shoot you."

"My goodness, what a relief that is!"

"He didn't intend to shoot anyone, and I think I can prove that."

Or at least create reasonable doubt.

"He's guilty, Sophie. I may be a liberal, but I believe in punishing criminals."

"I know he's guilty of something, just not attempted murder. And I know he has to do time. But when he went to the park that day—"

"Are you going to tell me he was crazy?"

"No, he's sane." Sophie paused, expecting to be interrupted. "Governor, I believe with all my heart that this boy deserves a chance to make a new life when he's done his time. But if he does thirty years—" The image of Donny came into her mind, beautiful, silent Donny. "It's too long, too long. He'll be ruined. His life will be over."

"That man Devane taught him how to shoot a gun? And then he left the gun around where the boy could find it and take it? Do you think he knew what the boy would do with it?"

"I don't."

Maggie leaned her head back and closed her eyes. "I wonder sometimes, will anything ever be simple again. You've worn me out, Sophie. The boy is sane; he steals a gun and shoots me. This is all we know, and then you bring me the story of sexual abuse and a cruelly unstable mother, a father driven away and afraid to come back—" She thought for a moment. "Perhaps, in a world of infinite wisdom and endless resources there might be a better way to punish him, but this is California and the world is not wise."

"Ma'am, I'm sorry, I—"

"Sophie, the people want revenge. My dear husband wants revenge."

"And you? Do you want it too?"

"Sometimes. I try not to go with the feeling but," she sighed, lifting and dropping her arms, "I'm not a saint."

"Have you read about restorative justice?" Of course she had, but Sophie had to keep talking if she hoped to engage the governor's interest. She spoke rapidly, conscious of the ticking clock. "The idea is that when a crime is committed the fabric of society is damaged, not simply a person or people. Like at Columbine. Kids and adults died or were injured and that was terrible, but the town itself was damaged too. And it still hasn't recovered. Punishment might satisfy the individual desire for revenge, but it doesn't do anything to heal a town."

"Now you're talking about the town?"

"SanSeb is always going to be known as the place where someone tried to kill the governor. But if you were to testify on his behalf at sentencing—"

"You want me to forgive him?"

Did she? All at once, Sophie wasn't sure of what she wanted. She felt awkward and ridiculous holding out her unreasonable request and expecting the governor to take it from her when it seemed now like a ludicrous gift from a white elephant sale, a picture of a rock star painted on velvet that she had convinced herself the governor would want.

"Forgive me, Governor. I've wasted your time."

"No, Sophie, you haven't. You've given me something important to think about. To ponder."

"The park's awful now. No one wants to go there. There's litter—"

"Enough. Here. Take my hand."

Sophie was close to tears but wouldn't cry. She would will herself into a dead faint before she'd let that happen.

"Robert and I have already talked about doing something for the city. We both believe in restorative justice and you're not the first person to contact me about this. We've had many letters from citizens asking us to do something, for some joint effort between myself, my family, and the city that would symbolize a new beginning. I appreciate your suggestion that we might begin by looking at Mission Park."

All Sophie could think about was getting out of the room and into her car.

"I also believe in the power of forgiveness, but as far as Donny is concerned, I'm not there yet. You and the prosecutor must arrive at some agreement. Donny must pay the price for what he did. Life is long and people change, but at the moment there is nothing you could say that would make me testify on his behalf."

47

Several days after her return from Sacramento, Alexander Itkin arrived in SanSeb—by limo from LAX—having concluded his expert testimony in Chicago. He spent three days interviewing Donny and administering several psychological tests. There was nothing left of Sophie's twenty-five-thousand-dollar retainer, and she sent Hamp to Salinas again. Afterward, she didn't ask him how he'd convinced Brad Crider to contribute another fifteen thousand to Donny's defense fund.

What Sophie had been told about the psychiatrist seemed to be true. He thought the world of himself and charged the moon and stars for his expertise; but he was diligent, and beneath his egotism, there seemed to be a genuine and caring man.

On the day he was to leave SanSeb, he and Sophie met in her office. He laid a thick binder before her. "My notes, transcripts, everything is in here. If you decide to go to trial and want me to testify, I'll rearrange my schedule. My report's been signed and notarized, so there's no question who wrote it." He paused, and as he looked around her office, Sophie glimpsed a likeable awkwardness.

"I don't see any ashtrays in here."

"All the office buildings are no smoking. You're in California, Alexander." An addicted psychiatrist: she reminded herself that despite this, he was still one of the best in the country.

He laid a packet of Marlboros on the arm of his chair. "I'm not going to tell you that Donny is mentally 'healthy,' but he's not legally insane in the sense that he doesn't know right from wrong. As far as that goes, he's as sane as you and me. He has what is known as borderline personality organization with a fairly typical though idiosyncratic identity diffusion."

"What does that mean exactly?"

"A very weak ego. Low tolerance for anxiety, lack of impulse control, and limited sublimatory channels." Sophie's frustration with the psychobabble must have shown in her expression, because Itkin laughed. "Here is what I would tell a jury were I to testify. We all need an identity, a sense of who we are, separate and different from others. Donny has very little sense of himself. It is perfectly human to have anxiety, anger, jealousy, those difficult or socially unacceptable emotions, but we learn to sublimate them, which means we channel the energy from them into socially acceptable activities. A boy who hates his father becomes a great football player. A neglected girl becomes a supermodel."

"A boy becomes a plantsman."

"Not simply a gardener." Itkin picked up the cigarette pack and put it down again. "In Donny's case, I think his green thumb may have saved his life, and perhaps on the unconscious level, he knew that. When his mother forced him out of the Boys into Men program, she was taking away the activity that kept him sane. I'm convinced that's what triggered his psychotic break."

"You said he's sane."

"Legally, he can differentiate between right and wrong."

"Now he can, but what about in the middle of a psychotic break?"

"First you must prove the break, and this is difficult to do in a case like Donny's."

Sophie said, "The day before he tried to kill himself, I questioned him about the abuse and he seemed to regress into a very childlike state. Using spilled cocoa like fingerpaint. Was he having a psychotic break then?"

"Perhaps. Of a sort." He turned the Marlboro box end to end. "More likely he was trying to escape you and your questions."

Listening to Itkin, Sophie recalled Maggie's question. Would anything ever be simple again?

"Did he actually want to kill Elena?"

"You mean by displacement? Again, it's possible. It's quite normal for an adolescent to have murderous feelings toward a parent. Surely you had some similar thoughts as a teenager?"

Sophie chose to regard his question as rhetorical.

"So what happened at the park? Did Maggie sort of become his mother?"

"Hard to say. But what is absolutely clear is that on that day, at that time, his already weak ego was fighting for its very survival. He would have felt it as survival of his very self, a matter of his own life or death. The need to act exploded out of him, shocking him into a break with reality."

"'Absolutely clear'?"

"To me. Perhaps to you. I wouldn't count on convincing a jury." He walked a few steps and stopped. "I wish I could have interviewed his mother. From Donny I have the picture of a severely narcissistic and sexually inappropriate mother, a woman without boundaries who is almost certainly a borderline personality herself. It would be interesting to know something about her background, but apparently she never shared her life history with Donny, which is rather strange in itself. He doesn't even know where she grew up."

"This is all in your report?"

"Of course."

A.J. Boyd had entered a plea of not guilty at arraignment. Perhaps he had intended to defend Donny on the basis of insanity. Now that this defense was out, would Donny's crippled sense of self, his sublimation, his psychotic break at least be enough to create a sympathetic jury? Sophie would have to convince them that he did not premeditate the shooting. If jurors really understood Donny they might resort to jury nullification—let their sense of social justice override the strict law of the courtroom.

"And what about Roman?" she asked. "How did he figure in?"

"Ah, the love object." He smiled.

"The man was abusing him. I don't take that lightly."

"Nor do I, Sophie." He knocked a cigarette out of the

pack and began to move it over and under the fingers of his right hand as he spoke, seemingly unaware of what he was doing. "It is a demonstration of how confused the boy is that he did not know the difference between Roman Devane's perverse attentions and a healthy, loving relationship. He idealized the pair of them, Devane and Iva, into the perfect family."

No matter how the judge instructed them, might the tragedy of Donny's life persuade them to find him not guilty? Did she have the courage to go to trial armed with such flimsy weapons: a damaged child, dreams denied?

For a moment sadness overwhelmed Sophie and it was difficult to speak. "Will he ever be willing to talk about it?"

"It's not a matter of willingness, Sophie. He isn't *able*. With therapy and time, maybe that'll change. But realistically? He'll go to prison and there will be no therapy, so I wouldn't bet on it. His denial is very deep. He unconsciously fears that if he were to acknowledge the abuse it would completely shatter what little ego structure he has." He stood up. Indicating the unlit cigarette between his fingers. "It is proof of the persistence of neurosis that I am unable to go more than an hour without one of these. Can we move our conversation out of doors?"

Sophie followed him into the hall. "And the gardening? How does that fit in?"

"Sublimation, as I said." He stopped at the top of the stairs. "You know, the longer I talked with Donny, the more I realized what an astonishing thing he did when he applied for Boys into Men. I had never considered gardening as being a talent in the same category as, say, dance or painting. His case is unique in my experience. The boy has a genuine talent, and an accompanying drive as compelling in its way as a dancer's need to dance, a painter's need to paint. His need to express himself provided the courage he required to make a break for freedom. One can't help but wonder what positive things might have happened if Roman Devane had not been a sexual deviant."

"Is all that in your report too?"

"Yes," the doctor said.

"It's so sad."

"No," Itkin said, starting downstairs, "it's life."

"And life is sad sometimes."

"I'm a scientist, Sophie. I don't see it that way. If I did, I wouldn't be able to do the work at all."

In the days that followed, Sophie often recalled her conversation with Dr. Itkin—not only as it applied to Donny Crider but often in connection to her own mother. During the run-up to the preliminary hearing and in the day-to-day business of her practice, Sophie and Anna were often together, and she caught herself reacting to her mother: begrudging her good ideas, resenting her advice, feeling trapped by her stalwart, positive presence. She wondered if Dr. Itkin would say that she was still trying to individuate from her mother. Sophie Giraudo, thirty-five years old, and caught in a maze she'd entered when she was still in diapers.

The date of Donny's preliminary hearing drew closer and tension in the office mounted; tempers sparked over mishaps as trivial as a misplaced phone number. Sophie caught herself about to flare up at Anna and managed to resist the impulse with the reminder that taking charge and showing love were the same thing for her mother.

In the middle of a disagreement, Sophie thought, *What old stuff this is*. Old and pointless and she was sick of it. She learned to apologize for her bursts of temper and unkind words, and her mother was always quick to forgive. Sophie found this very irritating.

48

On the day of the preliminary hearing in the case of *The State of California versus Donald Crider*, the parking lot and street in front of the courthouse were crowded with visitors and media. The line was long behind the scanning machines that checked briefcases, purses, and backpacks. Outside the second-floor courtroom, security guards searched those who wanted to observe the hearing. Some were court personnel and lawyers; many were reporters. The merely curious were present as well. There was a rumor that the governor would put in an appearance.

Sophie had arranged for Donny to be well dressed and groomed for his appearance. All that remained of his head-banging suicide attempt was a yellow bruise. When he was escorted into the courtroom, he was freshly shaved, his hair, though uncut, was clean and shining, and he wore a dark green crew-neck sweater and a new pair of chinos—a little large but Sophie had been guessing at his size when she sent Anna to buy them.

"When you walk into the courtroom, keep your back

straight and your head high," she told him the night before when she delivered the clothes. "And when you first walk through the door look right at me. Don't take your eyes off me. You might hear someone say something from the gallery, maybe your name, but don't turn your head. Eyes on me, Donny. Remember that."

The defense and prosecution tables were so close that Sophie could reach out from where she sat and almost touch the files laid out before Ben. She noted that despite the routine nature of the hearing he was wearing his second-best suit.

"Good morning, Counselor," she said. "You're looking snazzy."

He didn't even smile. "This is it, Sophie. Last chance to accept my deal."

"Attempted premeditated murder is no deal, Ben. We'd rather take our chances in court."

"You're going to regret it." He was disgustingly cocksure.

Two days earlier they had met in his office, a meeting initiated by Sophie in the hope that he could be persuaded to allow Donny to plead to a lesser charge. But Ben still wanted a big headline-grabbing sentence, a chance to grandstand and wave the flag and talk about the decline and fall of the Western world. He was unfailingly eloquent and persuasive when convinced of his own righteousness. She knew the way his mind worked. In Ben's thinking, Donny had already been sentenced and packed away to prison, and he, the triumphant prosecutor, had accepted a judicial appointment. When he finished shaving that morning, he probably looked in the bathroom mirror and said, *Good morning, Judge Lansing.*

He was staring at her now. "Why are you smiling?"

"Am I?"

He couldn't stand it when she seemed to know something he didn't. "This is the prelim, Sophie. No games. That kid beside you"—he lowered his voice and added a sneer—"Mr. College Prep, is going away."

Before Sophie could think of a comeback, Judge Hugh Arthur entered the hearing room by a side door, patting down his bushy gray hair—what court personnel called his "Scottish do." At the hem of his robe, Sophie saw the steel toes of his motorcycle boots. He spoke briefly, sociably, with one of the uniformed court officers and the court stenographer, then went behind the bench, where he stood for a moment, looking first at the crowded room and then back and forth between Sophie and Ben.

"Well, well. Together again, eh?" He didn't look happy about the day's work ahead. "Let's get this thing started. Mr. Lansing, is the prosecution ready?"

"We are, Your Honor."

"Defense?"

"We're ready, too, Judge."

"This is your moment, then, Mr. Lansing. Proceed."

Ben had organized his material well, knowing that Judge Arthur was a stickler for the efficient use of time. His first witnesses described the scene on the day of the shooting. Carmine, who looked at Sophie apologetically from the witness chair, had been the first person to run onto the platform after the shots were fired. Next a security guard, who'd been standing near the platform, identified Donny as the one who'd fired the shots. A third witness had seen Donny racing away from the scene, still holding the weapon. A police officer had tackled and cuffed Donny in the parking lot. It was to him Donny had said "I'm sorry"—not once but twice. A forensics expert showed that the two bullets recovered from the crime scene and the one taken from Maggie Duarte's back had been shot from the gun found beside the creek with Donny's fingerprints on it, and a detective testified to his confession in the police station. From time to time His Honor asked a question of a witness or Ben; sometimes he swiveled his chair and stared at the far wall; occasionally he took a note.

Sophie had made the tactical decision not to cross-examine these witnesses. Later she would study their uninterrupted testimony for weak links and inconsistencies that could help her when she questioned them during the trial. It was a long morning. After the lunch recess, Ben continued with his presentation and did not conclude until almost three p.m.

The judge looked at Sophie. "Ms. Giraudo, the government has eyewitnesses, forensics, and your client's statement that he was sorry and later his admission that he committed the crime. But you still want to go to trial?"

Not really.

"Yes, Your Honor."

He turned to Donny. "Mr. Crider, do you want a trial in this matter as well?"

Sophie had prepared Donny for this question. He nodded.

"Speak up for the record."

"Yes."

Arthur sighed. "Ms. Giraudo, your client has a right to a trial if he wants one, but—just for my own edification—can you tell me why you want to spend the court's time and the taxpayers' money this way?"

"With respect, Your Honor, I am prepared to present a vigorous defense of Mr. Crider."

"I'm sure you are," he said dryly. "And afterward the jury will find your client guilty. With all the evidence Mr. Lansing has, the jury will likely find him *very* guilty."

"Again, with respect, Your Honor, I'd never presume to predict what twelve fellow citizens will do." Someone in the gallery laughed. "As we know, they can be remarkably independent minded."

Judge Arthur sat back in his swivel chair and folded his arms across his chest, looking bad tempered. "What's going on here?"

Ben said, "May I approach, Your Honor?"

"I wish you would. Both of you." The judge put his hand over his microphone. "You know I don't like games and I don't like showboating. Why are we having a trial on this matter? Can't you two work something out?"

Ben looked offended. "Judge, this is a most serious crime, and I don't see any reason why the government should be forced to negotiate a plea when the question of guilt is so clear."

"What do you say to that, Ms. Giraudo?"

"The same thing as I did a minute ago, Judge. I will present a vigorous defense of Mr. Crider."

"Are you telling me you have evidence that he did not shoot the governor?"

Behind Sophie, the onlookers in the hearing room were growing impatient and began to whisper. "I'd prefer not to say at this time, Your Honor."

"I'll see you both in chambers!" Hugh Arthur said and hammered his gavel.

Hugh Arthur had been a judge in San Sebastian County for almost twenty years, and seniority had earned him the best office in the courthouse, a third-floor corner room with a view of the park.

"Sit," he said curtly as he removed his robe and hung it on a modern chrome coatrack. He spoke to the stenographer who had followed them into the office. "We're off the record here, Betts, but stick around in case we need to go back on."

The door clicked shut behind her.

"Now, listen up, you two." In the privacy of his own chambers, Arthur didn't bother minimizing his impatience. "You've tried cases before me plenty of times and you know I'm not a big cheerleader for plea bargains. But another thing I'm not cheering for is wasting the court's time. Especially in a high-profile case that's going to focus a national spotlight on this town."

He held up his hand, making sure he wasn't interrupted. "I know juries are unpredictable, Ms. Giraudo, and I know how you can dazzle them with doubt. You're going to be vigorous and all that, but in the end I also know that Donald

Crider is going to be found guilty. There will be no jury nullification in my courtroom."

"I'm not denying that my client shot at the governor, Judge Arthur."

"Shot her in the back as she turned to protect her child," Ben said. "Don't forget that part."

"But I have evidence that will show it was unlikely he premeditated to kill anyone that day."

"'Unlikely' isn't good enough," Ben said.

"Last time I looked, it amounted to reasonable doubt," Sophie said. "At the time of the shooting my client was under extreme emotional stress, Judge Arthur."

"I'm under extreme emotional stress right now, but I don't plan on shooting you, Ms. Giraudo."

"I'm relieved to hear that, Judge. I have evidence that prior to the shooting, Donny Crider had been the victim of sexual abuse for at least a year by a known pedophile."

"Why wasn't I told about this?"

"The defense isn't required to lay its case before you, Ben. And if you'd been at all amenable to negotiate, I *would* have told you."

"Will your client testify to the abuse?"

"He's not able to as of now. But even if he's not ready at trial time, I have testimony from other highly credible witnesses."

"That would be inadmissible, Judge."

Arthur looked at Ben. "I know it grieves you, young man, but so far as I know, I'm the only judge in this room. I'll determine what's admissible and what isn't."

Ben's face turned scarlet.

The judge looked at Sophie. "Tell me about your witnesses."

"One is Iva Devane, the pedophile's wife."

"Has this man been charged? Is he in our jail?"

"Not yet, Your Honor."

"Why not?"

"He's apparently gone into hiding. Both he and his brother—"

"Jesus, God, I don't want to hear about it!" Arthur lurched out of his polished oaken chair, strode across his office, and yanked open a cupboard door revealing a bar-sized refrigerator. He took out a small bottle of water and drank, crumpling the plastic in one hand when he was finished. "Why won't the kid testify? There's a lot at stake; does he understand that?"

"He's still in psychological denial about the abuse."

"*Alleged* abuse," Ben added.

"According to the psychiatrist who examined him, he may never be able to acknowledge what was done to him."

"Well, isn't that convenient." Ben's temper was gaining the upper hand, which was good from Sophie's point of view. Logic and clarity went out the window when he was mad.

"Are you going to tell us he's crazy, Sophe?"

"No, he's not legally insane, Ben. I'm not saying he is. But he's had a wretched life that's left him unable to deal with reality. He doesn't know why he fired the gun. He had no mens rea. No intent to kill. Certainly no premeditation."

"No jury's gonna fall for that kind of shit. You can't just pull a rabbit out of a hat—"

"I think you're wasting my time here," the judge said, but he didn't stand up and Sophie took that as an encouraging sign.

She reached into her briefcase and withdrew an inch-thick file.

"Donny's defense is all here, Your Honor. And it's compelling." She laid a smaller folder on his desk. "You'll forgive me, Judge Arthur, but I anticipated what your reaction might be today. I had my paralegal prepare a memo."

"A memo."

As protocol required, she handed a copy to Ben. "All the facts are here."

Doctor Alexander Itkin's report, statements from two neurophysiologists considered experts on adolescent brain development, Iva and Milo's unhappy tales, and statements from Jenna and the neighbor who had recommended Donny for Boys into Men. Sophie nurtured a seed of hope that by the day of the trial Maggie would have a change of heart and make an appearance, but there was nothing of this in the memo.

The judge looked down at the folder. If he'd begun to tug on his wild hair, his frustration would not have been much more obvious.

"This is preposterous, Your Honor!" Ben said. "Our justice system doesn't do trial by memo. Ms. Giraudo knows that as well as anyone."

"Stop bickering. You're not married anymore." Beneath

his tufty brows Hugh Arthur's eyes were like granite. "I'm going to say it one more time. Although this defendant has the right, I don't want this case to go to a jury. Is that simple enough? Could I be more direct? I do not want the vultures of the media descending on my courtroom. And if it's true that this boy's been abused by a pedophile, I absolutely will not help the tabloids get rich off his misery. Ben, from what Sophie says, I think she's got plenty to negotiate with." He thumbed through the report. "I'm sick of seeing this town's dirty laundry on the front page of the *LA Times* when I turn on my computer, and now there's this sex thing, and your client, Ms. Giraudo, is at the heart of it."

"Your Honor, what happened to Donny wasn't his fault."

"Did I say it was his fault?"

"No, sir."

"I just want you to know I'm sick of it."

"I understand."

"I hope you do." He opened another bottle of water. "Now, what would it take to make a bargain between you two?"

Sophie said, "Attempted murder without premeditation."

"Your Honor, Sophie wants you to let him out tomorrow, give him the key to the city. Poor traumatized kid. Well, I don't think so! I've been generous here. I could throw him to the feds under the Patriot Act if I wanted to."

"I think you're way too smart to try that, Mr. Lansing. Attempted murder, no premed seems fair. Add on time for grave bodily injury. Say fifteen years total. It's a violent crime so he'll serve at least eighty-five percent of the time.

Don't look so upset, Ben. Surely that's enough blood for you."

Sophie knew it wasn't the sentence that mattered to Ben at this moment. He had just realized he was going to miss out on the showcase trial of his career.

"Ben," she said, "this boy is not a criminal. Or a terrorist or a racist, and there was no political agenda. He's a boy who—"

"Save your argument, Ms. Giraudo." The judge picked up Sophie's draft brief. "I'm going to read this over carefully. Meantime, I want the pair of you to lock yourselves in a room somewhere and don't come out until you've reached an agreement."

He waved them out of the office.

49

Halfway through the plea negotiations that followed, Sophie realized that Ben might never forgive her for pulling the plug on his spotlight. By midweek he had agreed to reduce the charges against Donny to attempted murder, no premeditation, personal use of a firearm, and inflicting great bodily injury. In exchange, Donny would plead guilty. On Friday morning Judge Arthur sentenced him to fifteen years in prison. Afterward, Ben left the courtroom without speaking to Sophie. She had never seen him so angry. Maybe this case had struck the final blow to their relationship. There would be no more midnight visits or worried phone calls.

One day about six weeks later, Sophie was working a case that took her up to San Jose, and having a little time to spare as she approached Salinas, she decided to drop in on Brad Crider.

He was so like Donny that she would have recognized him as his father had they passed on a crowded street in a foreign city.

"I'm glad you came," he said, shutting his office door. "I've been meaning to write and tell you how much I appreciate what you did for the boy."

She noted that he didn't call Donny his son.

"The judge wrote to the prison office asking that he do his time in a minimum-security facility," Sophie said. "Somewhere there's a garden he can work in. He's no threat to anyone."

"My wife says I should write to him, try to build a relationship."

"I believe it would mean a lot to him."

He loosened his tie and pulled the collar of his bright white shirt away from his neck. "Is it true that Elena wasn't in the courtroom?"

Sophie nodded.

"Where is she?"

"Iowa."

Brad Crider was easy for Sophie to read. She knew he was a weak man, wracked by guilt, with no clear idea of what to do or the courage to face his choices squarely.

"Will you write to him?"

He would not meet her gaze. "I don't want to have anything to do with *her*."

"That would be up to you, but I doubt if she'll be back in SanSeb anytime soon."

"I don't want my girls dragged into this."

"Suit yourself, Brad. You're the one who has to live with the truth. That doesn't change just because you don't want to acknowledge it. But you should know, I told Donny that you paid for his defense."

"What did he say?"

"He's not much of a talker."

"That's how you survive around her. Shut up and wait for it to end."

Brad stared at his hands. Sophie knew that he was recalling the times he'd wanted to silence Elena with his hands around her throat. After so many years, she still aroused powerful emotions in him. At that moment Sophie was more certain than she had ever been that Dr. Itkin's diagnosis was right. Donny had seen Maggie Duarte, his mother's "astral sister," on the stage, and something sprang open inside him, liberating the feelings he'd so long repressed. For as long as it took to raise a gun, aim, and fire it three times, rage had blinded his reason. He saw his mother on that stage and his mind broke.

"Please write him, Brad. You can make a difference in his life."

He said he would try, but she thought he would more likely find excuses not to.

During the summer that followed, there were frequent updates regarding Governor Duarte's health. Called astonishing, called miraculous, her recovery was as remarkable as Anna had predicted. Then there would be reports of a relapse, a viral infection, exhaustion, followed by more astonishment and optimistic predictions.

Sophie didn't have much time to think about anything except her caseload. The publicity around Donny Crider's case had generated even more business than she had expected, and the office was growing. With her usual gusto, Anna tackled lease negotiations with the owner of the building, and in October the law offices of Sophia Giraudo would expand into the adjacent suite. Hamp was contented in his walk-in closet, but Clary required an office and Sophie was interviewing applicants for an associate position. The caseload threatened to overwhelm her.

At least once a day Sophie threatened to fire Anna if she didn't stop nagging and pestering and bugging her to slow down and eat three square meals a day.

When it was announced that Governor Duarte would address the state at six p.m. on the first Monday in September, Labor Day, Anna decided it was a perfect occasion for a family event, a gathering of the aunts and uncles and cousins. It was rare that the governor asked for special airtime, and in the days before the holiday everyone in and out of the media had an opinion about what she would say. Many thought she would announce her resignation, the challenge of recovery having proved too much for her after all. Sophie wondered if she was going to pardon Donny. Though it was unlikely, as unlikely as world peace breaking out, she was wishfully hopeful that it would happen.

50

Labor Day was one of the hottest days of the summer. The temperature dropped only a few degrees from the mid-nineties as the afternoon waned and family and friends began arriving at Joe and Anna's. The men wandered up to the olive grove, where they sat on benches in the shade, drank wine and beer, smoked cigars, and talked about Joe's Northside, baseball, and the price of olive oil. The women moved between the patio and kitchen, helping Mémé put the finishing touches on salads and side dishes, unwrapping their own contributions to the feast, and all of them keeping an eye on the dozen or so children. Teenagers, preschoolers, and an infant, they were all there, all making some kind of noise. Carmine and his same-age cousins stood at the grill, turning the chicken and sausages, talking sports and politics. Sophie had invited Tamlin and her family. Jimmy had to work, but the twins, Julia and Ryan, knew all the young cousins and fit in as easily as Giraudos and Marsays. Only Hamp seemed out of place, restless.

"You didn't have to come," Sophie told him. "You wouldn't have hurt my feelings—"

"I'm glad to be here," he said. "I just never have been much of a group person."

"That must be why I like you." They took their beers across the patio to a set of flagstone steps to the lower patio. Surrounded by oaks, the small space was in deep, cool shade.

"You went up to Santa Cruz last weekend. Did you learn anything new?"

"Yeah. Maybe."

When speaking of his daughter, Hamp always chose his words carefully, as if they were powerful enough to shape reality and he must therefore not make a mistake. Sophie had learned not to press him.

"I went up to the university. I thought I'd talk to the coach again, see if he'd heard any rumors."

Over the two years since Bronwyn had vanished, the coach's attitude toward Hamp and his search had gone from cooperative to impatient. During their last talk he'd told Hamp essentially the same thing his police officer friends already had: it was time for Hamp to start looking forward instead of back.

"The coach wasn't on campus, so I got to talking to a few of the students interning in the athletic office. Turns out one of them was on Bronwyn's floor in the dorm. She flunked out and just got reinstated. That's why I'd never questioned her before."

Sophie heard the restrained optimism in his voice and knew that he was trying hard not to hope too much.

"She told me that Bronwyn had made friends with a guy who didn't go to school. They'd met on the beach."

This might be his first real lead. "Did she know his name?"

"No. She and Bron weren't really friends. The only reason she knew anything about him was that he came to the dorm once, and afterward some of the girls were talking about it."

The laughter of the cousins drifted down the flagstone steps and Sophie knew that Hamp was wondering if, somewhere, Bronwyn was still laughing. "She said he was *way old.*"

To a college freshman, thirty might seem old. "What did she mean? Did you ask her to be more specific?"

"I did."

"And?"

"He had gray hair. The color of charcoal briquettes."

Tamlin called from the top of the steps. "Sorry to interrupt, you two, but the governor's ready to speak."

Robert Cervantes pushed the governor out before the cameras and microphones, carefully positioning her below the state seal of California and making no effort to hide her wheelchair from the cameras. Stepping back, he joined the dozen or so men and women who stood on either side of her. Everyone was smiling.

Anna looked pleased with herself as well. "Didn't I say this was going to be good news?"

Earlier, there'd been an argument about the likely content of the governor's address. Delio believed she was going to resign, the prospect of full-time work being too much in her condition. Another of Joe's brothers disagreed, and when he started to say why, Delio talked right over him. This had infuriated Anna, who had her own opinions. Sophie had tuned them out. Her mother and uncles would argue about any-thing. No wonder Ben had gotten on with them so well.

"Good evening, ladies and gentlemen, and thank you for permitting me to interrupt your holiday." Maggie was in a new chair, one designed for a woman of her diminutive stature. As it always had, her voice rang with the confidence she managed to make both assertive and feminine at the same time.

"I'm not going to keep you for long, but I want to talk about two things today. First, I am officially announcing that at eight a.m. tomorrow morning, I will return to work as your full-time governor."

Everyone in the family room cheered. On the television, Maggie talked over applause from the colleagues around her.

"Immediately following this address, I am releasing all my medical records so those of you who think maybe I'm not up to the job will be reassured. I feel terrific and I'm eager to get back to the hard work. And from now on, every time you see a picture of your governor in her chair, this beautiful, state-of-the-art, motorized and electronic chair, I want you to think of the millions of other physically challenged men, women, and children who live full and meaningful lives and enrich our society in countless ways."

Delio groaned.

"She's a politician," Anna said. "What do you expect?"

"I want to express my deepest gratitude to Lieutenant Governor Macklin for doing a fantastic job while I was recu-perating." She gestured for Macklin to stand beside her. "In this state it's possible to have a Democratic governor and a

Republican lieutenant. Some people say it's a bad arrangement. Unworkable. But the last few months have proved them wrong. Mark Macklin has been an outstanding leader during my recuperation, and I owe him an immense debt of gratitude. We all do."

Maggie led the applause this time.

"And now for the second matter."

Sophie thought she detected a hint of nervousness and looked at her mother standing at the back of the room to see if she, too, had noticed the quaver in the governor's voice. Anna raised her eyebrows and Sophie realized that she also thought there was a chance that Donny would be pardoned.

"Last week—very quietly, with my husband, Robert, no press or any of my aides—I visited Donny Crider in prison. We met in the warden's office. I wanted to look in the eyes of the boy who put me in this chair, to get his measure, you might say. Since the apprehension of Roman Devane, we all know the sordid details of Donny's life, too much, if you ask me. And I've learned other things about him, about his life before he quit school. I was curious to see what kind of boy it was who'd tried to kill me. I didn't have a particular agenda, but I felt compelled to meet him."

She spoke to the camera without notes, as if the viewers were all her trusted friends.

"Donny Crider is more comfortable with plants than people, and he doesn't use words easily. But he looked right at me and said, simple and to the point, 'I'm sorry I shot you. I don't know why I did it.'

"I looked at him and he looked back. It was quite ex-

349

traordinary, really. I guess you'd say it was one of those aha moments, because my reaction was a complete surprise. I believed him, my friends. I'm not going to tell you that I liked him or that I forgave him. I certainly don't admire him. But I believe he's sorry for what he did and, hard as it is for me to swallow his story, I think he spoke honestly when he said he didn't know why he did it. The government psychiatrist who examined him said in her report that he seemed to be completely disconnected from that act. Another psychiatrist said he had a psychotic break. Which I guess would explain why he was disconnected from the act. Honestly, I don't care anymore. For the first few months after the shooting, I let Donny rule my life. I was angry as hell with him and the sociopath who left a gun where he would find it. For a while, I *needed* to be angry. Especially in the beginning when I was in so much pain that I wanted to give up and die. Anger kept me fighting.

"But here's the thing about anger. If you hang on to it for too long, it starts to shrivel your heart. And so I have prayed on this. I have meditated on this. I've come to a place in my life when I'm sick of anger and I'm ready to put all of this behind me and get on with my life. I will not speak of Donny Crider again. I will not answer questions about the shooting. I've put the last five months behind me, and what I care about now is my family, this beautiful state, and every one of you. This is a golden state and I won't let the past tarnish it! Join me." Maggie held out her arms. "Together let us move beyond the events of last April and into a time of prosperity and generosity for all of us."

And that was that. The speech was seven minutes long, only a little more time than it took to sell a car during an NFL timeout.

As always when the Giraudo and Marsay families came together to celebrate, there was more than enough food and every dish was delicious so everyone had to taste each one and plates were piled high. Sophie could not swallow, but to avoid drawing attention to herself, she walked through the buffet line putting a little of this and that on her plate and carried it up to the top of the property, beyond the slope where the olives grew, to the line of oaks that marked the property line. She sat on the ground and stared out to the west at the streaks of violet, pink, and gold coloring the sky. Too many cars and people had combined to give Southern California the most beautiful sunsets in the world.

It was good news that the governor was going back to work. Sophie tried to feel happy for her, for all of them on that account, but her heart went out to Donny, locked up for thirteen years even with time off for exemplary behavior. She had known that yet nurtured a naïve hope of a pardon.

Maggie Duarte was extraordinary in many ways, a gifted and generous leader, but above all else she was a politician always reaching for the gold ring of another term or a higher office, seat, who knew what. She wouldn't forget Donny— the wheelchair guaranteed that—but neither would she let him hold her back.

She stayed on the hill until the sun set and a stiff breeze came up. Chilly, she took her uneaten food back down the hill and surreptitiously dumped her paper plate in the trash.

"It's a sin to waste good food, Sophia." Anna spoke more softly. "Wait a year and then petition for a pardon. Let things get back to normal."

"Great minds, Ma."

"You have to eat something. There's plenty left."

"No, I'm going for a walk." She didn't add that Hamp was going with her.

Sophie had avoided this block of Mariposa Street for more than twenty years. In that length of time, the pepper trees had grown taller and fuller, and in places their roots had pushed up the sidewalk like the veins on the back of Mémé's hands. Back when she had first explored the neighborhood, the houses and yards and lives of the inhabitants had not had time to blend. It was all too raw and new to be comfortable. Now a slight scruffiness made the street more settled and appealing. There were skates and trikes and bikes in the driveways, fairy lights in the trees, and the late summer lawns had gone from gold to brown, waiting for the fall rains.

She couldn't imagine her rapist in this homey neighborhood, but that was definitely his house across the street. The red Miata had been parked on that oil-stained driveway.

She stood in the fragrant shadows of a pepper tree where she had stood before, spying on what seemed like a perfect family.

"That's it. Across the street."

The street was lined with cars. Rock music played some-where and the smell of grilling meat was in the air.

"I think they're having a party," Hamp said. "Wanna crash?"

"City Councilman Jon Oldroyd lives there now." She had done a little research. "I went to school with his wife, Eve-lyn. They have four daughters. They bought the house eleven years ago from a real estate investor."

"And he bought it from...?"

"I dunno."

"Want me to find the guy?"

"I'm still figuring it out." She stepped back, deeper into the shadows. "All I know for sure is that I can't go on this way. I'm not a victim, Hamp. I know that with my brain. But in here"—she pressed her hand over her heart—"I still feel like one. I've felt like one since that night. And not just be-cause of the physical thing. That's bad enough, but instead of telling Ma and risking...whatever, I've carried his threats with me for more than twenty years. *More than half my life.*" In the breeze, the dry peppercorns rustled against each other and a few dropped to her shoulders with a touch as light as rain. She thought about the keys in her desk drawer. She imagined standing on the deck of the condo, drawing back her arm, and pitching them far out and into the dense scrub along Peligro Creek. The time was coming when she would be able to do that.

"I'm afraid there's only one way to put it behind me."

"Just say the word."

"Let's start with his name."

"What'll you do then?"

She shook her head. "I don't know. When I think about it I feel like throwing up."

"But you'll figure it out."

"Really? You believe that?"

He laughed. "I have no doubt about it, Sophie Giraudo. No doubt at all."

Author's Note

Dear Reader,

A while back, a friend asked me why I always choose to write about dark characters and events. She prefers stories where the characters go out of their way to understand each other, stay their hands before they slap, and apologize in time to save the marriage or the friendship. She would like me to write about good mothers and loving children who never stray too far from the well-worn path. But what stirs my imagination is the darkness in us all. What excites my imagination is exploring the lives of people for whom life is hard, the people who are easily despised.

Donny Crider is such a person.

He tried to kill a woman, and not just any woman, but the governor of the state. And half the town saw him. On the face of it, he's a despicable person and deserves to be punished. He's obviously guilty.

As the real-life attorney in many high-profile capital cases—Susan Smith, Jared Loughner, the Unibomber—Judy Clarke knows all about guilt and innocence. Sophie is a completely fictional character, but like Judy, she's a good listener and tries to reach beneath the superficial to understand her clients. In an interview for the *Huffington Post*, Judy Clarke said that most of the defendants have a history of "serious, severe trauma, unbelievable trauma. Many suffer from severe cognitive development issues that affect the core of their being."

Sophie knows that the traumas and issues of Donny's life don't make him any less guilty. But between the two extremes of letting him go free and sending him to prison for most of the rest of his life, she believes there has to be a middle ground that takes the facts of his life into consideration.

Judy Clarke is one of the bravest women I know. I wanted to show some of that courage in Sophie when she pleads for Donny before the governor and later when she stands up to Ben in the judge's chambers. Sophie isn't brave about facing her own problems, but when it comes to Donny, she's willing to fight.

I'm too much of a realist for fairy-tale endings; however, I feel cautiously optimistic for Donny Crider. I don't think the prison system will destroy him. He will pay for his crime as he should, but in the end he will walk into the world a free man, still young enough to follow his dream of becoming a plantsman. Or perhaps he'll buy a truck and start his own business, becoming the kind of gardener a homeowner can depend upon. Not quite a happy ending, but definitely a hopeful one.

Acknowledgments

With every book, the number of friends, colleagues, and advisors I should thank gets longer. It's begun to read like my e-mail's contact list and seems just as impersonal.

I can't name all the men and women at Grand Central who made this book possible from the first rough manuscript to the final beautiful book. Secretaries, administrative assistants, the receptionist at the front desk, the accountants, and editors and designers, all have played a role and I thank each of you for treating IN DOUBT with the care and respect it deserves. I thank Sara Weiss for her wisdom and thoughtful reading of the manuscript, Beth de Guzman for her ability to see books as both individual creations and as part of the larger marketplace. Thank you also to Marissa Sangiacomo, Brian McClendon, Bob Castillo, and Liz Connor.

Closer to home: As always the ladies of the Arrowhead Association helped me stick to my labors and held me up when I was falling down. Thank you, Judy Reeves, Carole Fegley, Peggy Lang, Susan Harmon, Susan Challen, and Betty Chase.

I particularly appreciate the help given me by Nancy Rosenfeld, who in her work as a defense attorney is smart, strong, and determined to protect the rights of her clients,

357

ACKNOWLEDGMENTS

many of them young and stripped of hope like Donny Crider. Nancy told me the law and she whipped up my imagination when it faltered. Any legal or procedural mistakes are mine.

Every day I am grateful for my family. Art, you rascal. Rocky and Matt, my bright stars. Mom and Margaret and Nikki. And the grands who, bless 'em, still want to spend time with Nana.

Reading Group Guide

In Doubt
Questions for Discussion

1. Elena says that she loves Donny. How do you think she would describe this love? Do you believe that Elena loves Donny?

2. Roman Devane claims to love Donny as well. Is it possible to love someone and still be a destructive force in that person's life?

3. Hamp is a loving father and yet he is full of guilt regarding his daughter, Bronwyn. Are his feelings reasonable under the circumstances? What will it take to make Hamp stop looking for his daughter?

4. In parent-child relationships, is there a difference between guilt and regret?

5. Anna is a loving parent but her controlling style of parenting grates on Sophia. How would Anna describe her parenting style?

6. How does Sophie's relationship with her mother grow and change over the course of the book? Why does that happen? What happens to Sophie that makes her see her mother in a different light?

7. Sophie had a troubled adolescence. At thirteen she was in full rebellion against her mother. As you read about this time in her life, did you empathize with her? Did you recognize yourself at all in her experiences? If you had been Anna, would you have handled Sophie differently?

8. Sophie's life has been marked by a horrific incident that she experienced in the house on Mariposa Street. She feels angry about what happened, but also guilty. Why? Is this a reasonable feeling?

9. How would you play out the scene with the man if Sophie had fought back more aggressively? How would her life have been changed had she done so?

10. Should Hamp help Sophie find the man who attacked her? What would you do if you were in her position?

11. In the course of her investigation of Donny's crime, Sophie comes to know him and to understand the factors that drove him to shoot the governor. Does Donny become a more sympathetic character over the course of the novel? Is he a danger to society?

12. Restorative justice is a theory that says, essentially, that in crimes of violence everyone is hurt: the victim, the perpetrator, and the community. In South Africa, Nelson Mandela argued for restorative justice to begin healing the wounds of apartheid. What do you think about this idea, and does it apply to Donny's story? When else in the past and where, in our own time, might restorative justice be applied?

Q&A with Drusilla Campbell

Q: What was your inspiration for this novel?

A: One of the women I most admire is an attorney named Judy Clark. Judy's clients are always the men and women who have committed unspeakable crimes—the boy who went on a shooting rampage in Phoenix, the Boston Marathon bomber, Susan Smith, and others. Judy is opposed to the death penalty and so committed to the principles of American justice that she is willing to face death threats and public insult to ensure that her clients get fair treatment. Her clients aren't nice people, and she's not getting rich doing this. She's doing what she believes is right, and that inspires me.

I was also inspired by the Jerry Sandusky case and other sexual abuse scandals in the news. I wanted to better understand the mindset of the victims and the selective blindness of those on the periphery of the abuse: the wives and mothers, friends and supervisors who looked the other way and kept silent.

Q: All of your novels wrestle with weighty issues and morally complex questions. What draws you to these kinds of stories?

A: I'm driven to make sense of the stories behind the tragedies that are everywhere in the news. Surrounded by media and blasted by opinionators, I sometimes feel like the events taking place across the country are happening right in my neighborhood. I didn't know anyone connected to the shooting at Sandy Hook Elementary but I still sat on my bed and wept for everyone involved. As I think back on that day, I believe I was also crying for myself and the people I love, for the sense I sometimes have that the world is out of balance. And yet, despite imbalance and pain, the life spirit persists.

On another occasion, I saw a piece in which Mrs. Sandusky talked about what a good man her husband is. Afterward I couldn't get her face out of my mind. I wonder why and how we deceive ourselves, why we keep secrets long past their pull date. It is miraculous that in the midst of bone-crushing pain, we humans continue to get up and eat breakfast, we laugh and write music and fix dinner. We have babies and mourn our dead. I write about weighty issues and morally complex questions because I want to understand how we manage to keep on doing it.

Q: How do you understand Iva's character? Is she a good person, in your opinion?

A: I don't think you can say she's either good or bad. She does what she unconsciously believes she must in order to survive. She loves Roman and trusts him because deep inside she knows that were she not to believe him, the foundation of her life would fall away. She'd go into emotional free fall and nothing in her life has prepared her for that. Blindness is safety for her.

Q: Do you have sympathy for Donny? Was he a difficult character to write?

A: He broke under stress and I empathize with that. I hope the reader does as well, but empathizing isn't the same as liking or excusing. Often we forget that. He was a difficult character to write because he was so shut down, lost to himself and to the world. It took the whole book for me to get to know him.

Q: Can you describe your writing process? Do you write an outline before you begin?

A: Writing a novel is a trip into a world I create in my head. It takes a big leap of faith to start that voyage and believe I can make a success of it. That being said, I don't like outlines even though they can provide a sense of security. I'm at my most imaginative when I know the beginning and the destination and leave room for side trips and dead ends. The most interesting trips are those that meander, right? My favorite way to write a novel is to have an idea, a character, and a central issue that hold my imagination. By the time I reach the end of the process, most of the meanders have been edited out. But they weren't a waste of time.

Without them I wouldn't understand the story I'm trying to tell.

Q: Of all the novels you've written, do you have a favorite?

A: No. When I'm writing a novel I feel like I've never written one before. I have all the same doubts and insecurities and panics as I did when I first started writing. I have favorite characters, however. Madora and Django Jones in *Little Girl Gone* and Merrell in *The Good Sister*. They are characters who spoke to me immediately.

Q: Did you always want to be a writer, or did you start off in a different career?

A: I've dreamed of writing books since I was about eight and a remarkable teacher encouraged me. Because of her I also wanted to be a teacher. Naturally, my parents encouraged me to be practical, so I put my dream away and taught elementary school for several years. I traveled around the world and the country doing that, but after a time I needed something else. I got an MA and worked for an NPR affiliate in Washington, D.C., where I interviewed a lot of writers. I saw that they were not so different from me, and I began to think I might be able to write a book after all. I began as a science fiction writer, moved on to historical fiction—what my husband called "sex, violence, and dress patterns." Though I was quite successful in that genre, historical romances were not what I wanted to write, and I returned to teaching when my children were small. For a time I was a professional shopper. Then I tried to be a limo driver, but that was a bust because I didn't know where the hot clubs and bars were located. I stoked my courage and tried to write the kind of book I liked to read. After three or four efforts, I sold one—*Wildwood*. That was about fifteen years ago. I still don't know where the bars and clubs are.

Q: What do you find to be the most challenging part of the writing process? What's your favorite part?

A: Until I get a first draft, I have no confidence that I will be able to translate the story from my imagination into hard copy. I struggle with the first draft, but once I've got a draft, no matter how messy it is, I am happy. I love the challenge of taking that discursive and unfocused mess and making it into something.

Q: What advice would you give to aspiring writers?

A: I'm surprised by how little and how narrowly most of my students read. There's a lot of nonfiction on their bedside tables, but not a lot of novels. I tell them that if you want to write stories, you have to read stories.

I do a lot of teaching now, as much as I can fit in. I love it. My students are almost always underpublished writers who've wanted to write a novel since forever. Their energy is exhilarating and over and over again I'm astonished by their great ideas. Then I have to do what I'm getting paid for, which is tell them the truth. That publishing is a hard business and getting harder every day.

That a writer must grow an alligator hide because rejection hurts like hell.

I tell them to find a way to be both a thick-skinned realist and a dreamer because writing is both a business and an art. First and last you have to write for your own joy and satisfaction. With that going for you, the criticism and rejection don't hurt as much. Battle scars prove you dared to step into the fight.

Q: Who are some of your favorite novelists? Have you read anything recently that you loved and would recommend?

A: I have what you might call a "heavy" reading habit. I was hooked by the stories of the Brothers Grimm and Hans Christian Andersen. Today my list of best-books-ever would include *Birdsong* by Sebastian Faulks, *Flight Behavior* by Barbara Kingsolver, and *Wolf Hall* by Hilary Mantel, but that's only one shelf. I've read *Girls* by Frederick Busch three times and probably will again. *Burial Rites* by Hannah Kent opened my eyes to a world I never knew existed. For the space of three days I was a beautiful, intelligent, and impoverished woman living in early-nineteenth-century Iceland. These days I'm reading E. L. Doctorow's *Andrew's Brain* and enjoying it now that I've caught the rhythm of the narrative. Dave Eggers's *The Circle* is so relevant and important that it should be read and discussed in high school classrooms.

The list goes on and on.

Q: Are you working on anything new at the moment?

A: I'm always working either on my computer, in a notebook, or in my head. I get an idea and I begin to think it both forward into a story with characters and backward into their history. I hitch a ride on both trajectories almost simultaneously and, usually after a week or so, I've lost interest and jump off. This can go on for a while and sometimes I think I'll never find my next story. This was happening to me recently, but then, just the other day, I thought of a family and a situation completely different from anything I've imagined before. I've been waking up at four a.m., thinking about it, unable to get back to sleep. This is a good sign.